SWEET TEMPTATION

Elizabeth felt her heart beat faster at Colchester's closeness. When he reached for her hand and started to gently stroke it she made no attempt to stop him. Then suddenly his arm was around her and she felt his fingers touch the side of her breast and she gasped. The next moment her head was tilted back and his warm lips were gently pressing on hers and she found her arms sliding automatically around his neck.

"I need you, Elizabeth," he murmured. "I would look after you, see that you lacked for nothing. I have a little house in Chelsea where we could meet, spend weekends together."

It would have been so easy for Elizabeth to surrender to this masterful male—but her mind overruled her heart as she declared, "I have never been so insulted in all my life. . . ."

COMING IN JULY 1988

Eileen Jackson
A Servant of Quality

Mary Jo Putney
The Would-Be Widow

Anita Mills
The Duke's Double

The New Super Regency
Edith Layton
The Game of Love

SIGNET REGENCY ROMANCE

The Willful Widow
Irene Saunders

A SIGNET BOOK

NEW AMERICAN LIBRARY

NAL BOOKS ARE AVAILABLE AT QUANTITY DISCOUNTS
WHEN USED TO PROMOTE PRODUCTS OR SERVICES. FOR
INFORMATION PLEASE WRITE TO PREMIUM MARKETING
DIVISION, NEW AMERICAN LIBRARY, 1633 BROADWAY,
NEW YORK, NEW YORK 10019.

SIGNET TRADEMARK REG. U.S. PAT.OFF. AND FOREIGN COUNTRIES
REGISTERED TRADEMARK—MARCA REGISTRADA
HECHO EN CHICAGO, U.S.A.

SIGNET, SIGNET CLASSIC, MENTOR, ONYX, PLUME,
MERIDIAN and NAL BOOKS are published by NAL PENGUIN
INC., 1633 Broadway, New York, New York 10019.

First Printing, June, 1988

1 2 3 4 5 6 7 8 9

PRINTED IN THE UNITED STATES OF AMERICA

Prologue

"AND TO MY barren wife, Elizabeth . . ."

He's talking about me, she thought as she gazed dispassionately at the unpleasant little solicitor, noticing how the seams of his too-tight breeches, already stretched to their utmost, threatened to burst as he leaned back in the large wing chair. His voice held more than a hint of malice, and his beady eyes gleamed spitefully as he paused, looking around and assessing the effect of her late husband's words on the somberly dressed gathering.

She could not help wondering what she had done to Josiah Jenkins, on his rare visits to the house, to warrant his obvious enjoyment of her embarrassment. No doubt Rupert had rehearsed him carefully, making sure his words from the dead would have the maximum effect. It had certainly been Rupert who had specified that the butler and housekeeper should be present for the reading of the will, though their bequests would doubtless be but a paltry sum.

Her stepson, Robert, now Lord Trevelyan, Fifth Marquess of Dewsbury, glanced up and caught her eye. He gave her a small nod of encouragement. She squared her shoulders, instinctively preparing to receive this final humiliation from the man she had married some three years ago. She reflected how fortunate it was that Robert and Sybil were married last month, for his father's death would have meant postponing the wedding for a year. Sybil was in her bedchamber today, feeling slightly unwell, but it was already quite clear that she would enjoy being the new marchioness.

Elizabeth felt a soft touch and glanced down as small, delicate fingers comfortingly stroked her tightly clenched fists. She looked into the gentle, faded blue eyes of Lavinia, her elderly sister-in-law, and her compressed lips relaxed into a faint smile.

It was strange how completely detached her mind felt, though her body involuntarily tensed as she waited for Rupert's last attempt to embarrass and debase her. At least this time it was out in the open—not just his voice shouting vile untruths about her so loudly that servants and family alike could not help hearing them through the closed door of the bedchamber.

What a pity he had not saved his shouting for this room, she thought. Two of its walls were lined from floor to ceiling with solid oak book stacks filled with rich, leather-bound volumes, and not a sound ever escaped into the hall and adjacent rooms. She always liked the library. In fact, when Rupert was away, it was her favorite room in the house—or rather, it was until today.

She glanced at the two servants standing uncomfortably with their backs close to the massive carved oak door, waiting to find out if their master for more than forty years had been more generous to them in death than he had during his lifetime. For a moment two pairs of sympathetic eyes met hers before the servants' heads lowered as though pulled by the strings of a puppeteer.

Beside the handsome fireplace, which bore the carved coat of arms of the Trevelyans, sat her lovely step-daughter. Just seventeen, only five years younger than Elizabeth herself, she had always seemed more like a little sister. At the solicitor's words, the girl seemed quite bewildered, turning questioning eyes to her brother, Gordon, who shook his head in disgust and glanced meaningfully toward their older brother.

"Let's get on with it, Jenkins," the new marquess ordered. "There's no point in prolonging the agony. I, for one, am anxious to hear our illustrious father's last commandments.''

Sitting up once more, Jenkins leaned forward and peered closely through an eyeglass at the document before him.

"To my, er, barren wife, Elizabeth,'' he repeated, "whose proven inability to produce heirs will surely prevent her remarriage, I generously grant the use of the London town house for the duration of her life, after which it will revert to the family estate. A moderate allowance is to be set aside for the upkeep of this residence, and she is to receive a personal allowance of two thousand pounds per annum so that she may maintain the appearance expected of the dowager Marchioness of Dewsbury.''

Pausing once more, Mr. Jenkins rustled the paper and peeked over it. Elizabeth felt a slight, uncontrollable flush tinge her cheeks as his gleaming little eyes met hers, but he was the first to look away.

He loudly cleared his throat. "The marquess added just one contingency," he murmured with satisfaction, then started to read once more. "In the event some penniless fool should think to marry her and live on my money, I will not tolerate this. Both the house and the allowances will immediately revert to the estate should she remarry.''

Other than meager bequests to the two servants, the balance of the estate, which was for the most part entailed, would now be in the hands of the new marquess, who would be responsible for his younger brother and sister. No provision whatsoever had been made for Lady Lavinia, who, as the spinster aunt of the new marquess, would have to trust to his generosity and to that of his young bride.

1

"I'M SO GLAD we came to town early, Lavinia. It will take all of two weeks to air this house out properly." Elizabeth Trevelyan sniffed daintily at the smell of damp and humidity that pervaded the dismal drawing room. "And I must get Pamela out of these awful dreary blacks and into soft pastels more suitable for a debutante."

Lady Lavinia's eyebrows raised a fraction. "Don't you think, my dear, that she should go into half-mourning for a few months?" she suggested mildly. "I know it's been a year since dear Rupert passed on, but . . ."

"One year, three weeks, and four and a half days to be exact," the young dowager said emphatically, "and I know one shouldn't speak ill of the dead, but we've all paid your brother more respect than was ever his due. I will go into half-mourning, but it's high time Pamela enjoyed herself, and I mean to see that her first Season is the happy, carefree time it should be for a girl of her age."

Lady Lavinia placed a gentle hand on her sister-in-law's arm. "I understand, my dear," she assured her. "You want her to have what you missed. You were but a year older than Pamela is now when your father brought you to marry Dewsbury."

"Sold me to Dewsbury, you mean, although I must confess he seemed perfectly charming when I first met him—as he appeared to most people outside the family." She looked thoughtful for a moment, then shrugged lightly, her usual bright smile reappearing. "But that's all in the past. Now we're free and we're going to take London by storm. We'll make sure Pamela falls head over heels in love and has all the handsome, eligible young men tripping over one another to ask for her hand."

"And what about you, Elizabeth? You're still young enough for romance yourself." The older woman sounded a little wistful.

"Oh, no, that's not for me. I'm going to be the young, sophisticated widow. Charming, witty, and with excellent taste, but a widow I'll remain. I've no intention of falling into that trap again!" Her eyes twinkled merrily despite her firm assertion. "Come along and let's find Pamela. The carriage will be outside soon, and you know how Tom Coachman will grumble if we keep the horses standing."

As she reached the door, she turned and looked critically at the solid, overstuffed furniture, its somber hues accentuated by a shaft of sunlight that succeeded in glinting through one of the heavily draped windows.

"It's a pity my husband's moderate allowance to maintain this place is so small. As it will revert to Robert eventually, I wonder how he would feel about paying for a little refurbishing?" she murmured thoughtfully. "He's alone in town, staying at his club, so I must invite him to dine tomorrow evening."

Madame Gerard's elegant establishment was set discreetly back from the main thoroughfare and looked more like an elegant private home than a thriving business.

"Are you sure this is the right address, Aunt Lavinia?" Pamela asked hesitantly. "It may have changed in the years since you were last in London, you know."

Her aunt smiled reassuringly. "Madame has come up in the world in recent years. My dear friend, Lady Clyde, told me that she is now the most fashionable modiste in town. I can't read that small brass plate from here, but I have no doubt it bears her name. She no longer has need to boldly advertise her services."

As the three ladies approached the pale-blue door, it was opened by a footman uniformed in the same shade of blue. They crossed the threshold, ready to begin their transformation from ladies in outmoded black to elegant members of the *beau monde*. Madame, a slim woman of middle years, elegantly gowned, immediately produced

ready-made outfits for each. These would be fitted and
adjusted by her staff, and available to change into by the
time she had decided how they were to be gowned for the
Season.

"I cannot permit you to wear those *vêtements affreux*
one more moment," Madame said, throwing up her hands
as if in horror. "If anyone should see you leaving, I would
be—what you say—ostracized." She shuddered drama-
tically.

Pamela made a sound strongly resembling a titter that
changed immediately into a hiccup as her Aunt Lavinia
gave her a warning pinch.

"The little one first, do you not agree, my lady?" The
bolt of French lace in the palest primrose that Madame
draped on the mannequin could not have been more
suitable, and Pamela's eyes filled with wonder as delicate
organdies, gauzes, muslins, and silks in the softest pastels
quickly followed.

They were soon intently selecting first the fabrics and
then the styles as the modiste, with deft fingers, draped
and pinned them to illustrate what she had in mind.

Elizabeth quickly realized that they could safely leave
themselves in the hands of the astute Madame Gerard,
who, she was sure, had never been more than twenty
miles outside of London in her life, but who had a
remarkable instinct as to what would look best on three
such different ladies.

They were sipping a most refreshing cup of tea and
nibbling delicate French pastries and cakes while
Madame checked the workmanship on the altered
garments, when there came a tinkle of the doorbell.

As the footman announced the Countess of
Colchester, Lavinia hurried forward with a little
exclamation of delight.

"Mildred, my dear," she cried. "I was hoping you
might be in town already."

The countess, Lady Beresford, a small, slightly
plump, but most attractive lady of about the same age
as Lavinia, held out her arms. "Lavinia, I'd have

known you anywhere, even though it must be twenty years since last we met. I wondered if we might now see something of you when I heard that Dewsbury had passed on. Where are you staying?''

''My sister-in-law kindly invited me to join her at the Dewsbury town house on Grosvenor Street. She is bringing out my niece this Season and, as you can see''
—she gestured ruefully toward her unfashionable attire
—''we only just arrived in town.''

With a more than interested gleam in her eyes, Lady Beresford glanced toward the two animated young ladies who were trying to hide their excitement as they discussed the accessories they would wear with the new gowns.

''Ah, yes,'' she murmured thoughtfully. ''I had heard, of course, that Dewsbury married a young chit before her come-out, then buried her in the country.'' She nodded slowly. ''She's not a classical beauty but very lovely in a special way, despite that drab gown she's wearing. She'll go over very well this Season, mark my words.''

''I hope you're right, my dear,'' Lady Lavinia said softly. ''She's inclined to be a little willful now there's no one to gainsay her, but a kinder, sweeter sister-in-law I couldn't have. And she deserves much better from life than she's had thus far. Come, let me make them known to you and you'll see for yourself.''

Elizabeth and Pamela made their curtsies as Lavinia introduced them, and Madame and her assistants faded discreetly into the background to get on with their work.

Briefly expressing her condolences on the death of Dewsbury, Lady Beresford joined them at the tea tray. ''You make an unusually young and lovely dowager, my dear,'' she said to Elizabeth. ''Is this your first Season also?''

''Yes, my lady. My father had decided I was to marry Dewsbury, so he saw no need to waste the funds on my come-out,'' Elizabeth said dryly.

''God moves in a mysterious way, my dear,'' Lady Beresford murmured as an idea formed in her mind. This might indeed be a fortunate meeting. ''I am planning a small dinner party next week, just some close friends who are in town a little early. You must come. I'll send you invitations as soon as I return. I am sure that Madame Gerard will have something suitable ready for you by then.''

Unaware that all the early arrivals in town were doing the same thing as they were—buying new wardrobes—Elizabeth felt somewhat embarrassed. She realized, however, that the party would give them an excellent entree into society, so she thanked Lady Beresford pleasantly. The conversation then continued mostly between the two older ladies as they reminisced about their own come-outs so very many years ago, and the fun they had, until Madame Gerard appeared to suggest that the ladies might like to change into their new garments while she attended to Lady Beresford.

Robert Trevelyan took one look at the town house, all the more gloomy because of Elizabeth's sparing use of candles, and he immediately agreed to release funds for some refurbishing.

"It must be twenty years since my mother did anything to this place, Elizabeth. Just go ahead and do what you feel is necessary to make it comfortable and attractive," he said, "and send the bills to me. You've never been extravagant, so I know you'll not go overboard, and you'll need to entertain quite a bit to bring Pamela out this year. I'm not like my father, you know," he assured her with a wide grin. "You needn't have gone to the trouble of making it look even darker than usual to convince me."

"Robert," she said, pretending to look innocent but unable to keep a completely straight face, "you surely cannot believe I would do a thing like that?"

"My dear Elizabeth, after living in the same house with you for four years, there's very little I don't know about you, and nothing I don't like. At one time, before I met Sybil, I even fancied myself in love with you." He touched her cheek lightly. "And you knew, didn't you, and somehow managed to turn it into a natural, brotherly regard?''

Elizabeth nodded, catching his hand and holding it for a moment before getting back to the matter at hand. "Even though you've not asked for it, I'll seek your approval for any large expenditures,'' she promised him, then smiled mischievously, "but I should warn you that I do not plan to let you have the house back for many years, so don't even think that I might remarry."

"I rather hope you will," he said quite seriously. "Not that I need this place, for Sybil has come into a much larger house just around the corner in Grosvenor Square. But you deserve some happiness after the way you put up with Father."

She laid her hand on his arm. "Don't, Robert. It's over now, and I don't want to talk about it anymore. It really wasn't my fault, you know. He just couldn't . . ." She broke off in embarrassment.

"I know," he said grimly. "And then he underestimated the Baxters completely, having them there at the reading like that. They'd cut out their tongues before they'd say a word against you."

"I know they would. But that nasty little man— Josiah Jenkins, wasn't it? If there's any talk about the will, it will be from him, not them." She shrugged lightly, deciding not to worry about it needlessly, then changed the subject. "How is Sybil and your new heir? Doesn't it feel wonderful to know that a part of you is already here to carry on the Trevelyan line?"

Looking at her warm, intense face, he shook his head a little sadly. "You should have had a child of your own, Elizabeth, and I sincerely hope that one day you will."

"Didn't you hear? I'm going to be the merry widow of the Season," she said, her eyes sparkling mischievously. "Your Aunt Lavinia is so cross with me she must have told you."

"I heard," he said briefly. "Just don't carve that in marble, that's all."

Elizabeth had stayed with him to discuss the house while he drank his port, and they now joined his sister and aunt in the drawing room, where tea had been served for the ladies. They had spent most of the day shopping for gloves, reticules, parasols, and so forth, and were quite relieved when Robert made his excuses and left them to retire early. Tired as they were, however, they would not make a move until Elizabeth had assured them that Robert had given her *carte blanche* to refurbish the house.

The following day, dropping off Lavinia and Pamela to look for slippers, shawls, and other accessories, Elizabeth took the carriage to the street where the best silk merchants and drapers offered their wares. The drawing room needed new hangings at the windows, as did the dining room and the three bedrooms they were presently using. In addition, the drawing-room furniture had to be recovered, as well as the dining-room chairs.

With a maid in tow, she went from merchant to merchant examining their materials and obtaining their prices until she found, down a side street, a smaller store where the fabrics were less expensive and the owner, a frail old man who looked as though he was in his seventies, much more obliging.

"If ye've the time, milady, t' come into t' back room where m' son an' one of 'is lads is just finishin' an order, ye'll see t' quality of work we do. Ramsbottom's our name," he said in a thin, reedy voice. When she nodded her agreement, he rose slowly and painfully. Bent almost in two as he leaned upon a stick for support, he eased his way past the heavy bolts of fabric and through an open door.

Millie, the maid, looked quite upset that her mistress would go into the actual workshop, but at Elizabeth's sharp glance she followed behind.

They entered a large cold room; its hardwood floor was bare but spotlessly clean, and sunlight poured through the many windows. Despite the open back door, the room was redolent of turpentine and varnish.

The younger man was carefully removing years of dust

and grime from the last two of a set of dining chairs, while his father put new covers on the rest. Elizabeth knew immediately that she had come to the right place. The reupholstered chairs bore almost no resemblance to the original ones. The only problem was that the Season would be over by the time the two men could accomplish the amount of work she needed to have done.

"We c'n do any job y' need, milady," the old man croaked. "I've seven sons all told. Lots o' mouths t' feed and lots of 'ands t' do t' work."

After the servile approach of the other merchants, Elizabeth found this family business much more to her liking. She quickly selected a couple of dozen bolts of fabric for them to bring to the house the next morning and give her a closer estimate of the cost.

When they returned to the main street, the coachman was still walking the horses and his worried look quickly disappeared when he saw Elizabeth's happy face.

"Let's go back to Oxford Street now, Tom, and if the ladies have had as successful a morning as I have, we may then go home for luncheon," she told him, "and this afternoon perhaps we'll . . . Oh, no, I forgot. We won't require your services again today." She had just remembered that a hairdresser recommended by Madame Gerard was coming this afternoon to cut and shape all the ladies' hair into more fashionable styles.

The Beresfords' town house was considerably larger than the one Dewsbury had given Elizabeth the use of. It was on the west side of Hanover Square, quite close to Bond Street, and the moment she stepped into the drawing room Elizabeth sensed the years of lovingly selected acquisitions that combined to give it an air of warmth and elegance. Just a touch of the current Chinese influence was evident in the wall hangings, a very beautiful black lacquer screen, and several delicately carved tables.

When the Trevelyans first arrived, Lady Beresford seemed somewhat flustered as she excused herself to give last-minute instructions to the butler, but when she rejoined them, her calm smile had returned and with her she brought a middle-aged gentleman who, from the warm glances they exchanged, it seemed safe to assume was a very close friend.

"I don't believe you will remember Sir James Moorehead, Lavinia," she said, bringing him over to where the Trevelyans were still standing exchanging pleasantries with two girls of Pamela's age and their mother, another old acquaintance of Lavinia. "He was here only for a few months when I first came out, then was abroad for a number of years."

She had just completed the introductions when there was a disturbance near the door, and a raucous female voice, raised in anger, could be clearly heard.

"You can just keep your hands to yourself, Minton. When I need your help to walk into a room, I'll ask for it. These legs may be a bit shaky but I can get around on my own."

Lady Beresford hurried to where a diminutive figure, her wrinkled face unnaturally white except for a circle of rouge on each cheek and a bright-red outlined mouth, leaned heavily on a walking stick. Her pale-blue gown, pinched in at the waist and the big skirt puffed over panniers, was outdated by at least thirty years. On her head she wore an enormous powdered wig, piled high and intertwined with pearls, feathers, and flowers.

The footman who had been trying to assist her stepped quickly back.

"There you are, Mildred." The woman's bright-blue eyes glared fiercely and her wig wobbled precariously as she lifted her head sharply. "I don't know what's happened to young ones these days. No manners at all! That grandson of mine should have waited to escort me, that's what he should have done. Where is he, anyway?"

"Now, Mama, don't get yourself so upset," Lady Beresford said soothingly, slipping a hand through her mother-in-law's arm. "Let me take you around and make you known to everyone, and then Lord Bridges will take you in to dinner."

A white-haired, bewhiskered gentleman wearing old-fashioned knee breeches stepped to the other side of the elderly lady and offered his arm, and the trio made their painfully slow way around the room, introducing the guests to the thrice-married Lady Butterfield, grandmother of the present Earl of Colchester.

As they progressed, the gentlemen moved over to the ladies they were to escort into dinner, and Elizabeth found herself taking one arm of Sir James while Lady Lavinia took the other.

"A last-minute cancellation makes me doubly fortunate," he murmured gallantly, and Elizabeth could not help wondering if that was why Lady Beresford had seemed a little distressed when they had arrived.

She was seated with Sir James on her right and a rather shy young man on her left who, it appeared, was a distant relative of Lady Beresford. The elderly Lady Butterfield was several seats away, but close enough for Elizabeth to hear most of that lady's tart comments throughout the meal.

"No respect for their elders, that's what it is," the old lady barked. "Mildred didn't bring that young whippersnapper up right. If my son hadn't died so young, he'd have had something to say about it. Going to his club to dine instead of helping entertain his mother's guests!"

Elizabeth felt no guilt about eavesdropping, as the voice was so loud anyone within ten feet could hear it clearly. She turned as she realized that Sir James had said something to her.

"I do beg your pardon, sir," she murmured with genuine regret. "I'm afraid I was air dreaming and didn't hear . . ."

"There's no call to worry yourself, my dear. I was just commenting on the fact that I met Dewsbury the other day and congratulated him on his recent acquisition of an heir. I thought he looked a little sly when he told me he was having dinner with 'the dowager.' " His kind eyes twinkled.

"Robert's always been like an older brother to me, and

he hated it when his father insisted he address me as mama. He's already returned to the country, as he dislikes town without Sybil." She was about to say how nice it was to see a love match these days when, once more, Lady Butterfield's harsh voice interrupted her thoughts.

"I wonder which chit he was dodging this time. Wants none of his mother's matchmaking, he says, as if it wasn't more than time he wed and bred a passel of brats of his own."

There was an unintelligible murmur of response and then the rejoinder, "Must have been that one that's longer in the tooth, over there in the lavender gown with the black hair. Mildred wouldn't dare try to match him with a chit straight from the schoolroom."

Elizabeth felt the color rush into her cheeks. Hers was the only lavender gown at the table.

"Now, don't you go taking any notice of what the old lady says," Sir James murmured. "You're far too lovely and, according to your stepson, too intelligent, to let the ramblings of a deaf old harridan like her upset you." He patted her hand in a fatherly way. "She's never happy unless she's stirring up some trouble or other," he added rather bitterly.

A grateful Elizabeth gave him her most brilliant smile. "You're too kind, Sir James, and Robert is also. If the Earl of Colchester did try to avoid me, he missed a delicious dinner in excellent company, and as we have never met, I can hardly be insulted."

Sir James' laugh was almost a guffaw. "Now, that's a whisker if I ever heard one. I guarantee that when he is finally introduced he'll get a very cool reception."

Elizabeth, ever honest, smiled a little sheepishly. "Well, his grandmama hasn't exactly made me anxious for that undoubted privilege. Perhaps it would help if you could enumerate his more pleasing attributes, if they exist."

"David is quite handsome," he began. "Blond hair and blue eyes. Much like his mother in looks, but much taller and without her delightful femininity, of course."

He seemed to be hesitating to say more, so Elizabeth prompted, mischievously, "How old is this so handsome rogue?"

"About thirty or thereabouts, and he's looked over every new crop of debutantes since he came into the title some nine or ten years ago." Sir James was obviously reluctant to put her in dislike of the younger man. "You might say his tastes have become somewhat sophisticated over the years, I suppose."

"I'm sure you might," Elizabeth retorted, privately thinking that the Earl of Colchester sounded like a too-good-looking, arrogant bore. "I'll be sure to steer my stepdaughter, Lady Pamela, out of his line of inspection when we finally meet," she said firmly. "His mother, Lady Beresford, seems a most charming person and my sister-in-law and she seem to have resumed their friend-ship, so I'm sure he'll not be able to avoid meeting me for very much longer."

"Once he does, my dear, he'll regret postponing the pleasure, I know," Sir James said with sincere gallantry. "His loss has certainly been my gain this evening."

Elizabeth warmly smiled her thanks, then excused herself to converse with the young man, newly down from Cambridge, who was sitting on her left.

2

DAVID BERESFORD, SEVENTH Earl of Colchester, was feeling a little worse for wear when he finally opened one reluctant eye. It was quickly closed again as it met the bright sunshine of an early-spring noonday.

"Barnes!" he started to shout, then shuddered as the noise reverberated around and around in his head. He heard a movement coming from the area of his dressing room. "Barnes." The voice was no more than a hoarse whisper this time. "Get in here and close those wretched curtains, if you know what's good for you."

There was no answer, but he heard the sound of rings being carefully drawn along rods. When he was sure the sound had stopped, he opened the other eye and this time he breathed a sigh of relief as he found the room in blissful shade once more.

"Now, Barnes, you can bring me something for my impossible head before it splits in two," he said softly, but not so softly that the waiting valet did not hear. He tiptoed forward carrying a silver tray on which a glass of some orange-colored concoction held pride of place.

After easing his master forward, he held the potion to his lips until the contents were drained completely. There was a groan from the bed as Barnes returned the tray and glass to the dressing room, then waited.

A full five minutes went by before there was a stirring from the direction of the massive four-poster bed.

"All right, Barnes, you can come out now—but quietly, and for heaven's sake leave those blasted curtains closed."

Both of the earl's eyelids were raised, if still a trifle

reluctantly, as though they were heavily weighted. They revealed a pair of startlingly blue eyes that were regrettably not shown to their best advantage at the moment, as their usually pure white background was decidedly blotched with pink.

The earl groaned as he jerked himself into a sitting position on the side of the bed, his bare toes making hard contact with the bedside table. With little heed for the unruliness of his mass of honey-blond hair, he dropped his head into his cupped hands.

"Why did I do it, Barnes? It's been so long that I'd completely forgotten how devilish awful this feels," he muttered.

"When I helped you up the stairs, your lordship, you said something about it being all Lady Beresford's fault. But how your dear mother could possibly be responsible, I just cannot imagine," Barnes said as he placed a wet towel over his master's forehead.

It was coming back to Colchester now. It had all started with a dinner party his mother was having; he'd rashly said he'd attend until she made a last-minute decision to invite an old friend from her youth . . . and two females, in town for their first Season. She had tried to insist that he do the pretty to one of them and take her in to dinner.

He'd become quite furious at his mother's latest matchmaking and finally stormed out of the house, heading for his club. As he thought about it, he could recall how upset his mother had been, see again the hurt expression on her face, and he knew that as soon as he could get into a little better shape, he must get dressed and go and make it up with her. She'd caught him on the raw, that's all, and hadn't deserved that kind of treatment.

In a little less than two hours, leaving an exhausted Barnes behind him to bemoan his fate, Colchester could be seen strolling along Brook Street in the direction of Hanover Square, dressed impeccably in skin-tight beige pantaloons, a blue coat made, of course, by Weston of Old Bond Street, and an exquisitely folded and starched white cravat. Only a very close inspection would have revealed that his complexion was still somewhat pale and his step not quite as jaunty as usual.

He ran lightly up the steps of Number Eighteen, and as an alert footman opened the door, he stepped inside, handing his hat, walking stick, and yellow gloves to the butler.

"Is Lady Beresford in the drawing room, Minton?" he inquired.

"No, my lord, her ladyship is alone in her writing room at the present time, attending to some correspondence, I believe," the unsmiling butler replied in a tone so correct that it implied a reproof.

With a nod of thanks and a sigh of relief that his grandmama was not with her, Colchester went in the direction of the writing room, knocked briefly on the door, and entered.

Lady Beresford had been sitting at a small mahogany writing table, accepting or regretfully declining a number of invitations she had just received. Despite his transgressions of the night before, she was delighted to see her son and rose to welcome him.

"David, how nice to see you. Do come in and sit here by the fire. Although the sun is shining outside, there's little warmth in it at this time of year," she remarked, holding out both hands toward him.

He took them in his, then leaned over and kissed her cheek. "Am I forgiven for upsetting your dinner arrangements last night?" he asked contritely.

She drew him toward the small, bronze-trimmed white marble fireplace. "Of course, my dear. I forgave you right away, but your grandmama is another matter. She was still commenting loudly on the behavior of youngsters today when the last guest left."

She sank into a comfortable green velvet chair on one side of the fireplace, and Colchester stood facing her, one elbow resting on the mantelpiece.

"What she really missed, of course, was your strong arm to help her down the stairs, David. She's getting more and more unsteady on her feet, I'm afraid, and more strange-looking in those gowns and wigs she's had since before your grandpapa died. At the start of dinner she was nodding so emphatically as she voiced her complaints, that her powdered wig, feathers, flowers, and all swayed like a ship at sea. For a moment I felt sure the entire monstrosity was going to fall slap into her soup."

She couldn't help but laugh at the recollection, and Colchester had to join in despite the discomfort to his still-aching head.

"It seems I missed an exciting dinner," he remarked with a smile. "My evening at the club was quite dull in comparison."

Lady Beresford, ever a doting mother, had not failed to see the signs of a night's overindulgence on her son's face. She was possibly the only person alive who was aware of the extreme sensitivity that her son's arrogant air concealed, and she realized how much their angry words had upset him. However, she was astute enough to press home her advantage when she could.

"While you are in so penitent a mood, I believe we should talk calmly and rationally about the growing need for you to marry and produce one or more heirs, David," she said seriously.

She saw he was about to interrupt and raised a hand to stop him. "No, my dear, hear me out for once. I know your grandmama's constant harping on the subject annoys you, but I have not spoken directly of it before, though I admit to pushing a few likely candidates into your line of vision."

Colchester affirmed this with a grim smile.

"Ten years is ample time for youth to have its fling, though the three years when you fought with Wellington cannot truly be counted," she conceded.

"How very generous of you, Mama," he murmured ironically, but Lady Beresford refused to be drawn.

"I will readily agree that I am too prejudiced in your favor to select a suitable bride for you, for no one would really be good enough for my son. However, if you wait much longer, you will end up with a June and January marriage, with too much age difference between you for you to have anything in common." Lady Beresford paused, waiting for some response.

"I cannot but agree with everything you've said so far, Mama," he said with maddening arrogance.

She sighed deeply. "Please believe me, that was the only reason why I wanted you to meet Lavinia's sister-in-law. I thought that at the age of twenty-three she might be a little more to your taste. She's not beautiful, but quite lovely in a vivacious kind of way. However, Sir James, who was one of her dinner companions, did say she was unusually outspoken . . . frank, I believe, was the word he used. And Lavinia, who loves her dearly, admits that she has become rather willful since she has been widowed."

He shook his head slowly so as not to disturb the equilibrium unduly. "Then I really don't think this willful widow is for me, my dear Mama. However, I do give you my word that I will earnestly try to find some suitable little thing whose blood will not dilute too much the Colchester brains."

"Really, David," she scolded lightly. "With that attitude you'll drive all the possibilities away."

"Not a chance, my dear Mama, not a chance. From my vast experience I can assure you that they'll all come running the minute I step into a room with you," he told her. "Don't look so surprised. I have decided I'll give it a month, and during that time I'll accompany you to every social engagement you wish. The only thing I ask is that you keep Grandmama out of my way."

As if on cue, there was the sound of a raucous voice still some distance away.

Lady Beresford rose. "I'll do my best, but you're going to have to put up with her for a few minutes now unless you want to escape through the French window." She kissed his cheek as he quickly bent toward her.

"Bless you, Mama. You're a mother in a million. I fail to understand how you've stood her all these years, but my head couldn't take that voice today." He blew her a kiss as he stepped into the garden and out of view.

Lady Beresford closed the French windows and turned to see what mischief her mother-in-law was about to make today, for she had realized for some time now that the deliberately rude, caustic remarks were a form of entertainment for a very bored old lady. Even more regrettable was the fact that as Lady Butterfield became more and more deaf, so the volume of her harsh voice increased.

The old lady had a daughter and a son by her two later husbands, but Colchester had been the first and most illustrious one—the most wealthy also—and it was to his residence she had returned each time she had been widowed.

"Where is he? Where's that son of yours?" Lady Butterfield entered on the arm of Sir James Moorehead, whom she had met in the hall. "Minton said the rascal was with you, and I'm going to find him and give him a piece of my mind." Releasing Sir James' arm, she tottered from one piece of furniture to another, looking around and behind each.

"It's good to see you, James." Lady Beresford extended a hand over which Sir James bent low, touching it with his lips before releasing it. His amused eyes flicked to the old lady and back, and he raised his eyebrows in silent questioning.

"Don't worry, she won't find him. He left through the garden," she silently mouthed, then failed to restrain what even in a younger person would have been a most unladylike giggle.

"She is such a trial to you, my love. Won't you change your mind and marry me by special license? If you don't want to send her packing, at least I'll be able to relieve you of some of the work and worry," he said softly, but he knew, before she shook her head with a sad smile, what her answer would be.

"What are you two whispering about over there? Are you plotting against me and hiding him? You never could control him, Mildred. Don't say I didn't warn you!" The wrinkled old face was screwed up in fierce anger, then suddenly her expression changed to a peaceful smile. As had happened many times before, she had completely forgotten what she had come in for. "Is Milton bringing tea in here today? How cosy. You will make sure there are plenty of maid-of-honor tarts, won't you? You know how I love maid-of-honor tarts."

Lady Beresford put her arms around the frail shoulders and steered her toward the door. "I think we'll have tea in the drawing room today, Mama. Let Sir James escort you and I'll just make sure Cook has all your favorites on the tray." Over her mother-in-law's head she smiled sadly at her good friend and whispered, "Bless you, darling."

The upper floor of No. 16 Grosvenor Street buzzed with excitement. Tonight was the first ball that either Elizabeth or Pamela had ever attended. The new gowns from Madame Gerard had arrived, and in addition to the two abigails Elizabeth had hired, the hairdresser who had cut their hair had returned to supervise the new girls' work.

In the master suite, Elizabeth was already dressed in a gown of pale-gray lace trimmed with seed pearls over a pearl satin slip. From the high waist fluttered ribbons of pearl satin and around her neck she wore a single strand of large and very lovely pearls, one of the few pieces of jewelry she had received from her late husband.

Lavinia, more excited than Elizabeth had ever seen her, had on a very stylish gown of black satin and wore a lavender lace cap on her gray curls. For the occasion she had decided to wear a necklace of amethysts.

"What a difference a well-styled gown makes, even though it is in black!" Elizabeth exclaimed. "You look most elegant, Lavinia, and the amethysts are just the right touch. But what happened to the lavender gloves you bought?"

"I thought they were a little too bright for a lady in mourning, my dear," Lavinia said, firmly. "I mustn't stray too far from tradition, or people may talk."

"Fiddlesticks! You've worn solid black for more than a year already," Elizabeth reminded her, "and what difference does it make if they do talk?"

"It makes a great deal of difference to me, and it will to you also, for the *ton* survive on gossip and rumor," Lavinia warned. "You look very lovely, my dear, and for someone of your age that gown is just right."

They waited patiently until Pamela's now-short coppery curls had been arranged to the final satisfaction of *monsieur le coiffeur*, and then that gentleman bounced into the bedchamber to comb some curls into place and thread silver ribbons and pearls through Elizabeth's black locks.

He had just finished when Pamela came running in, pirouetted around the room, then dropped into a low curtsy in front of Elizabeth. She was wearing the pale-primrose French lace, which set off her hair to perfection. At the sight of her, Elizabeth felt that all the work entailed in giving her a Season in town was very worthwhile. She could ot see how any man could help loving her on sight.

With not a little trepidation, the three ladies descended the staircase and stepped into the waiting carriage. Tonight was the ball given by the Earl and Countess of Bradenton, which marked the start of the Season.

Colchester noticed the vision in gray the minute she entered the ballroom, but as he knew none of the ladies she was with, he had no idea who she was. He had been standing to one side, some distance from the entrance, and was partially hidden by an orange tree in a large tub. From his vantage point he could clearly see her dancing eyes and lovely smile and he determined he must meet her.

The older woman, probably her mother, was taking the two younger ladies around to introduce them to her friends, and as the party moved down the room, it seemed to be gathering a cluster of eager young bucks in its wake.

To his mother's satisfaction, he had reserved dances with a couple of the young debutantes to whom she had introduced him. He had danced with one, who stepped all over his toes and blushed each time he looked at her. Now he realized that a cotillion was starting and he must claim the other one as his partner, but the problem was, which one of the chattering group was she? In the end he found out by a process of elimination as the chit in the pale-pink gown was the only one left when the others moved away to take up their positions.

He strolled unhurriedly in her direction and to his disgust, the young girl betrayed her anxiety by starting toward him. But at least this one danced well and he had to admit to feeling somewhat ashamed of himself. It wasn't her fault that she was so young and innocent. He made himself converse pleasantly with her, and after a stammering hesitation when she flushed a rosy pink, she made all the correct replies.

As he swung around he was surprised to see that the object of his interest was not dancing but standing at the side of the room talking to two young men, the older of whom he knew quite well. The minute this dance was over he must drift casually over and have his friend introduce him.

Elizabeth was thoroughly enjoying herself. She would have loved to dance. She had finally learned how from the dancing master she had hired to teach Pamela, and it would have been heavenly to drift around the floor to the strains of the small orchestra, but she knew that would have been going too far.

One thing she had refused to do, however, was to join the matrons and chaperons who were sitting together in an alcove, keeping a close watch on their young charges. Lavinia seemed happy enough in their company, for she had found a number of old friends and was eagerly catching up with them on the lost years. When they first arrived, she had caught a glimpse of Lady Beresford with Sir James Moorehead, but they had disappeared into a room at the side where she was told that card games were in progress.

So far she had felt quite comfortable, for there had always been two or three young men eager to stand and talk to her at the side of the room, and several had asked if they could sit a dance out with her on one of the benches in the bowers provided for the purpose.

The last dance finished, and Pamela, looking prettier than ever with an excited flush on her face, was led back to join her stepmother until the next one started. Pamela began to admire the unusual ball gown of another young girl, and when Elizabeth turned to see the lady in question, she noticed that the very handsome, very-bored-looking man who had glanced her way several times was now making his way toward her group.

"Lady Trevelyan, an old friend of mine is anxious to meet you. May I present Lord Beresford, the Earl of Colchester." (Afterward she could not remember who had made the introduction, but it had all been perfectly correct, she knew.)

His blue eyes seemed to hold a message that was just for her, and she felt the warmth of his hand right through her glove as he raised her from her curtsy. Somehow she recovered her breath and introduced him to Pamela, and then he was back at her side, asking for the next dance.

"I am sorry, my lord, but I am still not out of mourning for my husband, and to dance would not be quite proper," she explained, as she had done to a number of young men already.

"Then you must grant me the pleasure of your company for supper, my lady," he insisted with a compelling urgency.

Elizabeth felt strangely disturbed by the forwardness of his approach. She wondered if she had ever met him before for his name was puzzlingly familiar. Then her smile broadened and her gray eyes sparkled as she realized why. She knew who he was, but he had not the slightest idea who she and Pamela were! It might be amusing to teach this confident young earl a lesson.

"Why, of course, my lord, but we will probably be in a large party." She looked to where Pamela was surrounded by eager young men, then noticed that Lavinia had cautiously joined them.

The music started once more, and the group thinned as the dancers formed into sets on the floor. To her surprise Elizabeth found Colchester still at her side.

"As you have accepted my invitation to supper, would you care to sit this dance out with me, my lady?" He nodded toward a bench in a nearby bower.

"Of course, but I can hardly leave my sister-in-law alone. Lavinia, dear, may I present Lord Beresford, the Earl of Colchester. You know his mother well, I believe. My lord, Lady Lavinia Trevelyan." She had a difficult time concealing her mirth as he bowed low over Lavinia's hand.

He held an arm out to each lady to escort them to the bench, but Lavinia took pity on him.

"Thank you, my lord," she said graciously, "but I beg to be excused, for I must have a word with an old acquaintance before going in to supper. I'll see you inside, Elizabeth."

When he had made sure that she was comfortable on the bench, Colchester settled himself on the other end and turned to face her.

"Now, young lady, would you mind telling me what you find so amusing about me?" He sounded grim, but his eyes still looked warmly at her and there was a decided twitch at the corner of his mouth. She presumed he now had a very good idea of who she was.

"When you invited me to supper I could not help but recall hearing of your apparent reaction when asked to take me in to supper once before." Her eyes held a gleeful challenge. "According to your grandmother, you fled to your club in order to avoid doing so."

Humiliation replaced his arrogance of moments ago. This was no time to dissemble. "When you introduced me to Lady Lavinia, I realized who you were, but I had no idea that my dear grandmother had made you aware of my rudeness. Will you accept a most sincere apology, my lady, and let us start again?" he requested earnestly.

He meant every word, she knew, and instinctively she reached out a gloved hand to touch his. "Of course I will," she assured him. "It wasn't me you insulted, but some girl you'd never even seen. I will forgive you, but has Lady Beresford done so yet?"

"Of course. That's why I'm here tonight. But I had not thought my self-imposed penance would bring me so very much pleasure," he murmured softly. "May I take you for a drive tomorrow afternoon?"

Something about the way he looked at her set her heart beating faster and made her feel strangely warm inside. "Yes, you may, my lord," she said. "Do you know where I live?"

"I can find out easily enough, but perhaps you should tell me," he suggested.

She was having difficulty breathing again. What could be the matter with her? "My husband left me the use of the town house. It's Number Sixteen Grosvenor Street," she told him.

Suddenly realizing that the dance had finished and everyone was moving toward the supper room, he rose and offered her his arm. "I'll be there at two o'clock," he said with a pleased smile.

3

"YOU HAVE THE most bewitching smile and the most tempting lips that I have ever been compelled to watch and forbidden to touch."

His flowery words, delivered in a voice so quiet that Elizabeth had to strain to hear, sent a quiver down her spine, then an embarrassed warmth stole from her cheeks clear down to the tips of her toes. Was that really what he said, she asked herself, or did I not hear him properly?

By a maneuvering at which he was no doubt most proficient, Colchester had succeeded in joining the Trevelyan-Beresford party at supper, and yet seating Elizabeth far enough away from the others that he could converse with her without anyone else hearing.

To cover her embarrassment, she attempted to tease him. "My lord, are you sure my reputation will be quite safe if I go for a drive with you alone?" she asked with what she hoped was sophisticated raillery.

"You'll be safe enough in the carriage tomorrow, dear lady, but I won't prmise what might happen if you consent to walk with me in the garden this evening while the others dance their cotillions." Though his lips still smiled, his eyes had become even more blue and intense, almost as if they could see right through her.

"Then I must be sure to stay safely indoors, sir, for it would indeed be dangerous for me to catch a cold so early in the Season," Elizabeth quipped, with a little laugh.

"How old were you when you married Dewsbury?" The name felt unpleasant on his tongue, for he could not picture this charming creature wed to a man older than her father.

"Nineteen, my lord."

"Nineteen, David," he corrected her. "And you had your come-out the year before, when I was busy routing Napoleon?" He knew his mother had said it was her first Season, but it did not seem possible. She was far too assured for that.

She pictured how extremely handsome he must have looked in his scarlet-and-gold uniform. "No, sir, this is the very first time I have been to London."

"No, David. Say it, Elizabeth, please."

"But I don't know you well enough yet. Perhaps when we have seen more of each other . . ." She smiled gently to soften her refusal. Other than her childhood friends, she had never before called a man who was not a relative by his first name.

"Say it now," he insisted, "and then, when the others go back into the ballroom, we'll slip into the garden."

"No, my lord," she murmured regretfully. "Very definitely no. And I think that I should not spend any more of this evening alone in your company or people will start to talk. I am still in mourning, after all."

"Can you really tell me truthfully that you are sincerely mourning that old man?"

His words came too close to the truth, but his harshness hurt and she blinked back tears.

"I'm sorry, my dear. I had no right to ask that. Please forgive me," he said contritely, angry with himself for having spoiled their playful conversation, and hoping she would understand. When she smiled again he knew she had.

"There's nothing to forgive," she said lightly. "Why don't we join the others? I believe they're waiting for us."

They rose and went to where Lavinia and Lady Beresford were admiring the epergne in the center of the buffet table, its tiers intertwined with ivy leaves and bunches of grapes.

"It's such a pity you may not dance as yet, Elizabeth, but sometimes onlookers have more fun. However, at my age it's easy to say that." Lady Beresford smiled happily at her son. "You need not wait to take me home, as Sir James will do the honors, I am sure, and as I've been winning all evening, it may be very late before I leave."

They strolled back into the ballroom and this time Lavinia did not join the chaperons but led the way to some chairs conveniently placed far enough from the orchestra to be fairly quiet. Colchester sat with Elizabeth and Lavinia through the first dance, asked Pamela for the next one, and then graciously took his leave, reminding Elizabeth that he would call for her tomorrow at two.

"You seemed to enjoy Colchester's company a great deal, Elizabeth. Have you forgiven him so quickly for his rudeness the other evening?" Lavinia spoke quietly so as not to awaken Pamela, who, after the excitement of the ball, had fallen fast asleep in the carriage.

"His rudeness was to his mother, not to me, and she appears to have forgiven him," Elizabeth explained. "I found many of the younger men were rather immature. In comparison he was most refreshing. He's coming tomorrow to take me for a drive."

In the darkness Lavinia's eyebrows rose and she felt she must explain herself. "I know I'm not here to chaperon you, my dear, but there was something about his pursuit of you that made me feel I should stay with you after supper. I hope you didn't mind."

Elizabeth reached for her sister-in-law's hand. "Of course not, my love. He did seem rather interested in me," she said, knowing it to be the grossest of understatements, "and quite disappointed that I could not dance with him."

How shocked this sweet maiden lady would be if she knew he wanted to be alone with me in the gardens,

Elizabeth thought, and once again she felt a breathless excitement at the very idea.

Colchester arrived at the house a few minutes after two o'clock and instructed his tiger to walk the matched grays as, in his experience, punctuality was rarely a virtue of young and attractive ladies.

It came, therefore, as quite a surprise to him to find that Elizabeth was in the drawing room with Lady Lavinia, looking very lovely in a violet-colored bombazine gown trimmed with lavender satin ribbons. The brim of her violet velvet bonnet was lined with the same lavender, framing her black hair and showing off her fresh country complexion.

"I can see that the first ball of the Season did not prove too exhausting for you two lovely ladies," he remarked. "I stopped by to see my mama and found her still abed. But then I understand she severely trounced Lord Petersham in a game of whist that did not end until the small hours of the morning. Do you not play cards, Lady Lavinia?"

"I used to, but I can see that I will have to brush up on my card play if I am to remain in town for any length of time," Lady Lavinia told him. She turned to Elizabeth. "You were very wise, my dear, not to wear one of your muslins, for there's still a little chill in the air despite the sunshine. That outfit is just perfect for the day."

Colchester's approving gaze caused Elizabeth's cheeks to turn a rosy pink. His smile broadened. "I agree. Absolutely perfect," he said. "Shall we go?"

She left the room on the arm he held out for her, then allowed him to assist her into the waiting curricle. As he took the reins, the tiger jumped onto his perch behind and they set off at a moderate pace, Colchester silent for once as he concentrated on keeping a girm control of the fresh horses until they were clear of the traffic of Upper Grosvenor Street, had crossed Park Lane, and entered the park.

"Though you told me this is your first visit to London, Elizabeth, you seem completely at ease, so I assume that it is not your first ride in a curricle." He was delighted that she was not a scared ninny like so many of the young girls.

"Not only have I ridden in a curricle frequently, but I am also quite proficient at driving one," she professed proudly. "These past twelve months I have spent with my stepson and his wife. I believe you know Robert, the new marquess?"

Colchester nodded, as he could claim a slight acquaintance with him.

"After his father's death," she continued, "Robert made many innovations at Dewsbury House, and for his own pleasure he bought a curricle. Sybil was not in a condition to travel in it with him, so he used to take me for rides, and when I showed an aptitude, he taught me to drive."

"He did, did he?" Colchester sounded a little grim. "When I see him next I must commend him on his bravery. There are few men who would dare let a woman take the reins of any carriage, let alone something as light as this. I suppose you ride to hounds, also."

"As a matter of fact, I do when in the country. I have always been considered an excellent rider," she told him, turning cold eyes in his direction until she saw his teasing grin and she, too, had to smile. "Shame on you! You were deliberately leading me on to make me admit my indiscretions, sir."

"It was a temptation I couldn't resist," he admitted. He looked toward an approaching carriage. "As you have not as yet met very many people, I suggest you tell me when you want me to stop to speak to someone. I, on the other hand, know everybody, and do not intend to share you, so I'll just nod and drive by my acquaintances."

It was a delightful, sunny afternoon, and though so early in the Season, it seemed that half the *ton* had decided to take the air. Elizabeth sat back, happily oblivious to the stir she was causing, for Colchester had not been known to take any young lady for a ride in the park in many years.

"Is Dewsbury still in town?" Colchester asked.

"No. He came up on business when we first arrived, but he can't bear to be away from Sybil for very long, and he just dotes on his baby son, a delightful child who is the image of his father." Her face wore a happy glow as she remembered the youngster's antics.

"You seem to be fond of children, Elizabeth. I'm surprised you never had one of your own in three years of marriage."

"As my husband already had three grown children, it was of little importance to either of us," she replied rather abruptly.

It had been of importance, of course, but under the circumstances, quite impossible. A child would have pleased her husband, she knew, and it would have been someone of her very own to love, but as time passed and his children became fond of her, their affection had filled the void for her to some extent.

Dismissing thoughts of her late husband, she sat back and looked at the trees; some were already covered in light-green leaves and others just bursting into bud. She was enjoying herself enormously, for this was the first time in a while she had a chance to relax.

Since her arrival in London, all of her time and energy had been devoted to making the drawing room, dining room, and hall of the house more attractive, as quickly as possible, and in this she had succeeded beyond all expectation. The family she had hired had accomplished the renovations with unusual speed and expertise. The dark hangings and covers had been discarded, and in their place were soft pastel florals and stripes on light-cream backgrounds. Accumulated dust and grime had been removed from chair arms, sideboards, and tables, to reveal the mellow colors and rich grains of the woods. Carpets that had, over the years, achieved an indeterminate hue, had been expertly cleaned by other members of the Ramsbottom family, and their rich colors now graced the gleaming floors and complimented the glowing furniture.

Next would come the bedrooms, but first Elizabeth needed a rest, a time to enjoy herself, to breathe the fresh spring air . . . and to receive the flattery and compliments of handsome young men who would never know that this was the first time in her life she had listened to such delightful nonsense.

"Are you ladies taking a rest this evening, or have you accepted an invitation?" Colchester asked as they turned once more into Upper Grosvenor Street. "I don't recall where Mama said she was expected."

"We're to attend a musical evening at the home of Lord and Lady Jerome, I believe." She saw his pained frown. "I assume such entertainment is not quite to your taste, sir?"

He shook his head. "It is not the kind of thing I enjoy as a rule, but one never can tell. You know me a little better now. Do you think you could possibly bring yourself to call me David just once before you leave me?" he begged.

"I think so . . . David." She'd wanted to all afternoon, but hadn't felt she could until he asked her again. "And you now have my permission to call me Elizabeth," she told him with an impish smile.

"Can we do this again tomorrow afternoon?" he asked. "By the color in your cheeks it did you a great deal of good."

Apparently he would not attend the musicale even for her, but she was so glad he wanted to see her again. Not wishing to seem too eager, she nodded gravely as he helped her down from the carriage.

"Thank you, my dear. It was delightful. Two o'clock again?" he asked.

"Yes, David," she said, and turned to walk up the steps, not quite able to understand why she felt so light, as if her feet had wings. For once she failed to thank the footman who held open the door for her—she didn't even see him.

Colchester did come to the musicale that evening, accompanying his mother and Sir James Moorehead, and he made sure that they could all sit together, placing himself by the side of Elizabeth.

He took her driving the next afternoon, and for the next week he saw her at least once each day, either driving her in the park, having tea in her home when she was receiving, or at some affair or other at night.

Lady Beresford wanted very much to go to Vauxhall Gardens. She had been the previous year, enjoyed the music and, protected by her friends, the air of abandonment and gaiety seldom seen elsewhere. Lord Axminster, a good friend of Sir James, was to join the party and escort Lady Lavinia. His son, Michael, one of the young men who clustered around Pamela, would have the pleasure of escorting her. They were to take two carriages, Elizabeth going with the Beresfords in their carriage, and Lord Axminster taking his son and the two other ladies in his carriage.

The evening turned out to be quite balmy, and for once Elizabeth chose to wear black, a gossamer gown in gauze and lace, studded with silver glass beads, with a low neckline and only the tiniest of puff sleeves. Because it was a little more daring than she had envisioned it in Madame Gerard's, she had her abigail arrange a fine wool lace shawl over her head and shoulders in the style of a mantilla.

The Beresford party, by arrangement, arrived a little early and the coachman walked their horses while they sipped sherry in Elizabeth's drawing room.

"You look enchanting, *señora*," David murmured, noting her flush of pleasure at his words. "I have seen the mantilla worn many times, but never with such a devastating effect."

"I'd forgotten you were in the fighting in Spain and France. It must have been very exciting." She recalled how her stepson, Robert, had wanted to buy a commission, but his father would not permit it.

"I suppose it was, in a way," he said, serious now, "but it was also frightening, dangerous, and though necessary, very disillusioning." He stroked her cheek with his bare fingertip. "Some time I may talk to you about it, but not tonight. Tonight is a night for moonlight and magic and danger of another sort, unless we are very, very careful."

By now Elizabeth was used to feeling strange stirrings inside when David looked at her in a certain intense way, as he was doing now. "I've heard that Vauxhall Gardens are dangerous for an unprotected female alone, but you will be with me this evening," she said, opening the black lace fan she carried and looking at him over the top of it.

"Ah, yes, but who will protect you from me, my lovely Elizabeth?" His sandy eyebrows were raised over glinting blue eyes.

Lady Beresford interrupted them. "Are you ready, my dears? I understand that the Axminster carriage has arrived and we must be on our way. I'm sure my son has already told you how very charming you look, Elizabeth. Black looks better on you than it does on most people."

She motioned them to go ahead of her, and once everyone was settled, the two carriages started out.

They had reserved a box not far from the bandstands and were able to watch people in various styles of dress promenading by. After partaking of a light supper, Lady Beresford decided she would like to walk around for a while, and the party set out to stroll through the tree-lined, torchlit walkways.

"I believe we shall get the best view of the fireworks from over there," Lady Beresford asserted, and started out in the direction she was pointing, clinging firmly to Sir James' arm and tugging him along.

The crowds had already separated them from the others, but they had anticipated this and arranged to meet back at their box in an hour's time. Elizabeth became concerned, however, when she could no longer see Lady Beresford. "David, you're taller than me, can you see your mother and Sir James?" she asked a little anxiously.

"I think they went in this direction," he declared, steering her toward a narrower footpath to his left.

Suddenly, Elizabeth realized they were completely alone, and there was an expression on David's face that alarmed her. "Please let's go back, David," she asked as he drew her into his arms.

"In a moment," he murmured as his lips nibbled gently on hers, then captured them completely.

The warm feeling inside her had turned into a throbbing ache, and she no longer felt shame as her arms crept around his neck. Though she knew it was wrong, she wanted this sweetness to go on forever.

When he finally lifted his head, he was breathing heavily. He looked at the rapid movement of her breasts as she also fought for breath, her bee-stung lips, and the glow in her eyes. "You're right, my love, we must go back before I do something I shouldn't. Just tell me one thing, though. Didn't Dewsbury ever kiss you?"

"Not very often, and never like that," she whispered.

Colchester looked her over carefully, gently re-arranging the mantilla where he had pulled it out of place. As his fingers brushed her bare shoulders, she gasped. Finally coming down to earth, she picked a twig off his shoulder and straightened his cravat.

As they walked back to the still-crowded promenade, they suddenly realized that the firework display had been in progress for some time.

"I think we'd better make our way back to the box, my love, and wait for the others there," David suggested. "I, for one, have had all the excitement I can take for one night."

In complete agreement, Elizabeth slipped her hand

into his arm and allowed him to lead her back the way they had come, and in a few moments they saw the Trevelyan ladies, with their escorts, just a little ahead of them.

They entered the box together, Pamela quite excited at seeing her first fireworks. "Michael found the very best place to watch them from, Elizabeth. I wouldn't have missed it for anything," she chattered. "Aunt Lavinia said they were the best she'd ever seen."

Lady Beresford and Sir James arrived just then, and in the loud protestations of each that theirs had been the better location, no one seemed to notice how quiet Elizabeth and David were.

Soon the crowds started to thin, the entertainment was over, and the four couples headed back to their carriages. The Beresford carriage dropped Elizabeth off first, then headed for Colchester's lodging, but before he got out, Lady Beresford put a hand on her son's arm.

"I heard a rather disquieting rumor this evening that I think you should know about. Why don't you join me for breakfast in the morning in my bedchamber?" she suggested.

Colchester raised a curious brow but agreed to be there at ten o'clock.

"Will you have tea or coffee, my love?" Lady Beresford, looking very elegant in a pale-pink frilled wrapper, was seated at a round table by the window of her extremely feminine bedchamber, sipping her first cup of tea of the day. She pointed a dainty hand toward a cherry table that held china plates and several covered silver dishes. "And help yourself. There are braised kidneys, ham, bacon, poached eggs, toast . . ."

"Coffee for me, please, but at this hour I couldn't look a poached egg in the eye, Mama," Colchester protested, taking some kidneys and ham. "What kind of a rumor was it that you heard?"

She made no answer until he was seated across from her. "You seem to be more interested than usual in the 'willful widow,' as you called her once, if I remember rightly," she said. "Many of my friends have mentioned how special your attentions seem to be."

"I guessed it would be the *on-dit* before long," David said, sounding slightly bored. "I find her attractive and enjoy her company, of course."

"I'm afraid you're a little behind the times, David." Lady Beresford hated to be the bearer of bad news, but he must be told. "This week the *on-dit* is about Elizabeth Trevelyan and her late husband. The gossip is about Dewsbury's will, in which he apparently said she was barren, the implication being that he wanted more children and tried for three years without success. His ability is proven by his other three children."

"That's a rather strange thing to put into a will, don't you think?" he suggested, frowning.

"They say it was why he left her the use of the town house, that she'd not remarry, 'because of her proven inability to produce heirs,' or something like that." She saw him close his eyes as though to shut out the bad news, and knew that he must be in love with the chit. If it was true, it was a good thing he'd found out before it was too late.

Colchester rose to his feet, dropping his serviette on the table. "Would you excuse me, Mama? I find I'm no longer very hungry," he said, kissing her cheek lightly, then striding from the room.

When he saw Barnes' surprised face, he realized that he had walked the mile or so from the Colchester town house to his lodging quite blindly, lost in thoughts of Elizabeth. Until now he had not realized how deeply he felt about her, having known her such a very short time.

"I'll be in the library, Barnes, and I don't want to be disturbed for anyone," he said curtly.

On reaching that room, he closed the door, then removed his jacket, loosened his cravat, and checked the brandy decanter. Seeing it half-empty, he went to a cupboard and brought out a fresh bottle and a clean glass. He stretched out in an easy chair, glass and bottle beside him, then systematically emptied and refilled the glass until he could no longer feel the pain.

After the events of last evening, Elizabeth was looking forward more than ever to seeing David. She put on her prettiest lavender muslin gown and was waiting for him to call and take her for a drive, as he'd promised, at two o'clock.

When half-past two came, and with it calls from some of her aunt's and Pamela's friends, she escaped to her bedchamber, complaining of a very real headache. Lavinia and Pamela offered to cancel their plans for the evening, but Elizabeth insisted they must go without her, that all she needed was a good night's sleep.

By the following morning she had decided this must be David's way of telling her he regretted that kiss, and she had read into it more than he intended.

Determined not to sit around moping, she surprised everyone by coming down to breakfast, and if she was a shade paler than usual, it was thought that perhaps a trace of her headache still remained.

"I shall need the carriage this morning, for I've decided to call on the Ramsbottom family and get them started on refurbishing the bedchambers, beginning with the master suite. Did you plan to go out? Can I drop either of you anywhere?" Her voice was determinedly cheerful and her smile a little too bright.

"The master suite?" Pamela asked. "But that's your bedchamber. Where are you going to sleep?"

"In the room next to it. I've already got the maids busy on giving it a thorough cleaning and airing." She wrinkled her nose. "It smelled every bit as musty as downstairs did when we first arrived here, but I'll soon have it usable."

Neither of them needed the carriage, so Elizabeth made an early start, returning around noon with so many bolts of fabric it took all four footmen to carry them up the stairs to the master suite.

An hour later, the younger Mr. Ramsbottom knocked on the back door and was shown upstairs, and when the first callers of the afternoon started to arrive, Elizabeth, with her hair resembling a black mop head, and with smuts on her face, was helping him pull down hangings heavy with dust.

One of the callers was a rather pale-looking Colchester, who took a seat in the drawing room, accepted a cup of tea, and inquired after Elizabeth.

"I trust that she is not indisposed?" he asked Lady Lavinia, who had not herself seen her sister-in-law since noon.

"No, my lord. She was out most of the morning selecting fabrics to refurbish the master bedroom. I've sent word to her that you have called." Lady Lavinia was quite surprised that Elizabeth had not put in an appearance by now, but assumed her sister-in-law knew what she was doing. When he turned his attention to Pamela, Lavinia slipped out and hurried upstairs.

She found Elizabeth covered in a huge apron and a great deal of dirt.

"Are you not joining us for tea, Elizabeth?" she asked. "You know that Colchester has called, don't you?"

"Yes, I know, Lavinia, but I'm too busy to come down today. Please convey my regrets and tell him I'll see him next time he stops by." She turned around quickly, but not before Lavinia had seen the tears in her eyes.

Colchester did not appear at all put out by Elizabeth's message, stayed the usual length of time, and before he left, he invited Pamela out for a drive the following afternoon.

4

COLCHESTER WAS NOT present at the small dinner the Trevelyans attended that evening, and Lady Lavinia, seeing the strained look on Elizabeth's face, refrained from making any comment. Pamela had not, however, learned the art of tactfulness, and when they were in the carriage on their way home, she broached the subject.

"Have you and Colchester had a tiff, Elizabeth?" she asked forthrightly. "Before he left this afternoon he invited me to drive with him tomorrow, and I was wondering whether I should do so."

"Of course you should if you enjoy his company," Elizabeth replied, a little too quickly. "He has no particular obligation to me."

"But you've been together a good deal. I had thought . . ." She paused, as if wondering how to express herself.

"Whatever it was that you thought, it must have been your imagination," Elizabeth snapped, then saw the reproachful look in Lavinia's eyes. "I'm sorry, my love," she said, leaning forward and taking the younger girl's hand in her own. "I must have done too much work today, for I feel like a weary old crosspatch. The thought of sinking into my warm featherbed is most enticing."

Conversation was desultory at best after that, and when they were deposited at their front door, the three ladies were in agreement in their desire to retire immediately.

But once abed in the strange bedchamber she would be using until the master suite was refurbished, Elizabeth found it impossible to fall asleep. She told herself that it was the room, which had not quite lost its musty odor, and that she had become overtired by her exertions earlier in the day, knowing all the while that it was because of the wounded feeling deep inside.

If David's attentions had not been so pronounced when last they were together at Vauxhall, she might not feel so hurt at his failure to appear for the promised drive. Surely he could have sent word if something unforeseen had prevented his attendance.

This, of course, was the reason she had refused to see him when he paid a call this afternoon. For him to then turn around and invite Pamela to drive with him seemed to indicate his complete lack of regard for her feelings.

Well, if that was how he felt, she would not let him discover how much he had hurt her. There were plenty of other gentlemen who had been interested in her but had backed off when they saw Colchester's persistence. Tomorrow she would show him how little she cared, for she would be there when he came for Pamela, and she would look him in the eye, and she would . . .

At this point Elizabeth buried her head in the pillow and gave way to tears.

It was inevitable that Elizabeth and Colchester would meet some time face to face, and when they did, it was as though nothing had happened between them. They were extremely polite to each other, and as the days went by, he continued to call at the house, but now it seemed it was Pamela he came to visit.

Pamela had somehow overcome her habitual lateness and was always ready and waiting when Colchester arrived to collect her. By the time they returned, the drawing room was always filled, as it was this particular day, with several female visitors and an excessive number of gentlemen who seemed only too eager to pick up where Colchester had left off with Elizabeth.

"I understand you enjoy riding, my lady," Sir Edgar Lovell remarked as he bent low over her hand. "If you would care to join me one morning but have no mount,

I'd be delighted to bring a gentle mare along for you."

"You are too kind, my lord," Elizabeth replied sweetly. There was something a little too patronizing about Sir Edgar, but she did not intend to discourage him as yet. "I have been so busy that there has been little opportunity for early-morning rides, so I have not yet completely set up my stable in town. I do not believe, however, that I would be comfortable on a gentle mare, sir."

"She's used to a mount with much better performance, I'll be bound," Sir Charles Harkness interposed with a hearty laugh. "Better let me mount her when she's ready."

Colchester was standing with his back to the group surrounding Elizabeth, but at Sir Charles' innuendo he turned swiftly and glared so angrily at the speaker that Sir Charles muttered something unintelligible and moved to the other side of the room.

Too innocent to read any hidden meaning in Sir Charles' remarks, Elizabeth stared at Colchester with a look of surprise that quickly turned to scorn. How dare he show such disapproval of her acquaintances! She inclined her head, unsmiling, then turned to the door to greet a new arrival.

"Sir Archibald, how very nice to see you," she exclaimed as she moved toward the newcomer. "We quite thought you had forsaken us; it must be all of four days since you honored us with your presence."

The newcomer's chest puffed visibly at her words and he patted her upper arm in a familiar manner. "Been in the country on business, my dear," he volunteered. "Just got back this very morning and came just as soon as that valet of mine could put me to rights. Knew you'd be missing me."

He made as though to detain her, and Elizabeth's gracious smile appeared as she eased her arm out of his grasp and started toward another lively group when a maid appeared at his elbow with a glass of sherry on a tray.

"Not so fast, my dear lady." Sir Archibald Grover was not to be got rid of so easily. "Thought perhaps you'd like to step out into the garden for some air. A little stuffy in here after the country, you know.''

"What a good suggestion, sir," Elizabeth rejoined, "but I must first say good-bye to my friends."

Relieved that some guests happened to be leaving at that moment, she swept graciously into the hall to bid them *adieu*, then made her way to the small room she had set aside for her own use and sank into the comfortable chair by the fire.

It seemed to her that their friends had changed of late. When they first arrived in town, there had been quite a number of pleasant young men just down from university, and several quite charming ones a little older, always in attendance either here or at their friends' entertainments.

At about the time Colchester had taken her in dislike, these gentlemen had seemed to start drifting away and the older ones like Sir Archibald, Sir Edgar, and Sir Charles had taken their place. They were quite charming, of course, but they laughed a lot at their own jokes, which she did not find in the least amusing, and they frequently tried to touch her and to get her on her own.

Aside from Colchester and some of Pamela's true friends, their drawing room seemed to be filled each afternoon with these world-weary gentlemen. She readily admitted to herself that she flirted with them, sometimes quite abominably, but that seemed the only thing to do, particularly when Colchester was watching.

She was still pondering the matter some half-hour later when Lavinia came looking for her.

"You can come out now, Elizabeth," her sister-in-law said dryly. "They've all gone and it's time I went up to stretch out for a while and then change. Robert should be arriving at any time."

"Is this constant round of entertainment becoming too much for you?" Elizabeth asked, noting a slight strain around Lavinia's eyes.

"No, not at all. I haven't had such a good time since I was a girl. It's you I'm worried about. You're looking decidedly pale and peaky, and Madame Gerard will have to take in some of your gowns if you lose any more weight. Couldn't you leave some of the redecorating until the Season ends, perhaps?"

"No, I must do it now,' Elizabeth said sharply. "Robert will be able to see where his money is going when he comes. I hope he approves."

Lavinia moved toward the door. "He's sure to approve of the redecorating you've done, but I don't know how he'll feel about some of the so-called gentlemen we entertain these days." She looked grim. "I hate to appear critical, my dear, and I know you're enjoying some of what you missed as a girl, but must you make every dissolute rake in London welcome in your home? The way you flirt with them instead of sending them packing with their tails between their legs, I sometimes wonder who you're trying to impress."

"And I wonder where my meek little stepsister disappeared to," Elizabeth retorted, then regretted it, for she knew that Lavinia was right. "I'm sorry, my love. I know I wouldn't have allowed many of them in my home a month or so ago, but who would call if they didn't?"

She slipped her arm around Lavinia's shoulders and went with her to the upper floor.

"You don't have to take me on a tour of inspection," Robert protested. "I can see what a tremendous change you've made so far, and I know you've not spent anywhere near what I expected."

"Just come and take a look at the master bedroom suite and then we'll start dinner. After all, they're the rooms that will be of most importance to you and Sybil if you ever get a chance to live here," Elizabeth insisted.

The rooms were in a state of upheaval, but they stayed long enough for Elizabeth to ask Robert a few private questions.

"I know you've been out of town a great deal, but I've been wondering if anything has happened that I don't know about," she asked gravely.

"I've been here often enough to know that you've been

the subject of gossip almost since you arrived," he told her seriously, easing her into the one chair in the room that was still intact while he perched on the edge of the bed. "I wasn't unhappy when I heard that Colchester was interested in you, but now he's switched over to Pamela, I can't say I'm too pleased. She's far too too young and naïve for him."

Ignoring that remark for the moment, Elizabeth asked, "What kind of gossip has been going around?"

He sighed heavily. "I hate to tell you this—and I wouldn't now unless you had asked—but you're being called the 'willful widow.' "

"That's absurd," Elizabeth said emphatically. "I know that some of the old dowagers don't like it because I won't sit with them at balls, and don't approve of my going out of black so soon, but I've never danced, though I've longed to so many times."

"It's very difficult, I know. But gossip is what most of these old girls thrive on. You have been willful in that you've taken a sudden liking to having your own way since my dear papa passed on." He paused to smile grimly at her expression of indignation. "However, I don't believe that has anything to do with the name you've acquired. Think about it for a moment. It's a play on words, I believe."

Elizabeth did think about it. With her raised elbow resting on the arm of the chair, and her chin in her hand she pondered, then she suddenly realized. "It's the will, isn't it?" she asked.

Robert shook his head sadly. "I'm afraid it is, and the only way it could have got out is by that miserable little solicitor deliberately leaking it." He got up, then squatted on the floor by the side of her chair, looking at her very seriously. "When you first came here, everybody was talking about the beautiful, charming young widow, and though you said you wouldn't marry again, you were high on the list of prospects for some of the older bachelors with nurseries still to set up—Colchester, for instance."

"So that was why he suddenly stopped seeing me," she murmured. "He thought I couldn't give him the heir he must have. He could at least have told me."

Robert bent and kissed her cheek. "I'm sorry to bring you such news, but it's one of the reasons I came to town this time. The other is to see that slimy Josiah Jenkins, give him a piece of my mind, and take the rest of my legal business away from him."

"You'd already taken some of it away?" Elizabeth asked.

He nodded. "I'm sorry, love, but that's probably why he was so vicious."

Elizabeth rose slowly. "Let's have dinner. Lavinia and Pamela will wonder where we've got to. Let me tell them myself in my own way, would you?"

He offered his arm. "If that's what you want, my dear," he agreed.

The coming-out ball for the youngest daughter of the Earl and Countess of Bradenton was a lavish affair held in the magnificent ballroom of their Grosvenor Square town house.

Lady Lavinia had now become quite a good card-player, and at Elizabeth's insistence, she had joined her cronies in the card room.

Standing or sitting at the side of the ballroom was no longer a problem for Elizabeth, as there was always some rake or other, usually several, willing to join her; and though she laughed and flirted outrageously with them, it was nothing more than an act, for she was, in fact, becoming increasingly bored and was considering retreating to her parents' home in the country for a much-needed recuperation.

Colchester had seen her in the supper room, surrounded by the usual oafs who accompanied her wherever she went. He told himself he was thankful he had stopped his pursuit of her before she revealed her true colors, for he had watched her flirt with more than a dozen dandies and rakes. By comparison, Pamela was a much more sensible choice, but with a stepmother such as Elizabeth, her reputation was much in danger.

When Elizabeth stayed on, finishing her glass of ratafia

after the others left for the ballroom floor, he saw his chance.

"Madam," he started as Elizabeth suddenly became aware of his presence, "I have been meaning to talk to you for some time in regard to your wanton behavior."

Elizabeth, thinking at first he was coming over to ask her how she was, started at his words, then stiffened in anger. "I fear you must have had too much to drink at Lord Bradenton's private bar, my lord. Please excuse me."

She rose to leave, but he barred her way, holding her arm in a firm grasp.

"There is just one thing I would say to you, madam. I believe you have a care for your stepdaughter, despite your willful way. If you wish her to make a suitable, happy marriage, I would suggest you consider the damage you are doing to her reputation by your own questionable conduct."

A party entered the room and Elizabeth slipped out of Colchester's grip swiftly and brushed past him, then turned. "You are being most insulting, my lord. I would never harm Pamela. But can you say the same thing?"

He looked at her long and hard, then realized that people were watching and allowed her to walk gracefully away from him.

The room was hot and airless, for the Prince Regent was expected and, knowing his dislike of the night air, no one dared open a window. A cotillion had just started, so Elizabeth was sure that Pamela would be occupied for some time. Excusing herself from Sir Edgar's pawing attentions, she exited the ballroom in the direction of the ladies' retiring room, then took a narrow passageway and found herself at last in the garden, where she could breathe the sweet air.

Some torches had been lit on the pathways in case the romantically inclined chose to wander, and Elizabeth quickly found herself a secluded bench, beyond the range of a torch, and settled down to enjoy the evening air. She could hear faint murmurings and giggles, and was thankful that her iron-gray gown would not be noticed in the deep shade of the bench.

"So this is where you wait for me, my dear." Sir Archibald Grover, wandering through the gardens in search of some plaything, had found exactly what he wanted.

With a little squeal of dismay, Elizabeth jumped up from the bench, but Sir Archibald was too swift for her and in a moment she was held in a firm embrace from which she could not escape no matter how she struggled.

She felt his rough hand grasp the bodice of her gown, and she kicked with all her might in the direction of his pantaloon-covered leg. To her amazement the hand was withdrawn and she was miraculously free. A glance indicated, however, that Sir Archibald was firmly clutched in the grasp of someone much bigger than himself.

"If I ever see you try to molest this lady again, Grover, I promise you'll be in bed for a month recuperating."

The voice was unmistakably Colchester's. Elizabeth could not help wishing her rescuer had been almost anyone else but him. However, she was grateful and had to tell him so.

"Thank you, my lord," she said quietly. "It was foolish of me to wander out here alone, but I thought only to get some respite from the heat indoors."

As Sir Archibald slunk away, Colchester looked at her carefully to be sure she was really all right. Her gray eyes seemed huge in her white, frightened face, but he must have arrived in the nick of time, for she seemed to be otherwise unharmed.

"I don't think you'll have any more trouble with him, but if you do, just let me know and I'll deal with it," he said gruffly. She looked so small and helpless that all he wanted to do was draw her into his arms and comfort her. "Perhaps you'd better stay here for a few minutes longer until you get some color back in your cheeks, or there'll be even more rumors circulating about you," he suggested as he steered her to the seat she had previously occupied and sat beside her.

He was being kinder to her than he'd been since that night in Vauxhall Gardens, and Elizabeth felt her heart start to beat faster at his closeness. When he reached for her hand and started to gently stroke it, she made no attempt to stop him and then suddenly his arm was around her and her head had been placed on his shoulder in the most comfortable position imaginable.

She felt his fingers touch the side of her breast and she gasped, then the next moment her head was tilted back and his warm lips were gently pressing on hers most persuasively, and she found her arms sliding automatically around his neck.

When his tongue started to lightly tease the corners of her mouth, she heard herself making a sound that was almost a purr, and she felt sure he must be able to hear how fast her heart was pounding.

He raised his head at last. They were both breathing heavily and Elizabeth's eyes looked almost dazed.

"I'm not going to apologize," he muttered, "for I think you enjoyed that as much as I did. I don't know what it is you do to me. I've tried and tried and I can't get you out of my mind."

Elizabeth did not quite understand what was happening, but she was sure his kiss had not been something casual, stolen in the darkness.

"I need you, Elizabeth, more than I've ever needed a woman before," he murmured. "I would look after you, see that you lacked for nothing. I have a little house in Chelsea where we could meet, spend weekends together."

Something started to stir in Elizabeth. At first she couldn't believe that he was asking her to be his mistress. After moralizing about her behavior, he now was suggesting that she go further than even he had imagined.

Carefully she drew herself out of his arms. He watched her under half-closed lids as she stood, then drew herself to full height.

Taking a deep breath, she began, "My dear Lord Beresford, earlier this evening you soundly berated me for what you felt was improper behavior on my part. Let me tell you here and now that I have never been so insulted in all my life. Even Dewsbury at his worst had nothing of your gall, sir."

His eyes looked sad and his voice held a wistful note as he told her, "I intend no insult, my dear. If I could offer you more, I believe I would do so. Don't turn it down, please. Think about it awhile, for only an old man with children and grandchildren could wed you, and I can't bear to think of you with another old man."

Suddenly Elizabeth could stand no more. She was so angry she stamped her foot and regretted it immediately as her slipper was soft and the paving stone very hard.

"How dare you?" she protested. "How dare you say such things to me? You're so smug and self-righteous, but you don't know what you're talking about."

With a strangled sob, she swung around and hurried back to the ballroom.

Colchester stood in the shadow and watched her retreating back until he saw her enter the house. Without bothering to even thank his hosts or say any good-byes, he left the ball.

He hoped she would think on it carefully when she was over her first reaction, for tonight he had realized how very much he wanted her—and that was the only way he could have her.

After spending a sleepless night, Elizabeth realized that she couldn't face meeting Colchester right away, and decided to accept her mama's insistent invitation that she pay them a short visit. It was running away, she knew, but by noontime she had convinced herself that it was not a cowardly retreat but an organized withdrawal so she could reassemble her forces and then attack from a position of strength.

When she informed Lavinia of her plans, that lady secretly sent a note to her nephew, Robert, for she did not at all like the idea of Elizabeth hiring a post chaise for the journey, and she and Pamela would need the town carriage for their use in Elizabeth's absence. It was, in any case, too light a vehicle for such a journey.

5

THE JOURNEY FROM London to her parents' home in Warwickshire, not far from Leamington Spa, proved to be most tedious for Elizabeth, accompanied as she was by only a shy young maid. As Pamela and Lavinia had more need of the services of the abigail, she had selected the most likely of the new servants, but the girl was looking decidedly pale by the time they stopped at a coaching inn for the night.

The footman she had sent inside came back with a portly innkeeper.

"I have a very comfortable bedchamber for your use, my lady, and my wife has already started airing the linens," he assured her. "If you'd care to step into the private parlor, I'll bring you a mug of mulled wine to take the chill off, and I've some fresh salmon and a steak-and-kidney pudding straight from the pot, if it takes your fancy."

Elizabeth allowed him to help her out of the carriage and they entered a comfortable old establishment that appeared to be quite popular, as there were a number of tables occupied in the public dining room and loud voices could be heard from the direction of the public bar.

As she followed the innkeeper along the passageway, a tall figure in top hat and caped coat stepped aside to allow her to pass, then a deep voice called, "If it isn't Elizabeth Danville. It must be more than four years since I set eyes on you, my dear. How are you?"

"It's more than four, my lord," Elizabeth answered,

pleased to see an old friend from the days before she
was married to Dewsbury, "and I'm very well, though a
little chilled right now. Were you leaving?"

"I was just informed that the last private parlor has
been taken by a lady, and if you're the one, then
perhaps I can join you. I'm in a bit of a hurry, as I'd like
to get home before midnight." He was about
Elizabeth's age, boyish-looking still, and removal of his
top hat revealed a head of tawny-colored hair above
bright-blue eyes.

"Of course you may join me, George. I'd welcome
the company, for it's been a wearisome dull journey
thus far," she told him. "I'm going home to see Mama
and Papa, but I'd rather stay the night here than risk the
dangers of a journey after dark."

"Very wise, my dear," he murmured as the innkeeper
showed them into a cosy parlor. She removed her pearl-
gray velvet bonnet, and he suddenly became aware of
the fact that she was somberly garbed for a lady of her
age, despite the expensive cut of her charcoal-gray
carriage gown. "You're not in mourning, are you,
Liza? Seems like only a year or two since you left to get
married."

The sound of the nickname her friends had always
used brought a warm, nostalgic feeling to Elizabeth. It
had been a long time. A knock on the door heralded the
innkeeper once more, and she waited until he had placed
the mugs of hot mulled wine in front of them and left
the room, before answering her old friend.

"Just for your information, George, you are about to
dine with the dowager Marchioness of Dewsbury. You
were in France when my papa arranged the wedding, I
believe."

His eyes narrowed. "And Dewsbury was older than
Danville, according to what my mama told me when I
returned. Why did you let him do that to you, Liza?
You were no namby-pamby, shrinking female when we
used to race Tinker and Lightning. You took those

jumps as well, if not better, than John and Dick, and you were almost as good as I was then." He grinned, hoping she would rise to the bait as she always used to.

Elizabeth smiled sweetly. "I'm sure you recall the time you tried to jump Barnsley Creek because I had, and poor old Tinker just couldn't quite make it." Her laughter held much of her former mischief. "The water was low and you were covered from head to foot in black mud."

Unembarrassed, he joined in her mirth, then became serious once more. "You didn't answer my question, Liza. Why did you let him do that to you?"

She shrugged. "What else could I do, George? Papa was in dun territory and Dewsbury offered to bale him out. The twins were only twelve years old and Mama was constantly having fits of the vapors."

There was a knock on the door and the innkeeper entered once more, followed by a serving maid carrying a large tray, and steaming dishes were placed on the sideboard. He held up a warm plate with a flourish. "Would you like me to serve you, my lady, or would you prefer to help yourselves?" he inquired.

"We'll help ourselves, I believe." It was Sir George who answered. "And we'll have a bottle of your best French wine, if you please."

"Certainly, Sir George." With a bow the landlord hurried from the room.

By the time the landlord returned with the wine, George had placed a tempting plate of food in front of Elizabeth, and had filled a second, even larger one for himself. The hour was late, and they were both hungry, so they ate at first in comfortable silence, then Sir George's boyish face suddenly looked quite stern. "You know your papa's in the same straits again, don't you, Liza?" he asked, a little grimly.

Elizabeth stared at him in amazement. "Are you sure? Mama mentioned nothing about it when she wrote asking me to pay a visit." She frowned and took a sip of her wine. "When I come to think of it, though, she did sound rather insistent. But they know my situation. All I have is an annual allowance from Dewsbury and I've spent most of it in advance on gowns for the Season."

"He didn't leave you any money of your own, Liza?" George asked in some surprise.

Elizabeth's eyes looked wary for a moment. "No," she said. "He also left me the use of the London town house for the rest of my life, and both the allowance and the house are contingent on my not remarrying," she said quietly.

"You don't suppose your father's planning a repeat performance with you as the heroine once more?" Sir George eyed her closely. "Your mama told mine that he'd taken a number of trips into Wales recently."

"Wales?" Elizabeth asked disbelievingly. "Why on earth would he be going to Wales, of all places?"

"That's what I was wondering," George said, then placed a large hand comfortingly on hers. "It's probably nothing at all, so don't worry that very lovely head about it. You know, you grew into quite a beauty, Liza."

"Now, George, don't start that with me," Elizabeth warned. "You can't get romantic with someone who once put live frogs down your back. And what is more, I am by no means a beauty. By the side of my step-daughter, Pamela, I look almost a plain Jane."

George sighed. "That's the trouble with growing up with someone. They never forget all your old misdeeds," he said, studying her carefully. "Perhaps you're right. You don't have the features for classic beauty, but you're an extremely attractive woman, Liza." He rose. "If you'll excuse me for a moment, I'll see if the innkeeper has another bottle of this wine, and also try to get me a room for the night. If I'm successful, I'll escort you to your home in the morning."

"That's awfully nice of you, but you were trying to

get home by midnight tonight, weren't you?" she asked.

"That was before I found I might have the pleasure of such delightful company, my lady." He bowed low.

Elizabeth was gratified by her old friend's attention. "If it's not going to put you out too much, I'd be delighted to have your escort for the remainder of the journey. I'll not stay up much longer, though. The dinner and the wine have made me quite drowsy and I had thought of making an early start in the morning."

"What hour do you call early these days, Liza?" Sir George inquired, knowing that ladies of the *ton* frequently stayed in bed until noon.

"How does breakfast here at ten o'clock sound to you?" she asked. She had originally planned to leave much before that hour, but as he would probably stay up to finish the second bottle of wine, she did not want to rouse him too soon.

"Just right," he agreed. "I know an excellent inn where we can stop for luncheon and I'll have you home in the late afternoon."

The carriage turned off the highway and onto the private road leading up to Danville Hall. As they approached, Elizabeth viewed with rather mixed feelings the old manor house where she had lived for the first nineteen years of her life. She had only returned once before, a few months after Dewsbury had died, and she had spent some time this morning going over as much as she could recall of her conversations with her papa on that visit. He had been very concerned, or so she thought at the time, about how comfortably she would be able to live on the not-overly-generous allowance Dewsbury had provided.

Sir George Carlton's grave news regarding her family had come as surprise, for her mama had given no indication of monetary difficulties in her letter, though she had been most insistent that she pay them a visit. Because of Robert's generosity, she was arriving in the

splendor of the Dewsbury carriage, with its gleaming
dark-green lacquer and the family crest upon the door
panels. Tomorrow, after the coachman, footmen, and
outriders were rested, they would leave, and would
return for her whenever she sent Robert a note that her
visit was at an end.

As Sir George helped her to alight, the doors of the
hall were flung open and the twins ran down the steps
and into her arms, almost knocking her over with their
exuberance.

Over their heads she smiled ruefully at Sir George,
who had just declined refreshments. "I'll call on you
tomorrow morning early if I may, my dear," he said,
"and we'll go riding." Then he swiftly mounted and
with a brief salute galloped back the way they had come.

With Louise on one arm and Sylvia on the other, she
mounted the steps and entered the large hall.

"Papa's meeting with his man of business, and Mama
is having another of her fits of the vapors," Louise
informed her, "so why don't you come up to the old
nursery and have tea with us while you tell us all about
London?"

"Why not, indeed," Elizabeth said with a laugh,
thinking what a poor reception she would have had were
it not for her boisterous sisters. "If you'll give me a
moment to wash my hands and tidy myself up, I'll join
you there. Has my old bedchamber been made ready?"

"Oh, yes," they said in unison, and Louise added,
"The maids have been doing nothing else for two
days."

Elizabeth wasted little time in her chamber, for she
was as anxious to know everything that was happening
around here as the twins were to tell her. After dis-
carding her bonnet and tidying her hair, she splashed
her face with rosewater and patted it dry. The footmen
were already bringing in her baggage, so she instructed
Mary on what she should do, then walked along the
corridor to the old nursery.

The table in the window was laid with a fine tea of crumpets, with raspberry and strawberry jam, whipped cream, almond tarts, gingerbread, and rich plum cake.

Sylvia poured while Louise passed the cup to Elizabeth, and then they helped themselves to crumpets heaped with jam and cream. In appearance they were almost identical, with jet-black hair like their sister's, but their eyes were the brightest of blue. Sylvia was lively enough, but just a shade less exuberant than Louise, which was one of the ways their parents could tell which was which.

They were becoming very striking in appearance, though as yet only sixteen years old, and Elizabeth could not help but think how they would take London by storm when they had their come-out in two years' time. That was, of course, if their father's finances allowed them to do so.

"Will one of you tell me why Mama has the vapors again? Is she really ill or has something happened to upset her?" Elizabeth asked, grinning as both girls tried to answer her with their mouths filled with crumpets. "Don't choke. I can wait."

As usual, Louise spoke first. "Papa's keeping a tight hold on his purse strings again, and she can't have a new gown even though it's three months since she had one," she began. "We heard them having a big argument in Mama's bedchamber this morning, then Papa stormed out."

"I heard Papa say that you'd take care of everything, Liza, but Mama said you've scarce enough money to buy your own clothes at the price things cost in London," Sylvia volunteered.

"She's quite right, you know. Even though I'm in partial mourning, I had to have all new gowns for London," Elizabeth confirmed, "but when I was here a year ago, there appeared to be no problem. Have you any idea what happened?"

"Papa lost a lot of money at cards, then he played

again to try to win it back, but he lost that also," Louise said knowingly.

Elizabeth had to smile. "Now, Louise," she said lightly, "you know that Papa would be most upset if he realized you thought he'd done something like that. Where on earth did you get such a story?"

"She listens at doors," Sylvia interjected.

"I do no such thing, Sylvie. Was it my fault that I happened to be passing the drawing room when that awful man came to see Papa?" Louise asked. "And they shouldn't have shouted so loud if they didn't want anyone to hear."

Elizabeth passed her cup to Sylvia for a refill and helped herself to a piece of her favorite plum cake.

"Who was the 'awful' man?" she asked as a sinking feeling inside told her that Louise had the right of it. "And what did he want with Papa?"

"He was some kind of collector, he said, but I can't remember the word he used. And he said Papa would go to debtor's prison if he didn't pay up." Louise looked frightened. "Then Papa said he'd sell some jewelry and he went to London that day. That's when Mama had the vapors the first time."

"Stop looking so scared, the two of you," Elizabeth tried to cheer them up. "If Papa came back from London, he must have paid this man off, and all he has to do now is watch his pennies until more money comes in from the estates. This has happened before and it will probably happen again, but you two don't need money just yet, and Mama can manage without a new gown."

They looked much relieved and Louise asked the questions she'd been wanting to ask all through tea. "Are you seeing Sir George Carlton in London? Did he escort you here, and might you marry him, perhaps?"

"Of course not, to all three questions. Sir George and I have known each other practically since we were in leading strings, and he just happened to be staying at the inn I stopped at last night," she said, much amused at the conclusion they had jumped to.

"Did he ask you to have dinner with him?" It was Sylvia who wanted to know this time.

Elizabeth pretended to frown and ponder the question. "As a matter of fact, I believe it was I who asked him to dine with me," she told them, then laughed. "You see, I had reserved the last private parlor, and he was just about to leave when I arrived, so I asked him to join me."

Both twins looked disappointed, for they had been hoping a romance was brewing when they saw him ride up with the coach.

"But he said he was going to come to see you tomorrow," Louise stated with renewed hope.

"He was just being polite," Elizabeth told them. "He was anxious to reach home in time to change for dinner, so he wouldn't come inside, but it is usual, under such circumstances, for a gentleman to call the following day to assure himself that the lady is feeling no ill effects from her journey. It's similar to the way gentlemen call the day after a ball to be sure that the lady did not tire herself too much."

At the mention of a ball, two pairs of blue eyes lit up, and they spent the next half-hour asking her every question they could think of regarding the London Season. It had not occurred to them, of course, as it had to Elizabeth, that if their papa's pockets were to let, there would be no money for them to make their comeouts.

Dinner was an uncomfortable meal for Elizabeth. With Papa and Mama scarcely speaking to each other, it was left to her and the twins to keep up a light conversation. Her papa did, however, address Elizabeth when she first entered the room, dressed in one of her simpler gowns, a pale-lavender satin trimmed with dark-gray ribbons at the tiny puff sleeves, the neck, and cascading down the front from the high waist.

"You look very well, Elizabeth," he remarked, "and

do not appear at all fatigued after your journey. That's a dashed attractive gown you're wearing, but I'm surprised to see you still in mourning clothes."

"It is not out of respect for my late husband, I can assure you, Papa. Were I not living in London, I would have been out of mourning ages ago, but I did not want to occasion more gossip in the *ton* than I could help just at the time of my stepdaughter's come-out." Elizabeth noticed his frown at her first remark and continued to look him in the eye after she had finished speaking. He was the first to look away.

Elizabeth had visited her mama in her bedchamber earlier in the day, but all she could learn was that it was her papa who wanted her to come home.

She was facetiously wondering if he would like her to sell her fine gowns and give him the money, when he spoke to her again.

"I'd appreciate a private word with you in the library after dinner. You can have some tea in there when I have my port," he told her before lapsing into silence once more.

Elizabeth would have liked to have asked the twins if dinners were always as silent as this one, but the opportunity did not arise, for when her mother got up to go into the drawing room, her father rose also and escorted Elizabeth to the library.

Sir Edward helped himself to a generous glass of port, then went through the ceremony of preparing and lighting a cigar while Elizabeth waited impatiently to find out what this could possibly be about.

With puffs of smoke partially hiding him from her view, her papa finally addressed her.

"Dashed handsome young woman you've turned out to be, Elizabeth," he remarked, "and a good, dutiful daughter to boot. Raised the right way, that's what you were." He took a gulp of his port then reached for the decanter and refilled his glass. "While you've been gallivanting around London, I've been very busy these

last few months on your behalf. Can't say I don't look
out for my girl—no one can say that," he blustered.

He was obviously finding difficulty in getting to the
point, but Elizabeth really had been raised the right
way, so she waited in silence until he was able to say his
piece.

"I've found you a wonderful husband, my dear," he
said finally. "Not a marquess this time, but an earl with
twice as much money as Dewsbury had. You'll not have
to worry about clothes or jewelry; he'll dress you like a
queen. What do you say to that, eh?" He looked across
to where she sat calmly watching him.

"I don't want another husband, thank you, Papa,"
Elizabeth said softly.

"Of course you want another husband. Never heard
such nonsense," he was pretending outrage, almost
shouting now. "A young woman of your age can't
spend the rest of her life alone. I've arranged to take
you to see him. Pack a few pretty gowns and we'll leave
tomorrow afternoon. Wanted to take your mother
along, too, but she's not been feeling well lately."

"Where does this earl reside, Papa?" Elizabeth
couldn't keep the touch of sarcasm out of her voice.

"West of here a ways," he said. "We'll have Cook
pack a hamper so we don't have to stop at some squalid
inn and pay good money for inferior food."

Elizabeth almost laughed out loud. He didn't even
have the blunt to pay for a meal and probably intended
to drive through the night also.

"That's settled, then," he said firmly. "Just be ready
by two o'clock, for you know how I hate waiting
around while women preen their feathers."

"Nothing's settled, Papa." Elizabeth did not raise
her voice, but spoke slowly and clearly. "As I told you,
I have no intention of marrying again, so I will not be
traveling with you to see any prospective husband either
tomorrow or any other day. Now, if you will excuse me,
I will retire to my bedchamber."

As she rose to leave he glared at her, then snarled, "Sit down, my girl, I haven't finished."

Wearily, Elizabeth sat and waited for whatever else he had to say.

"This is the last chance I have to recoup my losses. He's an older man, not looking for heirs, and he's agreed to settle twenty thousand pounds on me the moment the vows have been exchanged. Without that money this family will starve to death," he said as Elizabeth sat unmoved.

"It won't be for too many years, the man's sixty-five already, so he'll be gone in a year or two and you'll be a very rich widow," he pleaded. "You can't let your family down for the sake of just a few years."

"You've already had your few years, Papa," she said, feeling her disgust rise. "You have the estates. There's more than enough income from them to keep the family in food and clothing. It's a good thing the estate is entailed and not yours to gamble away also."

"Only the hall and a few acres are entailed," he told her bitterly. "The rest of the estates have been sold to pay our debts. And who's been telling you lies about me gambling, I'd like to know? Got into some financial difficulties, that's all, like many another before me. No fault of mine," he claimed, blustering again. "Let's have no nonsense now about your not marrying again. Just you be ready by two o'clock, like I said, and I'll overlook your impertinence this time."

"Don't bother ordering out the carriage, for I'm not going with you, Papa," Elizabeth said sadly, and she got up once more to leave the room.

'You've got to come with me. Don't you understand? You're my last hope." He grabbed her shoulders and shook her. "Willful, you are, and disobedient, too. I never thought a daughter of mine would treat me like this after all I've done for her."

His grip on her slackened and somehow Elizabeth managed to pull herself out of his hands and ran from the room, not stopping until she was safely in her own bedchamber with the door locked and bolted. She half-expected him to come pounding on her door, but though she listened carefully, there was no sound to indicate that he had followed her.

Fortunately, she had told the maid she would not need her services this evening. She felt herself shivering, so she undressed swiftly and slipped under the warm covers, but her mind was too active to sleep right away.

Why had she not realized that her father's trips to Wales had been for such a purpose? After all, he'd made many trips to see Dewsbury before he had everything arranged four years ago. Even when he'd said he wanted to see her in the library, she had never dreamed that he was trying to marry her off again. No wonder her mama didn't want to talk to her. She knew what her husband was planning again, and couldn't warn her.

Exhausted, Elizabeth finally fell into an uneasy sleep, with no one to see her tossing and muttering as she dreamed Dewsbury was still alive, lying in the bed beside her and cursing her for something she didn't understand.

6

ELIZABETH AWOKE AS the first light of morning seeped into the room, and she thought at first that she was ill, for every bone in her body seemed to ache. As she became more conscious, however, she realized that her head was the culprit. Its throbbing had prevented her from sleeping soundly and left her exhausted.

Suddenly everything came back to her; the gloomy dinner last night, and the conversation with her papa in the library afterward. She knew there was nothing he could do to make her remarry, but the years of doing her father's bidding had left its mark, and she shuddered at what might have happened if she had been unable to fight him.

The room seemed airless and she threw back the covers and swung out of bed, shivering as she washed herself thoroughly in the cold water that had been brought the night before. Taking a black velvet riding habit out of the armoire, she quickly dressed, pulled on her riding boots, and opened her door to see if anyone was about. Hearing nothing, she ran swiftly down the stairs and out to the stables.

At this hour there was just one sleepy stable boy on duty, and Elizabeth, hearing a whinny to her right, turned to see a magnificent black stallion matching her gaze.

"What a beauty you are, sir," she said softly, "and you want some exercise just as much as I do."

"I wouldn't take 'im, milady," a young voice piped at her elbow. " 'E's not settled in properlike yet."

"Where are Ginger and Ladylove?" Elizabeth asked, seeing neither of her two favorites in their stalls.

"Master sort o' swapped 'em, milady, for Goliath 'ere. E's got good bloodlines, master says, but 'e's not a lady's mount, mum." The boy looked worried, for there was nothing else in the stable for her to ride other than a couple of ancient mares. She wondered what the twins were doing for mounts.

"Saddle him for me," she ordered.

"Don't think 'e'll take to a sidesaddle, milady." The boy was making a last attempt to stop her.

"That's all right. This skirt is full enough to ride astride. Saddle him," she ordered once more.

Obviously wishing someone else had been around who could countermand her order, he took out the stallion and slowly saddled him.

"I'm taking him out today, not tomorrow," Elizabeth said dryly. "I could have had him saddled myself five minutes ago."

Once mounted, she started to enjoy the morning. Goliath was quite spirited, but he'd probably been closed up in the stables too long. She cantered down the lane, then decided to let him have a gallop along the path that ran alongside the woods. Too late she realized that he was eager to go into the woods, and she soon found he was too strong for her—she simply couldn't hold him. Letting him have his head, she leaned low to avoid low branches, hoping that he'd tire before he caught a foot in a hole and stumbled. Then out of the corner of her eye she saw the white tail of a frightened rabbit as it ran toward the path.

Elizabeth had only enough time to feel Goliath's head come up as he reared violently, then she felt herself flying through the air toward a clump of trees.

"What do you mean you can't find her anywhere? She can't have just disappeared. And which twin are you, anyway?" Sir George Carlton was unusually irritated when he had arrived to go riding with Elizabeth and no one knew where she was. "Did she go for an early ride, perhaps? Are any of the horses missing?"

"The only one missing is Goliath, and Papa allows no one to ride him except himself, so she can't have gone riding. And I'm Louise, Sir George." She turned to look down the lane. "Goodness, there's Goliath now. Papa must have been thrown again."

"Papa's in the dining room with a headache and a bad temper, Louise. You don't suppose Elizabeth saddled him herself and took him out?" Sylvia had come from the direction of the house to join her twin.

Without a word, Sir George mounted his chestnut gelding and took off down the lane. When he came to the path by the side of the woods, he remembered it as a favorite spot of Elizabeth's for a good gallop in her younger days, and he soon spotted hoof marks in the soft earth. Recalling that he had seen some small scratches on the stallion's sides, he rode slowly into the woods, coming to a walk as he picked his way along.

Once he thought he heard something, but continued when the sound was not repeated immediately, then he heard the sound again, something like a low moan. Dismounting, he tied his horse to a stump and walked back.

He almost missed her as she lay in a dark thicket, the black of her riding habit blending with the shadows, but when another faint moan sounded, he was beside her, gently turning her over to see what condition she was in.

"Can you hear me, Liza?" he asked softly.

"Yes." Her voice was barely a whisper.

"Can you tell me where you hurt, love?" he urged.

"My head."

George's gentle fingers searched and found a fast swelling lump on the side of the temple.

"Do you hurt anywhere else?" He ran gentle hands over her as he asked, all the while watching her face to see if she winced.

"No, it's just my head," she moaned.

"Listen, Liza, I'm going to go back to the hall to get help. I won't be gone more than five minutes." As he spoke he started to get up.

"Don't leave me," she pleaded.

He knew he could carry her, for she was quite small and dainty, but he was frightened of doing her further injury. When she tried to lift herself up, he made a quick decision. She might hurt herself more if he left her. First he untied the gelding. It was known in the neighborhood, so if it didn't follow him, it would soon be found and sent home.

"Put your arms around my neck and see if you can hang on," he instructed as he slipped his own strong arms beneath her and raised her from the ground.

By the time they reached the hall, his muscles ached abominably, but he wouldn't allow anyone to take her and he carried her up the stairs and into the bed-chamber.

"Oh, dear." Lady Danville fluttered over her eldest daughter. "Do you think there is anything we should do before the doctor arrives? Someone went for him and he will be here momentarily."

Sir George had loosened the tight neck of her riding habit. "No, my lady, she's got a nasty bump on her head, but she is conscious, or at least she was when I found her." He turned as Sir Edward stormed into the room.

"Where is she? I'm going to give her a piece of my mind, taking out my stallion against my specific orders," he shouted.

Sir George stepped in front of him. "I think you'd best leave that for later, sir. She's in no condition for scolds right now." As he spoke, he was steering Sir Edward out of the room, then, firmly closing the door behind her father, he came back to see how Elizabeth was.

"Thank you . . . George," she murmured, to his profound relief, as he'd been unsure up to now if she knew who he was.

Once the doctor arrived, he examined her carefully in the presence of her mother and the girls' old nanny, and pronounced her suffering only from a slight concussion. Lady Danville had gasped when she saw blood on her daughter's thighs, and fearing internal injuries, the doctor had checked very thoroughly. Had she been a single girl, he would not have been at all concerned, but he knew her to be a married lady. He left with a puzzled frown on his face and instructions that she should stay in bed for a few days and be kept absolutely quiet. He promised to stop by the next day.

Tired after the events of the morning, Elizabeth had fallen into a light sleep and awoke to the comforting sight of Nanny sitting by the side of her bed, her knitting needles clicking away.

"Where were you yesterday, Nanny?" she asked.

The elderly woman's kind face broke into a big smile. "Why, I was just visiting a friend in the village, Miss Elizabeth. I came looking for you this morning, but you'd already gone out on that awful wild horse."

"He's not awful, really. He's just in need of a good, strong master, that's all." Elizabeth looked to see if there was anyone else in the room, then said, "Listen, Nanny, promise me you won't leave me alone with Papa. If he should tell you to leave, just slip into the dressing room, please."

"If that's what you want, missy, that's what I'll do," she promised. "You seem to be feeling a bit livelier. How's your head?"

Elizabeth grinned faintly. "Sore, but it was my own fault. I need another favor. If Sir George Carlton stops by, I must see him."

"Doctor's orders were no visitors, missy," Nanny said, doubtfully.

"I know, but he's different. He's the one who came looking for me and I must thank him." Elizabeth had always been able to persuade Nanny to help her.

"All right. As a matter of fact, I believe he's still here, for he did say he would stay until you finally awoke, to be sure you're all right. Proper worried he was." She smiled kindly. "Do you want me to fetch him?"

Elizabeth smiled and nodded slightly, and the old lady went out, returning almost immediately with George, who had a broad grin on his face.

"I knew I'd get to see you if I waited long enough. You really had me worried, Liza."

Elizabeth glanced to where she could see Nanny busying herself in the dressing room. "Listen, George," she whispered. "I need your help."

"Of course, love. Is something wrong?" he asked.

"Yes. As soon as I'm over this, I must get away—get back to London," she said softly. "The Dewsbury carriage was to have started back this morning. If it has, could you send someone after it and have them turn around and come back to wait for me at the Golden Lion just outside the village?"

"Of course. I'll go myself to be sure it's done properly, and I'll alert the landlord at the Golden Lion to take good care of them. What's the matter, Liza? Can you tell me?" He had realized at once that there was something seriously wrong and was eager to help.

"He's trying to marry me off again. I've said no, but I'm a little afraid, so I want to get away from here as soon as possible." She put a finger to his lips as she knew instinctively that he was about to emote something profane.

"You can trust me," he said quietly, then more loudly, "I'd better get out of here before Nanny throws me out, as she used to when I was a lot smaller." He bent swiftly and placed a light kiss on Elizabeth's cheek.

Nanny bustled forward. "I certainly will throw you out, young man, big as you are, if you get my patient excited. Just look at those flushed cheeks." She shooed him out of the door and closed it firmly behind her.

As Nanny settled down again by the side of the bed and picked up her knitting, she said, "It's funny, you know, Miss Elizabeth, most people go a little deaf as they get older, but I'm not one of them. And I can hear whispers louder than normal voices. You can trust me, too, my dear. I'll not let anything happen to you."

To Elizabeth, the journey back to London seemed to take no time at all, though doubtless the coachman and outriders would not have agreed with her.

Lady Lavinia and Pamela were a little surprised that she had traveled all that way for so short a stay, but she told them nothing of what had occurred, simply saying she had accomplished all that was needed. If they noticed the bruise on her head, concealed by a slight change of hairstyle, they made no mention of it.

Plans for the evening were to attend a musicale where Lady Porchester was presenting her protégée, whom she considered to be a gifted soprano. Although Elizabeth did not yet feel completely recovered, she decided she should put in an appearance there, but not go on to the ball Lady Lavinia and Pamela were to attend later.

Refusing the assistance of the abigail lest she notice and talk about her bruised forehead, Elizabeth dressed slowly and carefully, selecting a gown that fastened with tiny buttons down the bodice that she could step into rather than pull over her slightly aching head.

As they entered Lady Porchester's ballroom, now covered with rows of small gilt chairs, Elizabeth heard the orchestra tuning up and knew she had made a mistake in coming, but it was too late now. She sighed heavily.

"Are you sure you feel quite well, Elizabeth?" Lady Lavinia asked. "You've been very quiet ever since you returned to town. Perhaps the journey was too much for you; you looked quite exhausted when you came in last night."

Forcing a bright smile, Elizabeth reassured her. "I'm feeling fine, my dear Lavinia, really I am. I will confess, however, that the thought of listening to the squeal of those strings and the high notes of the probably screechy soprano does not quite put me in high alt."

"Then you'd better sit at the end of a row, near one of the doors so that you can creep out quietly if you should feel the need," Lavinia suggested. She raised her head and smiled at someone just behind Elizabeth. "Good evening, my lord. As you can see, my dear sister-in-law has returned from her visit."

Elizabeth was startled when she turned around and found herself face to face with Colchester. She dropped him a curtsy and he held her gloved hand just a little too long as he bent over it.

"I trust you had a pleasant stay with your family, my lady, though I had thought it was to be of a longer duration," he said, his eyes seeming to mock her. "Don't tell me, for I know it already. You could not bear to be away from such charming company a minute longer than necessary."

Elizabeth laughed softly, hiding the effort it cost her. "My lord, you have found me out. I simply could not bear to be away from my dear friends, so I just turned around and came back."

"I trust you will be going on to Lady Mansfield's ball afterward?" he asked. "And though I know you will not dance, I beg that you will allow me to sit out at least one with you?"

Before Elizabeth could answer, Pamela interposed, "My stepmama has decided to go directly home from here, my lord. Perhaps you can persuade her to change her mind and join us."

Lady Porchester was signaling for everyone to take their seats, and Elizabeth was grateful to find herself sitting at the very end of a row, with Colchester nowhere in sight.

As the music started, she realized what a mistake she had made in coming this evening. Her temple started to throb, and each time the soprano tried to reach a high note, she felt it like a knife cutting into her head.

As all eyes were on the makeshift stage, Elizabeth slipped quietly through the door to her left, which led into a small conservatory, and then into what appeared

to be a sitting room. She made her way past the potted
orange trees and flowering shrubs, anxious to get as far
as possible away from that dreadful noise. On entering
the sitting room, she closed the door quietly, then made
for a large wing chair by the fireplace into which she
sank gratefully, closing her eyes and resting her aching
head.

Colchester had been most distressed when he found
that Elizabeth had suddenly left for the country. His
suggestion had not been as improper as she so obviously
believed, for there were many widows of good family
who enjoyed such liaisons, a number of which lasted for
many years. Providing they were conducted with the
utmost discretion, society turned a blind eye and both
parties were still accepted as members of the *ton*.

After her firm rejection, he should, of course, have
discontinued his efforts, but he felt an urgency about
her that could not be controlled, and if he could not
marry her, he was determined to entice her into his bed
some other way.

His request to sit a dance out with her had been but
one way to maintain contact with the elusive widow,
and only their hostess's insistence that her guests take
seats immediately had prevented him from pursuing this
further.

He was less than enthusiastic about muscial evenings,
but was still trying to satisfy his mother's urgings, and
thinking to slip out of the room for a while once the
program started, he also had selected an end seat just
four rows behind Elizabeth. When he noticed her slip
out of the room quietly, he saw his opportunity to talk
to her once more.

After waiting five minutes, he quietly rose and exited
through a different door to the one Elizabeth had used.
Unlike her, he knew the house well and guessed that she
would be in either the conservatory or the room beyond.
He could not find her in the first chamber, but he

noticed the door at the end was closed and surmised that she was in the sitting room.

He made not a sound as he turned the knob and stepped into the room, closing the door quietly behind him. She looked so very vulnerable, resting there, that he almost turned around and crept out without disturbing her. He walked toward her and had turned to draw a chair close to hers when he heard her gasp.

"Don't be afraid, my dear." He tried to sound reassuring. "I just want to talk to you for a few minutes to try to make you understand that my offer was not intended to insult you in the slightest."

"Oh, no!" The pain in her head, which had eased somewhat, now started up again, and she unthinkingly pushed the hair away from her temple, revealing the dark bruise.

He was on his feet in a moment, bending over her, and not realizing what she had done, she shrank more deeply into the chair.

"Stop behaving like a shrinking violet, you silly girl," he snapped in his concern. "Let me see that bruise on your head."

His fingers were gently moving the hair away and he cursed softly. "No wonder you couldn't listen to that caterwauling in there! How did you do this?" he demanded sternly.

"I was thrown from a horse," she told him, "and had a slight concussion, but it's all right now except for occasional headaches."

"Would you like me to let your sister-in-law know and take you home?" he asked solicitously.

She shook her head, then winced at the effort. "They don't know anything about it, and I'd rather they did not. Would you mind opening the door, though, for you are putting me in a most compromising position?"

Without a word Colchester walked over and opened the door wide, then came back and sat in the chair beside her. The music could still be heard, but only faintly now.

"While I was away, I thought about your suggestion, and though I now realize that it is not really unusual, I'm afraid that I could never consider anything of the kind," she said quietly. "Please don't try to persuade me, my lord, for I shall not change my mind."

He looked at her long and hard. "I can see now that you won't, and I wish with all my heart that I could make the more traditional offer you deserve, but I must produce at least one heir, and . . ."

"And you heard some unpleasant gossip about my husband's will, decided I could not fulfill your needs," she said scornfully, "and dropped me like a red-hot coal."

He flushed. "I know I owe you an apology, but I came the next day to offer one and you refused to see me."

Her head still ached, but she had to get a few things off her chest. "At the time I knew nothing about the rumor, my lord, but you could have at least questioned me about its authenticity." Her eyes flashed angrily.

With a sardonic expression he asked, "Could you suggest how I might phrase such a question?"

It was Elizabeth's turn to be embarrassed, and she looked down to her lap and watched as his large bronzed hand covered hers.

She looked into his eyes and the tenderness in them made her heart flutter. "I don't know whether I'm b-barren or not," she said bravely. "You see, I never had the opportunity to find out."

Colchester racked his brain to find a tactful phrasing of his next question. "Do you mean that you're still a virgin? He was being purely malicious because of his own inadequacy?"

She nodded. "That's right," she said. "And if you still have doubts, you might try talking to my stepson, Robert, for though we have never discussed it in detail, I'm sure he is aware of the circumstances."

They suddenly realized that the music had stopped and even the clapping was tapering off.

Colchester was on his feet in a flash. "I'll slip out the back way before anyone gets here. You'd better rearrange your hair if you still don't want anyone to see that bruise," he said. "I'll be out of town for a few days, but I'll see you as soon as I get back."

He hurried toward the other door as footsteps could be heard approaching from the conservatory. Elizabeth rearranged her hair as best she could without a mirror, then smiled wanly at Lady Lavinia as she entered the room.

"I'm so grateful for your suggestion, Lavinia," she said with a rueful smile. "I have been resting in here and now I think I'll call for the coach while you have refreshments. I'll send it right back here to take you on to the ball."

Lady Lavinia reluctantly agreed.

Later, it was a very thoughtful Elizabeth who allowed herself to be undressed, and slipped into bed. She was still wondering if she'd done the right thing as sleep took over.

It was unfortunate that Dewsbury preferred to stay at his country estate, Colchester thought as he rode out of London. But if he wanted any peace of mind, he had to meet with him and find out as much as possible about the relationship between the old marquess and Elizabeth. To enter into a marriage, knowing in advance that his bride could never produce an heir was inconceivable to him, no matter how much he might desire the chit. That he would have her, one way or the other, there was no doubt in his mind, for he could not ever remember wanting a woman so much.

After spending the night at an excellent inn, he set forth once more in the best of spirits to ride the few remaining miles, and it was not long before he found himself approaching the house.

Luck was with him, for Dewbury had been just about to leave for the day for a tour of his estates with his steward.

"Come in, my dear fellow," he said warmly. "What brings you to this part of the world?"

"I was just passing this way, Robert"—Colchester tried to sound casual—"and thought I'd stop in to pass along Elizabeth's best wishes."

Noting his visitor's serious expression, Dewsbury canceled his tour and took him into the library, calling for a fresh decanter of brandy. His first thought had been that Colchester was here to ask for Pamela's hand in marriage, but he dismissed that quickly as Elizabeth would surely have warned him of any serious suitors.

"And how is my stepmama faring? I'm curious as to why she made the journey to her parents' home and stayed only three days. Did she give you any explanation?" Dewsbury asked.

"I didn't feel it my place to ask her and she volunteered no information. However, she had a nasty bruise on her head the other night and said she'd taken a fall from a horse." Colchester noted the other man's puzzled look.

"That's dashed strange in itself, David. Elizabeth's horsemanship takes some beating by men, never mind women. I must find out what happened. We all became very fond of her when she was here, you know." His tone held almost a note of warning.

Colchester took a sip of his brandy, then carefully placed his glass on the table. "I have a very awkward question to ask you, Robert. Elizabeth suggested to me that you might know the answer. I only hope you will not find it offensive, but the matter is of the utmost importance to me."

So that was it, Dewsbury thought. Elizabeth must have strong feelings for this man to speak to him at all on such a matter. He decided to make it easy for both of them. "I can tell you in a few words, David. My father was impotent in his later years. In his frustration he blamed her, and he did it very loudly from their wedding night onward."

"Then the rumor concerning the will was not true?" Colchester asked.

Dewsbury shrugged helplessly. "The rumor was accurate. Possibly spread by the miserable little solicitor my father used. He read the will to all of us here in this room." He paused thoughtfully. "My father was not quite the charming gentleman he seemed to be to the rest of the world. We all heard him shouting at Elizabeth, telling her it was her fault, that she ought to be able to do something to help him. Even Pamela heard, though she didn't understand what she was hearing. Only days before he died I heard him call her his vestal virgin."

"You have no idea what a relief this is to me, Robert," Colchester said, "and I promise you it will go no farther than this room."

"I take it you want to wed the 'willful widow,' as I've heard her called. Does she want to marry you? She told me not very long ago that she had no plans to ever marry again." Dewsbury smiled sardonically.

"I know, but I'm hoping I'll be able to persuade her otherwise. As you must realize, I have to marry someone soon, and she's by far the most desirable candidate I've seen." Colchester felt he had revealed enough of his feelings already.

"I wish you luck, David. She's a very lovely lady, and though you don't need them, you have my blessings. I think you would probably be very good for each other."

Although he was warmly invited to spend the night, Colchester stayed only for luncheon, then started the journey back to London and Elizabeth, his heart much lighter than it had been on the outward journey.

7

THE TREVELYAN LADIES were at home, entertaining callers for tea, and an almost completely recovered Elizabeth was seated by the large urn, pouring and handing dainty cups of the finest oolong to exquisitely dressed Corinthians and dandies for conveyance to equally fashionably garbed ladies. It was a warm day and the windows and doors were open wide to let a breath of fresh air into the high-ceilinged drawing room.

As she glanced around the room, Elizabeth felt well satisfied with her efforts. Instead of the dark greens and browns that must have been there for more than two generations, light greens and beiges made backgrounds for soft rose, lemon, and azure-blue flowers. The last time Robert had visited he had declared it money well spent and thanked her for what he knew had been a great deal of effort on a home she did not own.

As if drawn by a magnet, she looked toward the open door just as Colchester appeared there. He did not at first see her, and she wondered whom he might be looking for as his eyes searched the room. She forced herself to look away, not wishing him to realize that she had been anxiously awaiting his return to town ever since their unconventional conversation at the musicale.

"Good afternoon, Elizabeth."

She started at the sound of his voice, then, quickly recovering, smiled graciously. "Good afternoon, my lord. May I pour for you?" She held a delicate china cup in her left hand, and as he reached for it, she chuckled softly. "Come, now, don't be bashful, sir.

84

When did you last drink so bland a beverage? You'll find sherry on the sideboard behind Sir Geoffrey Wadsworth.''

"I'd much rather drink tea with you than lose my place by your side for the sake of a drop of sherry. You're looking very well. Are you completely recovered from your fall?" he asked with what appeared to be real concern.

Her hand went instinctively to her temple. "Thank you. I'm feeling fine, and there's only the slightest trace of a bruise remaining.''

He seemed like a mischievous schoolboy for a moment. "Look, if I drink this wretched tea, will you let someone else do this and come for a drive with me? I've got to talk to you.''

Her gray eyes sparkled and her lips quivered as she tried not to laugh out loud with joy. "I can't just get up right now and walk out of here with you," she remonstrated. "What would people say?''

"Who cares what they say?" he retorted, wickedly grinning at her.

"You cared a great deal a few weeks ago when you berated me soundly for my wanton behavior.''

"I was a fool, an idiot, and I was very jealous of all the men you were flirting with. Forgive me?" he pleaded, but laughter still sparkled in the depths of his eyes. "If you wish, I will go down on my knees right here and now to beg for your pardon.''

"My goodness," Elizabeth said with a roguish smile, "if you do, I promise that half the people here will rush off at once, eager to impart the news of your downfall. They'll tell their friends they witnessed your proposing to me, and you'd have a hard time refuting something they saw with their own eyes.''

He gazed at her so strangely that Elizabeth started to go warm all over. "What if I did not wish to refute it?" he asked softly.

"Then I would say you had better behave yourself,

my lord," she scolded lightly. "This is neither the time nor the place for serious conversation."

"I agree with you completely. But what am I to do when you refuse to come for a drive with me?" He gave an expressive shrug of his shoulders and looked at her beseechingly, though laughter still lurked at the corners of his mouth.

Elizabeth glanced around the room and saw several elderly members of the *ton* eyeing them with considerable interest.

"Why don't you go and talk to my sister-in-law, and charm some of the other ladies before we have all London talking about us?" Elizabeth suggested. "We are expected at Lady Jersey's for dinner tonight, but I will be home quite early, as I have been confining my activities to one engagement each evening. Would you care to pay a call tomorrow morning about eleven?"

He screwed his brows into a deep frown, but Elizabeth was watching his lips and their twitching gave him away. It was almost her undoing as she could nearly feel, once more, their warm pressure, and she gasped a little as her heart seemed to skip a beat. His expression changed and she was sure that, in some strange way, he knew exactly what she was thinking. She blushed furiously.

"I would much rather pay a call when you return this evening," he said sensuously, "but I'm sure you would not permit it. If I go and do the pretty to these ladies, may I return in about an hour and speak to you privately before you go up to change?"

Elizabeth strove to regain her composure, but her cheeks were still quite rosy, making her look very young and appealing. "Very well, my lord," she said a little breathlessly. "For just a few minutes only."

With a satisfied grin, he made her a deep bow, then crossed the room to greet Lady Lavinia.

Elizabeth had made no mention to Lavinia or Pamela

of the visit Colchester had arranged, for memories of her hurt and embarrassment over his failure to keep his previous appointment still lingered. When they went up to rest before changing, she made an excuse to see Cook, then returned to the drawing room and sat studying the toe of her dainty slipper as though seeing it for the first time. She almost jumped as the door bell sounded, but by the time the butler had announced Colchester, she was able to walk quite calmly across the room to greet him.

He kissed her hand, then led her to a couch, taking a chair across from her and pulling it closer, his manner serious.

"Thank you for permitting me to call at such an unusual hour, Elizabeth," he began, then came straight to the point. "I met with Dewsbury and at my insistence he spoke confidentially of your relationship with his father. He gave it as his firm belief that the marriage was never consummated because of his father's inadequacy. He feels the ugly rumor concerning you must have been started maliciously by the solicitor."

Elizabeth nodded. "I think it must have been him, for the servants would never have tried to hurt me," she said quietly.

He reached for her hand and she allowed it to stay in his, but it did nothing to ease the trembling she felt inside.

"I would like to first be sure you understand the reason for my earlier suggestion, which I know you found so very improper," he said earnestly, his eyes never leaving hers. "Unless I produce an heir, the Colchester title and much of the property that has been in direct line for hundreds of years will, at my death, go to a remote second cousin who has no interest in the family or its traditions."

"That would break your mother's heart if she were alive to see such a thing happen, I know," Elizabeth agreed quietly. "I was deeply insulted when you first made the suggestion, but after our last conversation I did understand the reason,'' she assured him, ''although I could never be a party to such an arrangement.''

He reached for her other hand and now held both tenderly in his own large, warm, bronzed ones.

''After my conversation with Robert, I know that if you remarry you will give up this house and your allowance, my dear, but if you marry me, I promise you will come to know how insignificant that loss really is. I am one of the wealthiest men in the kingdom and will instantly settle on you unentailed property that would keep you in comfort should anything happen to me.'' He leaned closer until his face was no more than a foot away from hers. ''Please say you will marry me, Elizabeth. I want so very much to make you my wife.''

Ridiculous tears of happiness sprang to Elizabeth's eyes. She hadn't dared allow herself to believe that he would ever marry her, but now she knew it had been the only thing she wanted since that first ball when he had not known who she was.

She nodded. ''Yes, David, I will marry you,'' she said with a little sniff as the tears threatened again.

She didn't see him move, but suddenly he was beside her on the couch and she was cradled in his strong arms. ''Don't cry, my love,'' he murmured, wiping one tear away that had fallen on her cheek. ''You've just made me the happiest man in the whole of London.''

He kissed her eyelids and her cheeks, then his searching lips found hers and his kiss set her afire. There was nothing angry about him this time as, softly and persuasively, he coaxed a response from her and she found her own lips seeking his in an unbelievable joy and passion.

He was the first to hear the loud cough Lady Lavinia made as she entered the room and closed the door behind her. He withdrew his lips, but continued to hold Elizabeth firmly in his arms as, flushed and confused, she tried to pull away from him. Still holding her tightly, he rose to his feet and Elizabeth found herself erect, but pressed close to his side.

"Lady Lavinia, please be the first to congratulate me. Elizabeth has agreed to become my wife," he said proudly.

He reluctantly released Elizabeth as Lavinia rushed over to throw her arms around her sister-in-law in a big hug; then, as she hesitantly held out a hand to him, he pulled her into his arms.

Breathless with excitement, she said, "This is wonderful news! I had feared at one time . . . But never mind that now. I am so happy, for I knew from the start that you were made for each other."

With another warm embrace for Elizabeth, she exclaimed, "I must go and tell Pamela right away. If you're still going tonight, you'd better come and dress, Elizabeth, for we're due to leave in an hour."

As Lavinia left the room, Elizabeth turned back to Colchester. "I really should . . ." she started to say.

He smiled softly. "I'd better leave, for if I take you in my arms again I won't be able to let you go. I'll send an announcement to the newspaper tonight, and if I may, I'll call on you in the morning to make plans for an early wedding. It can be as big as you like and wherever you wish as long as it is soon."

He pulled her against him, kissed the tip of her nose, then turned and left the room.

Elizabeth stood for a moment, trying to collect her thoughts. She really would have preferred not to attend Lady Jersey's dinner this evening, but could hardly back out at the last moment. She decided, however, not to say anything to anyone there, and hurried from the room to let Lavinia and Pamela know her decision.

"You wish to be married in two weeks?" Lady Lavinia was quite surprised at the haste. "But you can't possibly get all your clothes together and make all the

arrangements in so short a time, my dear. You know
what they say about marrying in haste.''

Elizabeth laughed softly. ''I'm not going to repent
this marriage, Lavinia. I couldn't, for I'm so excited
and happy about it I could burst. David doesn't want to
wait even two weeks, and I've bought all the clothes
these last few months that I could possibly need.''

''Well, if you plan to get married in gray . . .''
Lavinia shrugged helplessly and shook her head.

''Madame Gerard will make my gown in time, and
it's to be in the palest-blue satin with a long train. David
and I stopped at her establishment this morning when
we went for a drive,'' Elizabeth reassured her sister-in-
law.

''What about your mama and papa? Will they be able
to arrange for a wedding reception at such short
notice?'' Pamela asked.

''Don't you start, Pamela.'' Elizabeth sighed. ''I
keep telling you, it will be very small, at the village
church, with just Lady Beresford and Sir James, the two
of you, and one or two of my friends from home.''

''How about David's grandmama, Lady Butterfield?'' Lavinia asked dryly.

''Oh, God forbid, Lavinia. Can you imagine that
loud voice of hers and the things she says? We'll make
the excuse that it's too long a journey for a woman of
her years.'' Elizabeth shuddered as she recalled the only
time she had been in the old lady's company.

''Lady Beresford,'' the butler announced loudly, and
Lavinia moved forward to greet her old friend, then
brought her over to Elizabeth.

They looked at each other for a moment, then Lady
Beresford held out her arms. ''Elizabeth, my dear, I am
so happy you've consented to wed my son at last,'' she
said with a twinkle. ''He's been behaving like a bear
with a sore head ever since he met you. I know he'll
make you happy, for he's got a loving heart under that
arrogant air he adopts.''

"I'll make him happy, too, I promise," Elizabeth
assured her.

"I know you will, my dear. I always hoped for a love
match for him, but was beginning to worry as the years
went by and he seemed to care for no one." She patted
Elizabeth's arm, then turned to greet Pamela.

Once again, Robert had sent a carriage for their use,
and it was piled high with boxes and packages when the
three ladies started out for Warwickshire a week before
the wedding.

Her wedding gown was everything she had wished,
but Elizabeth had received a big surprise when a whole
new wardrobe of gowns was delivered with it. David
had decided he could not live with his bride dressed in
lavenders and grays, and had ordered gowns in every
color of the rainbow, with all the accessories to match.
Although Elizabeth had thought it a little high-handed
of him, she said nothing, as she was secretly tired of
wearing such dull shades and delighted to be out of
them for good.

Lord and Lady Danville received them warmly when
they reached Danville Hall, where rooms had been prepared for them, and all arrangements made for the
small wedding in accordance with the letter Elizabeth
had sent.

Lord Danville could not have been more pleased, of
course, for he was completely aware that his daughter's
fiancé was an extremely wealthy man. He planned to
have a long conversation with him when he arrived the
day before the wedding. Colchester would, of course, be
staying at the Golden Lion and not in the same house as
his bride.

It was to be an early wedding, and immediately after
the wedding breakfast, they planned to leave for the
Colchester family seat, near Oxford, and would arrive
there easily before nightfall.

Lady Beresford and Sir James Moorehead, who were

staying at Danville Hall, arrived in the early afternoon
of the day before the wedding. Elizabeth was in the
drawing room with Pamela, admiring the delicacy of
her needlework, when their carriage drew up to the
front door, and she casually glanced toward the
window.

"Oh, no," she moaned. "I knew that everything was
going too smoothly. What are we going to do with
her?"

Pamela looked at her inquiringly. "What on earth is
wrong?" she started to ask as she peered through the
sheer curtains, then murmured, "Oh, dear, I see what
you mean."

"I must wait here to receive them," Elizabeth said
with a heavy sigh, "but I would really appreciate it if
you would go quickly to find Mama and ask her to have
another room readied right away. Tell her the rose room
would be the best one as it's next to Lady Beresford's in
the east wing. And ask your Aunt Lavinia to join me as
soon as she can."

Pamela, vastly relieved to escape from the drawing
room before the guests came in, gave Elizabeth a
grateful smile, then hurried away.

A few minutes later the butler announced, "Lady
Beresford, Countess of Colchester, Lady Butterfield,
and Sir James Moorehead, my lady."

"Thank you. You may show them in here and bring
tea and refreshments right away," Elizabeth told him,
then rose to greet her guests.

"I trust you had a comfortable journey," Elizabeth
said as Lady Beresford entered first, then Lady Butterfield followed on the arm of Sir James. "We were just
about to have tea, and I'm sure you'll find it more than
welcome after the dust of the road."

The tiny figure looked a little less incongruous than
when Elizabeth had seen her last. This time she wore an
old-fashioned carriage gown in dark green, edged with
ermine, close fitting to a low waist, then billowing forth

over heavy padding at the hips. Perched atop her powdered wig was what appeared to be a huge purple saucer filled with yards of yellow and pink ribbon, and also edged in ermine.

Clinging to Sir James, she proceeded slowly across the room; then, as she came close, she raised her walking stick and pointed it directly at Elizabeth, her bright-blue eyes gleaming.

"Is this the one, Mildred?" she bellowed. "Is this the one that's going to leg-shackle my grandson?"

Lady Beresford, looking very apologetic, hurried forward. "Yes, Mama, this is Lady Elizabeth, David's fiancée. You must have met her before, if you recall, at a dinner party I gave."

She steered Lady Butterfield to a comfortable chair close to the tea table on which a maid was already placing platters of dainty sandwiches and pastries.

Elizabeth moved over to where the tea service had been placed, and started to pour while Sir James handed the cups around. At the sight of the food, Lady Butterfield appeared to have forgotten about Elizabeth and concentrated on tasting every item on the table. Even when Lady Lavinia and Lady Danville entered the room, she paid them little heed, continuing to sample the pastries and loudly guzzle her tea.

After greeting Lady Lavinia, Lady Beresford moved over to Lady Elizabeth.

"David is going to be very angry with me," she said softly, "but there was nothing I could do short of tying her onto her bed. She was bound and determined to see David married. I hope you will not be too unhappy, my dear Eliz—"

A raucous voice broke in. "Unhappy? What's that about her being unhappy? She should be the happiest gal in England." The old lady glared in their direction, wrinkling the withered face even more, but as Elizabeth smiled at her, the frown disappeared and she once more turned her attention to the array of food before her.

"Luckily, she forgets what she was saying much of the time," Lady Beresford murmured even more quietly than before. "I'll stay close to her and try to stop her being too outrageous."

"Don't worry about it, my lady," Elizabeth said, suddenly seeing the humor of the situation. "As it's just family, nothing she says can do any damage, and it will make a fine story to tell to our grandchildren."

When Colchester reached Danville Hall, the ladies were still dressing for dinner, as he had expected, but he had come somewhat early in response to a brief note from Lord Danville, which had awaited him when he arrived at the inn earlier in the day.

He was shown immediately into the library, where Lord Danville awaited him, a glass of brandy in hand.

"Come in, my dear boy, and help yourself to a drink before the ladies come down. Haven't met her yet, but I understand that grandmother of yours is a bit of a terror." Danville laughed jovially and patted his future son-in-law on the back as though he had known him for years.

"I hope you do not mean to imply that Lady Butterfield is here, in this house?" Colchester asked. He had intended to refuse the drink, but Lord Danville's confirmation decided him to accept the offer and he poured himself a small measure.

"Sit down, sit down," Danville urged. "It'll be the best part of an hour before they join us."

Colchester sat down in a leather wing chair and waited for Danville to come to the point.

"Must say, Elizabeth's done me proud. I had a good marriage all arranged for her a month ago, but she'd have none of it. That daughter of mine had something better in mind, I can see that now. Always was a good girl, looking out for her old father, my Elizabeth was." He eyed Colchester, wondering how much he dared ask.

"Just what do you think Elizabeth had in mind, sir?" Colchester asked, his voice dangerously soft.

"Why, the same arrangement as I had for her with the Welsh lord, of course." This was the tricky part and Danville felt a little uneasy, but he thought he could pull it off. "I've had some setbacks these last few years. Poor crops, managers robbing me left and right, you know the kind of thing."

"I'm afraid I don't," Colchester drawled. "Tell me about it."

Danville laughed uneasily. "You're a man of the world, Colchester. A man after my own heart, I can sense that. You wouldn't let your wife's father lose all he had, that I'm sure." He didn't like the way Colchester said nothing, but maybe it was a good sign. He went on, "The Welshman had agreed to give me a fresh start with twenty-five thousand pounds." He wondered if he'd made it too high. The Welsh lord had offered twenty, but he had nowhere near the wealth of Colchester.

Colchester put his glass carefully down on the table before turning to look Danville in the eye.

"He was either a fool, or else an old man seeking to buy a young bride," Colchester said slowly. "She's not yours to sell anymore, Danville, and if I ever find out that you were the cause of that bruise she had on her forehead, you'll be sorry you ever told me about your trading practices."

Danville started to bluster. "That was her own doing. I'd no part in it. She took out a stallion she'd no right to ride and he threw her," he said.

Getting to his feet, Colchester looked down on his future father-in-law, then walked to the door. "I intend to forget this conversation ever occurred, sir, and I would advise you to do the same," he said, then opened the door and left the room.

The ceremony was simple and very beautiful, as the couple were married before their close families and many of the villagers, who filled the pews in the rear of the old church. Sylvia and Louise made striking brides-

maids in their identical gowns of palest lemon. They had
fallen in love with their new brother-in-law, believing
him extremely handsome and charming, and he in turn
had found them delightfully refreshing.

Elizabeth felt happier than she had ever been in her
life as she caught a glimpse of David before slowly
walking down the aisle on her father's arm. David had
seemed rather quiet and thoughtful at dinner the
evening before, but when he had slipped the ring on her
finger, he had squeezed her hand gently and gazed at her
lovingly.

Lady Butterfield had dined in her room the night
before and had been silent at the wedding ceremony, but
when they returned to the hall and were seated at the
wedding breakfast with their families and a few close
friends, her loud voice was suddenly heard by all as she
called to her grandson.

"Are you sure she's a good breeder, David? She looks
a bit narrow to me." She gave a loud cackle, then
turned back to her food.

In the silence that followed, Louise's giggle sounded
quite loud and Elizabeth's cheeks seemed on fire. She
couldn't look at David, but she could feel his eyes on
her as he put a hand below the cover and grasped hers
firmly.

"Don't let her embarrass you, my love," he said so
softly that only she could hear. "Lift your head and
look at me . . . please."

Slowly, she raised her head and what she saw in his
eyes made her go even pinker, but he leaned toward her,
taking her chin in his hand and placing a soft kiss on
each of her burning cheeks, then one on her rosy lips.

The toasts seemed endless, but they finally finished
and Elizabeth was able to return to her old room and
change into a carriage gown for their journey to
Oxford. A few minutes later, he helped her into the
carriage, sat down beside her, and they were on their
way.

8

"IF I WERE you, my dear, I would put my head against that pillow and sleep for a while, for it'll be almost nightfall before we reach the castle," Colchester advised, "and you must have been up since dawn, being primped and bathed and fitted into that gorgeous gown that made you look more angel than woman."

"Thank you, kind sir." Elizabeth smiled, happy that he had been proud of her. "But how about you, David? It's not much fun for you to travel all the way with a sleeping bride."

"It will be even less fun, and will add nothing to my prestige, if my bride is so tired that she falls asleep when I try to make love to her tonight," Colchester remarked dryly.

Elizabeth blushed. "I hadn't thought about that, David. I am rather tired, so if you're sure you don't mind . . ."

For answer, Colchester reached across and carefully removed the hat pins that held an exquisite concoction of peach and turquoise lace and feathers on her head. "Now," he said as he lifted the hat and placed it on the opposite seat, "just settle back and have a nice nap, my love, and I'll wake you before we get there."

As soon as she was settled comfortably in the corner, he dropped a kiss on her lips and marveled at the ease with which she fell into a deep sleep. She looked, to him, to be no more than the nineteen years she had been when she was first married to Dewsbury, and he wondered if this was because she was still such an innocent.

When he had initially informed his mother that he was to marry Elizabeth, she had expressed dismay. As it was she who had first heard the rumors about the young widow who was so closely connected with her good friend, Lavinia, she felt guilty about causing her son unhappiness. He had assured her, however, that the whole thing was a case of spite from the grave, and so she had given the marriage her blessing, agreeing that Elizabeth had both the breeding and beauty to give her the kind of grandchildren she craved.

His grandmama had not really been terribly outspoken except for that one occasion during the breakfast, which had embarrassed Elizabeth for but a moment. All told, he felt that the wedding had gone extremely well, being marred only by the avariciousness of Elizabeth's father, Sir Edward Danville, but he believed that gentleman had been effectively put in his place. When the time came, he knew he would have to provide dowries and pay for the twins' come-outs, of course, but they were so delightful it would be a pleasure.

The countryside seemed to be flying by as the carriage made excellent time, stopping only for a change of horses at the inn where he had fresh cattle from his own stable waiting.

He was glad that Elizabeth did not awaken until they were only a half-hour from the castle. Then she stretched her arms like a warm kitten, blinked her eyes open, and smiled affectionately at him.

"Did I sleep very long, David?" she asked. "I feel so beautifully rested."

"You had a very good sleep, my love. We'll be home inside a half-hour, and one of the outriders has gone ahead to make sure everything is ready when we get there. I know Shackleton, that's the butler who has been there since before I was born, will have the household lined up for his new mistress's inspection." He gave her a devilish grin. "Now, aren't you glad you had a good rest first?"

Her eyes opened wide in mock horror. "Oh, dear," she said, reaching for her hat. "There's no mirror and I'll never get this on straight without one. What will they think about a mistress with a crooked hat?"

"They'll think I've lost my touch if I can't put a lady's hat on straight." He grinned. "I'm quite sure that every one of them remembers more about my exploits than I do."

"Shame on you, sir," Elizabeth scolded mischievously. "I just hope they don't think you couldn't wait until tonight."

Colchester roared with laughter. "Elizabeth, I am so grateful I married you and not some eighteen-year-old chit with more hair than wit. You're good for me, you do realize that, don't you?"

"I hope so, David," Elizabeth said seriously. "I very much want to be."

The sun had already set and little could be seen in the twilight as the carriage drew up in front of a huge house, from the front door of which a number of footmen came running.

Colchester was right, of course. The staff were lined up in the great hall in order of rank and Shackleton introduced the male servants, who bowed in silence, while Mrs. Fowler, the housekeeper, introduced the equally silent females, each of whom gave a little curtsy.

When they had been dismissed, Mrs. Fowler escorted Elizabeth to her bedchamber, where warm water, soap, and towels were ready for her to freshen her hands and face before joining Colchester, who was already seated at one end of the very long dining table. He rose as she entered the room and motioned to Shackleton, who was about to seat her far away from him at the opposite end.

"I prefer not to have to shout at Lady Beresford, Shackleton. Let's move the place setting down here," he said, picking up some of the cutlery and a napkin and placing it to his right. Shackleton brought the remainder of the setting while Colchester seated Elizabeth, and the first course was then served.

"Is this really a castle, David?" Elizabeth asked. "I always associated castles with a dragon and a moat, but I saw neither as we approached."

"You didn't notice the turrets and the holes for the archers to shoot through?" Colchester asked with a wicked gleam in his eye. "I don't believe there ever was a moat, though it may, of course, have been filled in during the last hundred or so years. But the turrets are real and some might say that I'm the dragon, for I do breathe fire and fury when I'm not instantly obeyed."

She laughed. "I never saw anyone look less like a dragon than you, and the way Shackleton looks at you it's obvious you've never breathed fire and fury at him. But it will be a marvelous place to bring up children," she said, then looked a little self-conscious.

He reached for her hand, now adorned with his diamond wedding band and the ruby ring he had given her when they became betrothed. "Don't feel embarrassed with me, darling, for there's no need. It is a wonderful place for children, and ours will be as happy here as I was, I'm sure."

He squeezed her hand gently, then allowed her the use of it to continue her meal.

"Of course, it isn't a castle really, but apparently there was an eccentric ancestor who decided he was going to turn it into one, and it was he who added the turrets and then named it. Fortunately, the earls who came later were more interested in their own comfort and it is less drafty and more livable than most houses of more recent vintage." He had dismissed the servants between courses, and he now refilled Elizabeth's wine-glass himself, then raised his own. "To you, my dear. May you always be as lovely as you look tonight, and to us, to our happiness together for many years to come."

Elizabeth gladly drank to that, then asked, "Shall we be spending most of our time here, or will we be mostly in London or one of your other homes?"

"I don't know. I really hadn't thought about it, but this is the finest of the country houses I inherited. It is

very large, though, and there are two wings that I don't
recall ever being used. I think you'll enjoy this place,
though I must admit I've spent very little time here these
last few years." He smiled warmly at her. "I think it's
something we'll have to think about when we're a little
more used to each other's preferences."

The dinner was quite delicious, although later
Elizabeth could not recall what she had eaten, for it was
so exciting just being with David. When they were
finished, she excused herself and went to her bedchamber to prepare to retire, leaving him sipping a glass
of port before joining her.

Mrs. Fowler had picked out a suitable maid to assist
her mistress until she hired a proper abigail, and she
found the girl already in the bedchamber. The maid had
finished unpacking and had almost put everything away
except for the prettiest of her nightgowns, which she
had laid across the large four-poster bed.

"I'm afraid I don't remember your name . . ."
Elizabeth started to say as she closed the door.

"Jeannie, milady," the girl said quickly with a little
bob. "I hope I've done it right for you."

She seemed anxious and Elizabeth quickly reassured
her that all was as she wished. "You may help me
undress, Jeannie, then I think that will be all for
tonight," she told her.

"Wouldn't you care for me to brush your hair,
milady? I'm very good at it."

Elizabeth looked a little doubtful, then decided to
give her a try, hoping she would not be too rough, as
many untrained maids were. To her surprise, Jeannie
was, as she had said, very good at it, and she found the
gentle rhythm so soothing she almost fell asleep.

After she had dismissed Jeannie, she sat at her
dressing table for a while, sadly remembering her last
wedding night, but not at all worried that there might be
any repetition. She was sure that David felt as she did,
and had no fears that he might be cruel or impatient
with her. Uncertain whether to wait for him here or to

get into bed, she finally decided on the latter course and climbed quickly in. Even if she should fall asleep, it would be very nice to have him waken her, she was sure.

As she lay between the cool sheets, her eyes half-closed and her head softly cradled in the large feather pillow, she heard a faint sound, then watched intently as the door separating their chambers slowly opened. His face was in shadow, but she saw the gleam of his maroon brocade dressing gown where the firelight caught its silky texture.

He approached the bed, his hands slowly untieing the cord around his waist as he came, then he reached down to draw back the covers and shrugged the gown from his broad shoulders before sinking down onto the bed, as naked as the day he was born.

Elizabeth could feel her heart start to pound wildly as he turned toward her, then leaned farther over and placed warm, comforting lips on her trembling mouth. One strong arm pulled her closer while gentle fingers stroked the nape of her neck and massaged her back, soothing the tension from her body.

"We've got to get you out of this gown, my love," he murmured, his breath caressing her cheek as he spoke.

"There's a bow you untie at the neck and then it just drops off," she whispered, and a second later she felt the garment loosen. A few sharp tugs and it was off and tossed onto the floor.

His hands seemed to be everywhere, stroking and exciting her as his lips nibbled down the length of her jaw, her neck, her shoulders. She gasped as they fastened on the tip of a breast and she felt a response surge from deep inside of her.

Instinctively, her hands reached out for him, caressing his velvety soft skin and exploring the cordlike muscles that tensed at her touch. Her fingers, tracing patterns in the silky hair of his chest, found and circled the hidden nipples, and when she heard his sharp intake of breath, she knew that she had given him pleasure.

His own hands, which had been still for several

moments, went into motion once more, sliding between her thighs and caressing her tender flesh until she moaned with desire. Then his mouth silenced her, his lips parting hers and his tongue entering her mouth, urgently searching all the little crevices until her head swam and she could feel nothing except a fire that started somewhere inside and seemed to consume her.

Suddenly she felt a sharp pain and cried out. She clung to him, instinctively arching to meet him as he moved rhythmically inside her. She gasped out loud as waves of pleasure shot through her, carrying her higher and higher. Finally, his whole body shuddered and he collapsed on his side, pulling her with him.

One of her arms was trapped under him, but she did not mind the discomfort. She still felt a little sore, but with it had come a strangely triumphant feeling that she was finally a complete woman.

His breathing was steadying now, and his eyes, which had been half-closed, opened wide to study her face.

"I know I hurt you, my love," he said, his voice like a caress, "but I promise it won't hurt anywhere near as much next time. I'm sure it was very different from your experiences with Dewsbury."

"Must we talk about it?" she murmured.

He touched the tip of her nose, then her lips. "I think we should, my love, and get it out of your system once and for all."

"He never took all his clothes off, but came to bed in his nightshirt, and I always wore my gown, and he would hold me and sort of rub against me. Then, after a while he would start to get angry with me and pace about the room shouting." She shuddered.

He pulled the covers over her. "Are you cold, love?" he asked solicitously.

"No, it was just the remembering, that's all," she explained.

"He didn't beat you, did he?" The thought had only just occurred to him.

"No. That is, only the once, and afterward he

attempted to explain that he was trying to see if it would help, but after that I was always worried he might do it again."

He pulled her close to him and held her tight. "You should be glad it didn't help, or life would have been a great deal worse for you." He tilted her chin and captured her lips in a long, comforting kiss.

Elizabeth had no way of knowing what time it was when she awoke, except for a faint gray light that could be seen through a chink in the curtains. From this she assumed it must be close to dawn.

It was probably the sound of David's steady breathing in the bed beside her that had awoken her, for she was unaccustomed to sharing a bed with anyone. The fire had long since gone out, and she was hoping that no one would come to light it again, for she would have been quite embarrassed to be found in bed with her husband. Dewsbury had never remained in her bed-chamber for very long.

Even in the dim light she could see how handsome David looked and how somehow vulnerable when his cynical blue eyes were closed and his mouth was relaxed in sleep. A surge of pure joy swept through her as she realized how much she loved this comparative stranger, and how she looked forward to getting to know him better each day.

"Is it morning?" His sleepy voice disturbed her revery.

"How do you do that?" she asked, delighted that he was awake.

"Do what?" He blinked and pulled her into his arms.

"Open one eye and not the other," she said, laughing. "I've never been able to do it." She screwed up her face as she made an attempt to copy him.

"That, my dear, is a habit acquired through vast experience. When one has a reluctance to rise too early, it's better to open just one eye to the unpleasant shock of daylight, rather than shock them both at once." He kissed her eyelids, then the tip of her nose, and finally placed a gentle kiss on her soft lips. "Are you sore this morning, love?"

"I don't think so," she lied resolutely as his hands stroked her body and started a tingling feeling within. "Will you be very busy this morning, darling, or will you have time to show me a little of the estate?"

"I must see my man of business this morning, but this afternoon I think we could go for a drive if the weather is favorable. You'll probably wish to go over accounts and menus and such with the housekeeper this morning anyway," he said practically.

"Of course. I hadn't thought about that, but it should be done as quickly as possible. Is it a well-run house?" she inquired.

"Well enough, I suppose, but it needs a woman's touch to see that everything is done to perfection, and the chef needs to be apprised of your favorite dishes, of course." He bent over her to nibble gently on her ear.

"You're going to spoil me if you're not careful, and I'll get heavy and matronly," she protested mildly.

"I'd like nothing better than the opportunity to spoil you a little, my love, but as to getting heavy, the only way I want to see you heavy is with my child," he told her. "Should you start to put on excess fat, then I'll have to chase you around the bedroom until it disappears. I can show you some delightful ways to exercise fat away."

This time his lovemaking was gentle at first, then became even more passionate than the night before, and she realized how much he must have been holding back so as to hurt her as little as possible. After only the slightest discomfort at first, Elizabeth experienced a torrent of feeling beyond anything she had ever imagined, and as she drifted into a shallow sleep afterward, she knew she must be the happiest bride ever.

* * *

When Colchester awoke for the second time, Elizabeth was still sleeping, and he crept out of bed quietly so as not to awaken her, then entered his own bedchamber, where his valet waited.

When he was dressed and his toilette completed to his valet's satisfaction, he returned to Elizabeth's chamber, but was disappointed to find that she had already left the room and was presumably having breakfast below.

The bed was still in disarray, the covers swept to the foot and the pillows still bearing the indentation of their heads. His eyes fell on something white peeping out from under the bed, and he stooped to pick up Elizabeth's gown, which he had discarded in his passion the previous night. As he bent down and his eyes were level with the mattress, it suddenly occurred to him that he could see no blood on the sheets.

Clumsily, he pulled the covers off altogether. The sheets were crumpled, but as pristine white as they had been the night before.

He could still hear his valet fussing in the next room, so he sat on the edge of the stool, looking blindly at the reflection of himself in the dressing-table mirror. He had an unusual ability to recall events in detail, and as he thought back, he realized that he had not met with the resistance expected when deflowering a virgin. And Elizabeth had foolishly admitted to him that she did not feel sore, though she had shown enough of feminine wiles to cry out at the crucial moment.

The gnawing feeling of hunger that had plagued him when he had first risen disappeared completely. He had been deceived by a beautiful, conniving witch who had taken from him his chance to produce an heir! He wanted nothing more than to wring her beautiful neck, but knew that if he did so he would surely hang, and she wasn't worth that.

Jumping to his feet, he flung himself out of the room and down to the stables, where he had his favorite hunter saddled in a fraction of the usual time, and rode off at a gallop.

* * *

The closing of the door to David's room had awoken
Elizabeth, and she had just slipped out of bed when
Jeannie entered with warm water and a cup of hot
chocolate.

She could hear sounds from the next room as she
dressed; then, reluctant to interrupt David and feeling a
few hunger pangs, she left her bedchamber and went
down the massive staircase into the great hall. A
footman showed her into a small dining room where the
smell of bacon and hot bread coming from under
covered dishes was tantalizing, and she decided to start
breakfast before David came down.

By the time she was nibbling toasted bread topped
with preserves and sipping fragrant coffee, she became
concerned. She had looked forward to having this first
breakfast with David and could not understand where
he could be. A place was set for him, with a newspaper
close by, so she reached over and glanced at the newspaper to pass the time until he arrived.

When the door opened, she looked up quickly, then
tried to hide her disappointment when it was only the
housekeeper.

"I thought you might want to go over some of the
accounts, milady," Mrs. Fowler said, "and then I could
show you the kitchens, pantries, laundry, and so on."

"Of course, but I was waiting for the earl to have
breakfast . . ." Elizabeth began.

"No point in waiting for him, milady. The earl left in
a great hurry more than half an hour since," Mrs.
Fowler said, looking a little disapproving. "Didn't say
when he'd be back, neither."

Elizabeth forced a smile. "Very well, Mrs. Fowler.
Let's start on the accounts first," she said quietly.

She spent most of the morning with the housekeeper,
inspecting the vast kitchens and service rooms, hoping
that David would return and wondering what could
have caused him to leave without letting her know.

Before luncheon she went back to her bedchamber to

tidy herself a little. As she put up a hand to fix a loose
pin in her hair, the door burst open and David stormed
in, not the David who had made love to her last night
and this morning, but a stern stranger with angry blue
eyes, heavy brows, and a face of thunder.

Shocked, she glanced at the riding whip he still
carried. He followed her gaze, then flung the whip
away. "Don't worry, ma'am, you might deserve it but I
would never allow you to drive me that far," he said.

She raised worried eyes to his cold face. "I don't
understand. What have I done, David?" she asked.

"Played me for a fine fool is what you've done, my
chaste virgin," he sneered. "And Robert Trevelyan
must have been in league with you, or did you convince
him, also, with your honeyed lies?"

She shook her head. "I don't know what you're
talking about, but I would like an explanation," she
said coldly.

"You know full well what I'm talking about, madam,
but just so there are no more misunderstandings, I'll
spell it out for you," he snarled. "You swore to me that
you were a virgin, that Dewsbury had been inept, unable
to perform, and had never enjoyed that chaste little
body."

"Of course I did. It was true," Elizabeth protested.

"It was a lie!" he said with emphasis. "A damned,
evil lie to get me leg-shackled. And if you lied about it,
there could have been only one reason: because you're
what he said—barren."

He walked toward her, his face so filled with anger
and disgust that it took all her courage to stand her
ground and not step instinctively back.

"Why are you saying this, my lord? What makes you
think I had done that before?" she asked, not knowing
quite how to phrase it.

At any other time her words would have amused him
by their innocence, but he was too angry to even notice
them. "There was no blood on the sheets, for a start.

Don't you know that knights of old used to hang the bloody sheets from the flagpole to let all know their bride had been a virgin?''

Elizabeth was quite well-read, and she did remember something of the sort, but surely, she thought, there must be an explanation.

"You cried out at the right moment, but not because it was your first time. It was all a careful piece of acting, wasn't it, Elizabeth?" He reached out and grasped her shoulders, pulling her toward him and giving her a little shake, "Answer me, dammit!"

Her eyes filled with tears, but her pride would not let them escape. "All I know was that it hurt," she gasped.

He let go of her. "You mean you pretended it hurt," he said scornfully. "It's done now, and you got what you wanted yesterday—a young, rich husband. But you'll not gain much by your deceit. There'll be none of my property settled on you now. You fooled me into buying a new wardrobe for you, but you'd better make it last, for the next clothes will be a long time coming."

Elizabeth's eyes flashed in anger. "I didn't ask you to buy any clothes for me. You were the one who had them made up and delivered to my home," she said hotly. "And as far as I'm concerned, you can take them and sell them back to Madame Gerard. None of them has been worn except the wedding gown, and you can take that back to her also, for I never want to see it again."

With an oath, he swung around and headed for his own room, slamming the door behind him.

Elizabeth sat down, distractedly fingering her gown until she realized it was one of the ones he had bought her. She had donned it earlier to please him, knowing he didn't wish to see her in lavender or gray.

She walked over to the bed and tugged on the bellpull. It was a good thing she had brought with her those despised gowns that she had paid for herself. From now on she would wear nothing else!

9

ELIZABETH DID NOT see Colchester again until she took her place for dinner at the foot of the dining table, a distance of some twenty feet from him. He rose as she entered, and looked directly at her, his face stern and his eyes unyielding. This evening there was no last-minute change of place setting to bring her to his side, and the meal was partaken in total silence save for murmured responses to Shackleton and the footmen.

Elizabeth was more than a little hungry, as she had forgone luncheon and spent the afternoon unpacking what she regarded as her own gowns but had thought never to wear again.

After one look at her mistress's grim face, Jeannie had not uttered a sound when instructed to take the garments of more somber hue, press them, and put them in the armoires in place of those of every shade of the rainbow that Elizabeth was now carefully folding and packing into boxes.

By the time her gowns were all pressed, Cook had been ready to serve a nice tea, but Elizabeth would partake of nothing more than a cup of the delicious brew while she worked.

With a shake of her head, she continued folding and packing the gowns when Jeannie begged, "Won't you take a rest, milady, and let me finish the task?" The little maid could not understand how her mistress could bear to pack away the beautiful garments, and asked, "Are they to go in the attic until you're out of mourning, ma'am?"

"It would be best if you have Mrs. Fowler check with the earl to find out what is to be done with them,"

Elizabeth had replied. "Until he gives instructions, they may be placed in any empty chamber, but I do not wish to see them here when I return."

When it appeared that Colchester had finished his meal, Elizabeth rose. "You may send tea to my bedchamber, Shackleton," she said clearly, then walked slowly toward the door, secretly hoping Colchester would call her back, but the only sound she heard was the tap of the stopper against glass as he helped himself from the decanter of port.

On reaching her chamber, she realized how very tired she was, but did not immediately change out of the gray silk gown she had worn to dinner, just in case her husband should decide to join her for tea. Perhaps the port would put him into a more mellow, forgiving mood, she thought.

When more than an hour had gone by and the tea was completely cold, she rang for Jeannie to assist her out of her gown and into the large, empty bed. Tired as she was, however, she could not fall asleep, and was still tossing and turning when, some two hours later, she heard movement and the murmur of voices in the adjoining room. She tensed, waiting until there was complete silence once more, before she relaxed and fell into a troubled sleep.

As Elizabeth moved slowly through one of the two long galleries, with its ornate paneling and magnificent plasterwork ceiling, massive marble fireplace, and gilt-framed portraits of the former Earls of Colchester and their families, she found it exceedingly difficult to relate her previous housekeeping experience to a residence of such vast proportions.

"How many bedrooms did you say are kept in readiness, Mrs. Fowler?" she asked.

"There are one hundred and ten in all, ma'am, but only fifty are ever used these days, with twenty kept aired and ready at all times for visitors and their servants," the housekeeper told her. "That's not counting the schoolroom and the nurseries, of course, ma'am, and it's there you'll find your pretty gowns when you should want them," she added, her plain face showing not a sign of curiosity.

"Were those Lord Beresford's instructions?" Elizabeth could not help but ask.

"Yes, milady," Mrs. Fowler said calmly, as though the nursery was the usual place to store clothes.

Elizabeth shivered slightly as the portrait of a tall, blond earl, dressed in a lace ruff, doublet, and hose, seemed to gaze accusingly at her, and she turned and moved toward the door.

"One thing I'd like you to do for me, Mrs. Fowler, is to find me a small sitting room, on the ground floor not too far from the kitchens, where I may keep the household accounts and also use it as a writing room," Elizabeth requested. "With all the rooms this place has, there must surely be something suitable."

The housekeeper nodded. "There's a very nice one in the back, looking over the kitchen gardens, milady, that the Dowager Lady Beresford used when she resided here. You'd want to change the furnishings to your taste, of course."

"I've no wish to incur any unnecessary expense," Elizabeth said hastily, mindful of Colchester's last remarks to her.

"With all the furniture in this great place, you've got more to choose from than in a London warehouse, ma'am. All it will cost is a little elbow grease for the moving of it," Mrs. Fowler assured her, "and it will be good to see the footmen do some work for a change."

Elizabeth privately agreed, for it seemed they did nothing but stand at their posts all day long, and there were a great many of them.

"They'll soon have more than enough to do, never fear," Elizabeth said, "for I see many things I want to change, but for now I'll just take a look at the room if it's convenient, Mrs. Fowler."

The housekeeper led the way down the elaborate staircase and toward the back of the house, opening a door into a most attractive room of medium proportions, with an Adam fireplace, light paneled walls, and an interesting ceiling decorated in a soft pastel motif. The furniture was scaled down, for use by a lady, and the floor was thickly carpeted in a rich shade of blue.

Elizabeth walked over to the French windows, opened them, and at once the perfume of a rose garden wafted in.

"This is perfect for my use," she said as she turned around to Mrs. Fowler, breaking into her first, stiff smile of the day. "I'm so glad you remembered it. I will start here early tomorrow morning, and now I think I will go for a walk. The fresh air is most inviting."

"The room will be cleaned and made ready for you, milady, and a walk will do you a world of good. Best stick to the path that leads down to the stream, though, for you mustn't get lost your first time out." With a curtsy, Mrs. Fowler left Elizabeth and hurried toward her own domain.

It took but a few moments for Elizabeth to change from house slippers to ankle boots and pick up a shawl to wrap around her shoulders should the breeze turn cool; then she slipped out of the back door, passed the tall hedges until she saw the path that had been visible from her new writing room.

She followed the path as it hugged the edge of the woods, pausing to watch a pair of white-throats busily building a nest in the branches of a low tree. Careful to stay within sight of the footpath, she picked her way between bushes to where she could see small crab-apple trees covered with crimson buds and pink blossom and, beneath them, a carpet of wild hyacinths. Stooping, she gathered a handful, enjoying their woodsy fragrance, then headed back to the path.

Now her step was lighter as she continued toward the

stream, its gurgle growing louder though the water itself had not yet come into view. She loved the countryside, had sorely missed it when in London, and now determined that she would spend her afternoons outdoors as long as the weather permitted. If she devoted her mornings to household duties, her days would be satisfyingly filled and she would be in a better frame of mind to face Colchester's stern silence at dinner. She still hoped, however, that tonight he might address a few pleasant words to her.

There was a flat-topped boulder on the bank of the swiftly flowing stream, and she sat herself carefully down on its smooth surface, resting her back against the trunk of a nearby oak tree, and watched the frogs, both large and small, hopping about in the sparkling water. From the direction of the woods a cuckoo piped his sweet note, and Elizabeth, feeling more calm and peaceful than she had in the last thirty-six hours, closed her eyes and let her sleepless night take its toll.

She woke with a feeling that someone was watching her. Even before she raised her eyelids she could sense another presence, then she heard the slight snort of an impatient horse. Startled, she opened her eyes to find Colchester, sitting astride his chestnut gelding and watching her closely, with an almost wistful expression on his face that quickly disappeared when he realized she was awake.

In her confusion the bunch of wild hyacinths dropped from her lap and she bent to gather them up again, hoping that by the time she raised her head once more either her rosy flush or her husband would have departed.

"Have you nothing better to do, madam, than to spend your time sleeping in the woods like a country bumpkin?" he asked coldly. "What if some tramp had found you, or a poacher?"

"He'd probably have been pleasanter company than you, my lord," Elizabeth snapped with a toss of her head. "And as for something better to do, I'm certainly not going to trouble myself with household matters when you refuse to even clothe me," she lied, hoping he had not observed her touring the castle with Mrs. Fowler, or he would know she was not speaking the truth.

"So that's why you packed all those new clothes away and told Mrs. Fowler to ask what was to be done with them—so that everyone would believe you had to stay in mourning because I wouldn't buy you more gowns," he growled, his scowl deepening. "Well, you can get them unpacked again, for I'll not sit opposite you every night in those funeral rags."

As soon as the words were out, he wished he could take them back, for he bitterly regretted having mentioned her gowns the previous morning. He was not a mean man and he had seen the hurt in her eyes before she lashed back at him.

"Then perhaps it would be best if my supper were served in my bedchamber, sir, so that you need not see me at all," she countered aggressively.

"Whenever I am in this house for either luncheon or dinner, you will join me, whether you wish to do so or not," he pronounced sternly, then decided that the matter of the gowns was best dropped, for even in mourning gowns she looked very lovely. "But you may wear whatever you choose, for it is of little concern to me."

The gelding was becoming impatient once more, and easing his tight hold on the rein, Colchester swung around and headed at a fast pace for the castle.

Elizabeth watched them until they rounded the edge of the woods and were lost from her sight. She did not know what to construe from her angry exchange with him. She would have dearly loved to take advantage of his avowal of unconcern and appear at dinner tonight wearing the outfit she had bought for bathing at Brighton, but decided it might be distinctly dangerous to push him too far.

Placing her shawl around her shoulders, for there was

now a distinct chill in the air, she walked slowly back to
the castle, thinking sadly how, a mere few days ago, he
would have scooped her up in front of him and carried
her back in his arms.

Elizabeth had now been in residence at the castle for
more than six weeks, and though her husband never
made any comment of either approval or disapproval,
she knew she had made a vast improvement in its
condition.

The pleasant smell of beeswax filled the air inside, the
rich leathers and fine woods of the furniture glowed,
and silver and brass fixtures gleamed brightly in the
light of the candles' dancing flames. Bowls and baskets
of fresh flowers and foliage brightened almost every
room and hallway. An airy arrangement of tigerlilies
and asters had been placed in the center of the dining
table, and through it Elizabeth could look at Colchester
while he ate, without appearing to stare.

Colchester was, however, in a quandary. Dinner had
become the high point of his days. Though he would not
give Elizabeth credit for it, the quality and variety of the
food, enriched with delicate sauces and side dishes, had
improved beyond belief lately. But no matter how the
food tasted, it would have meant naught were he unable
to see Elizabeth's beauty each evening, and he resented
the bouquet for cutting off a part of his vision. How
could he order the flowers removed without letting her
know how much he enjoyed just watching her?

He spent his mornings with his agent, John Bingham,
going over improvements to be made to the tenant
farms, but there was a limit to how many innovations
might be discussed and how much work in progress
could be checked upon. He had never paid so much
attention to detail before, and though nothing was
actually said, he could tell that John was wishing he
would leave him alone to get on with his routine work.

In the afternoons, when the weather was fine, he rode

over the estate, stopping for a word with any tenants he met, most of whom had known him since he was a young boy. He never went right up to the stream again, but he frequently saw Elizabeth in the distance as he approached the house, and wondered why she had never asked him for a mount and gone farther afield.

When he questioned Bob, who had charge of his stables, he found that she frequently visited the horses, knew them all by name, and had once indicated a wish to ride, but when advised that a groom must accompany her, she had not brought up the subject again. Tonight was as good a time as any, he thought, to mention it to her.

"For someone who rides as well as you, Elizabeth, I'm somewhat surprised that you have never asked to be suitably mounted. Are my stables not to your liking, madam?" His tone was the deliberately cool one he had come to use with her to hide the feelings he could not prevent.

"On the contrary, my lord, you keep an excellent stable, but once I realized I could not ride alone here, I lost interest," she replied in the bored voice she reserved for her conversations with him.

"The accident at your parents' home must surely have pointed up the dangers for a woman riding alone," he snapped. "There are always plenty of grooms eager to accompany you, I'm sure." As soon as he said the words, he frowned, realizing he had no wish to see her riding out with a young groom.

"But I am not eager for their company, my lord. I have ridden alone on an estate all my life, both at Danville Hall and on the Dewsbury lands, and if I cannot do so here, then I would rather not ride," she said firmly, a defiant look in her eyes.

This was the general tone of all their conversations now, she thought, but at least they no longer sat through dinner in silence. But any discussion, no matter how mild, took on the dimensions of a quarrel when the words had to be almost shouted in order to be heard at such a distance. Tonight's argument was of little importance to her, however, for soon she would be unable to ride, if what her body was telling her were true, and if her recent stomach upsets were not caused by her heartache, but by the new life growing inside her.

She had the strange feeling, sometimes, that if she ordered her place moved closer to his, smiled, and spoke more gently to him, he would be most receptive, and more normal relations would be resumed, but she was too hurt by his continued absence from her bedchamber to be the one to make the first move.

It had not occurred to her when she married Colchester that she would be completely dependent upon him for everything, though she knew that the town house and her allowance would revert to Robert. The unentailed property that he had said he would settle on her as soon as they were married had not, to the best of her knowledge, been put in her name, so she was penniless, as she had been in her previous marriage. But at least she received an allowance before.

Her pride would not let her discuss with Colchester either his promise of property or the need for some money for personal items, and as she became certain that she was expecting a child, her resentment and bitterness toward him grew, and the chance of a reconciliation diminished.

It came as no surprise, therefore, just three months into their marriage, when one evening, after partaking of his first sip of port, Colchester told her of a decision he had reached.

"I will be leaving for London in the morning," he said abruptly, "for I have urgent need to finalize some business there."

"You will be staying in Hanover Square, my lord?" Elizabeth asked, not sure whether she felt pleased or unhappy about his sudden journey.

He shuddered visibly. "Definitely not. I have not

stayed there since my grandmama moved in." He grimaced. "Shackleton has the address of my lodging in town, should you need it."

Elizabeth had a strange feeling that he was moving out and leaving her in the castle. "Will you be gone long, sir?" she asked in as cold a tone as she could summon.

"At this time I cannot say, madam. But surely, under the circumstances, my presence or absence can be of little concern to you?" he suggested with a tight smile.

Elizabeth rose to leave him to his port. Inclining her head, she murmured, "As you say, sir. Give my best wishes to your mother when you see her."

She walked swiftly, head held high, out of the room and up the great staircase, and it was not until she reached her own bedchamber that she let go. Then she collapsed on the bed, sobbing softly, sure in her own mind that he was leaving her for good.

When she calmed a little, she gave careful thought to whether she should tell him of the child she was carrying. It was impossible at this stage to discern any outward sign of it once she was fully clothed, for the high-waisted gowns concealed all but a slight additional fullness in her breasts.

When it occurred to her that, as he thought she was not a virgin, he might think the child was not his, she decided against saying anything to him at this time. She realized she was more easily upset now than she had ever been before, and though she had become accustomed to their verbal sparring over the dinner table each evening, she feared that a violent disagreement might upset her enough to lose the baby, and she wanted this child very much.

She lay awake until she heard him moving about in his chamber and, for once, did not rise the next morning until she was sure he was gone from the castle.

10

COLCHESTER HAD WATCHED Elizabeth's face closely as he announced his intention to leave for London the next day. Could it have been his imagination, or did he really see a trace of sadness in her expressive gray eyes? he wondered. If it had indeed been there, it was gone in a flash, replaced by her usual icy indifference toward him.

Once he was settled in his London lodging, he hastened to Hanover Square to pay his respects to his mother, but for once he did not walk the short distance, for he was not eager to meet acquaintances and become involved in lengthy explanations as to the whereabouts of his bride.

"David, my love, how delightful to see you." Lady Beresford held out her arms to her son, who hugged her warmly and kissed her cheek. "Is Elizabeth resting after the journey?"

"My bride did not accompany me, Mama. I am sure I will be able to accomplish my business here and return to the castle before she misses me," he said, believing his words to be true even if he stayed away a dog's age.

Lady Beresford's eyes brightened. "She isn't, perhaps, increasing already, is she?" she asked hopefully.

"No, she is not," he snapped as she touched on a sore subject. "It's just that she has much to do at the castle and preferred not to leave at this time," he went on in a more conciliatory tone.

His mother sat down in her favorite chair and motioned him to a love seat opposite.

"Since you two left, Sir James has been trying even harder to persuade me to marry him, and I am almost at the point of agreeing to do so. How would you feel about it, David?" she asked, a worried frown creasing her brow.

"I'm in favor of anything that would make you happy, Mama. But what would you do about Grandmama?" Colchester asked. "He's not willing to take her on as well, surely?"

"She's the only reason I've been refusing him for the last twelve months, but surprisingly, he is willing to live here at first and help me with her. That is, of course, if you and Elizabeth do not mind. He has a perfectly good house here of his own, and we would move into it right away should you and Elizabeth decide to come to town." She raised questioning eyebrows, waiting for his views.

"Not and leave Grandmama behind, I hope," he growled. "But there's no reason whatever why you should have to take her with you. She's not even a relation of yours."

"I know, but Sir James handles her so very well, and he really doesn't seem to mind. He's a good, kind man, you know, and I could do a lot worse, David." Her face showed some of the relief she was feeling now that she had brought up the subject.

"I can think of no one I'd sooner see looking after you, Mama, and you've got to give him points for persistence. By all means stay here for now, and by the time Elizabeth and I come back, we'll have found some solution." Colchester grinned. "Are you going to have another society wedding?"

Lady Beresford laughed. "Of course not, silly. Now you're in agreement, he'll probably get a special license and we'll have a small country wedding and announce it on our return."

"You didn't seriously think I would object, did you, Mama?" Colchester was amazed at the very idea.

She looked a little sheepish and said, "It does seem strange, but as head of the family, you should give your blessing, I believe."

Colchester came over to his mother, took her hands in his, and kissed her. "Sir James is a fine gentleman and I'm sure the two of you will be very happy. If it's needed, then you surely have my blessing." He looked at the little clock on the mantelpiece. "Now I must run if I'm to get my business accomplished. Don't look for me for any social duties as I'm not planning to mix with the *beau monde* on this trip."

Lady Beresford rose to see her son out. "I understand, dear. You want to get back to your beautiful bride as soon as possible, and I can't blame you for that." She looked thoughtful, though, as she watched him run down the steps, for she knew her son very well and she was sure something was making him most unhappy.

On leaving Hanover Square, Colchester proceeded directly to the office of his solicitor, where he made arrangements to have the property he had promised settled on Elizabeth. He had thought long and hard on this, but finally decided he must in all conscience keep his word. He was leaving tomorrow to check on some land he owned in Dorset, and would be gone about a fortnight. On his return he would make it a point to come by the office once more and append his signature to the document.

He looked neither to left nor right as he left the offices of his solicitor, having accomplished what he had set out to do. Should anything happen to him, Elizabeth would not find herself in the kind of embarrassing situation that Dewsbury had devised, and she would have ample funds to give the twins their come-out when the time came.

"David, my pet." Deep in study, he still instantly recognized the lilting, sultry voice and swung around.

"Why, Angelique, this is a surprise! But you're in black, my dear. Did something happen to the marquess?" he asked, knowing the lady's husband to be frail and elderly.

She lifted her heavy veil and pressed a dainty kerchief to first one eye and then the other. "He passed away just two months ago, may God rest his soul," she sniffed, "and I have been so very lonely. Seeing you like this has made me feel so much better, however. You will join me in a glass of sherry, David, won't you? It will be like old times."

When he did not immediately refuse, she took his silence for assent, linked an arm through his, and guided him toward the nearby town house she had so recently inherited.

At the age of thirty-three, although admitting to no more than thirty, Angelique Preston was still a very beautiful woman, with her lustrous black hair and golden eyes. She had first met Colchester some twelve years ago when he was not much more than a boy, but though he was infatuated with her, she knew his family would never permit her to join their ranks.

A year later she married the old marquess, and periodically she had still met with Colchester, for her husband was not difficult to deceive. As the years went by, however, she realized that Colchester's feelings had changed considerably. He was now a man of the world and she just one of a number of women who received his favors from time to time.

No sooner was the old marquess buried, however, than she began looking for Colchester once more, for she had decided long ago that he would make her a very satisfactory second husband, and the influence his mother had exerted on him as a raw youth was no longer effective. All she had to do was rekindle in him the fires that had once burned for her so brightly.

But the news she had heard some six weeks ago that Colchester had finally married and was living in the country came as a terrible shock. Worse still, her informant advised her that it was a love match and that his bride was a beautiful young widow.

As they entered the hall of her home, Lady Preston divested herself of her bonnet and shawl, then led the way into the drawing room, which was rather dark and gloomy, unfashionably furnished with heavy draperies and dark woods of an earlier time. Refurbishing her inheritance in a lighter style was clearly not one of Lady Preston's priorities.

"How long will you be in town, my lord?" she asked as her butler poured drinks for them, then left the room, closing the door firmly behind him.

"As long as it takes to conduct a small business transaction," he replied. "I must say, Angelique, that, like my wife, you look extremely well in black."

"Thank you, David," she said, looking reproachfully at him. "I had heard, of course, that you did not wait for me, but married a widow. Is she very lovely?"

He smiled grimly. He had not forgotten how willingly she had cuckolded her husband with him and with others of his acquaintance. Could she seriously think he would ever have married a woman like her? There had been a time, of course, when, as a callow youth, he had thought her the most exciting woman he'd ever met, but he had quickly grown up. Now he had no intention of discussing his wife with her.

"Of course. Would I marry anyone who was not?" he asked with a supercilious smile.

"Well, I've no doubt I shall see her for myself, as we're bound, sooner or later, to run into each other at some crush or other," she said lightly. Then a happy thought crossed her mind. "She is with you in town, of course?"

He took a slow sip of his sherry. There was no point in evading her question, as she would find out eventually. "My wife has much to do making Colchester Castle to her liking. On this occasion she preferred not to accompany me to town."

Sudden excitement turned her golden eyes to amber. "Indeed, my lord. So you're all alone in town. How very interesting," she said huskily. "Do you have plans for the evening, or would you care to join me for a light supper? My chef is French and can, no doubt, provide something to please the most exacting palate."

Why not? he thought. He was reluctant to either dine alone or join his bachelor friends at his club, for he had no taste for the none-too-subtle hints and questions that would be asked.

"I am leaving town early tomorrow morning for a couple of weeks," he said, "and had planned a quiet dinner and an early night."

Lady Preston's voice grew even huskier, and she lowered her gaze lest he see the triumph in her eyes, for he knew her very well indeed. "Then of course you must dine here, dear David," she murmured, "for I cannot wait a fortnight to show you the wonders my chef can perform."

It would have been difficult to refuse, even had Colchester wanted to, and so he graciously consented to share a meal with her.

"I must say, my dear Angelique, I am delighted that you are in considerably more affluent circumstances than when first we met," Colchester remarked. The delicate poached salmon, venison pasties, sweetbreads, roast beef, jellies, and cakes, served with hock and Madeira, had put Colchester in a mellow mood, as Angelique had planned. "Your chef is a jewel beyond price and must cost more than the rest of your kitchen staff put together. How on earth did you find him?"

Angelique smiled, quite satisfied with her evening's work. "My stepbrother, Trevor, found him for me, helped him escape, or some such thing. I am well-pleased with the gratitude he shows." Her wide eyes and deprecating shrug prevented him from questioning her further. "As I have tempted you away from your club this evening, David, could I offer you a game of piquet?

We are both much more accomplished, I am sure, than in those wonderful days when we used to practice piquet . . . and other things?'' she murmured with a heavy sigh.

Before dinner she had changed into an evening gown of black lace, cut so low at the neck that, if she took a deep breath, her ample, lily-white breasts were in danger of being completely revealed. Colchester needed no reminder of how round they had been, and how deliciously soft to the touch. His gaze was drawn to them like magnets and it took determination to lift his head and look into her softly appealing, golden eyes.

She had looked exactly like that when she told him she must marry the marquess, he remembered, and instantly the spell was broken. "A game of piquet would be an excellent ending to a delightful evening,'' he told her with an amused smile, and he did not fail to notice the way she flounced away to get the cards, disappointed that her efforts had come to naught.

He won the game easily, refused a nightcap, and prepared to leave, pecking her cheek lightly when she offered her lips for a good-night kiss. His lodging was only a short distance away, and he stepped out briskly, swinging his cane high and relishing the cool night air. He would see her again, for he had enjoyed himself immensely once he realized what her little game was. It was strange, though, for he'd have imagined she would have been looking for another husband rather than a lover at her age.

Lady Preston arose at an unusually early hour the next morning, and even before she finished her hot chocolate, she sat down at her writing table and composed a short note, requesting a certain gentleman to attend upon her within a few hours. After carefully sealing the note, a groom was ordered to deliver it immediately and to wait for a reply.

Having accomplished as much as was possible for the time being, she ordered a light breakfast, then rang for her abigail to help her bathe and dress.

Breakfast was the first to arrive and her ladyship took one look at the poached egg she had ordered, poked it with her fork, and started to scream. "Just what do you call this? I asked for a soft poached egg, not a lump of rock."

The pretty young maid who had brought it was new, and she had just reached the door when she heard her ladyship's scream. Lady Preston threw the plate just as the maid turned around, and she caught the full force of it in her face.

"Get out, you're fired," her ladyship shouted as the girl stood for a moment, transfixed, while blood from her gashed cheek mingled with egg yolk and ran down her face, staining her white collar. Then, with a little sob, she ran from the room.

A few minutes later an older woman in a plain dark dress entered, accompanied by another maid with a dustpan and broom. While the maid cleaned up the mess at the door, the older woman walked slowly over to Lady Preston.

"There you are, Yates," her ladyship said, angrily panting for breath. "You certainly took your time in getting here. Where were you?"

"I came as fast as my swollen legs and feet would carry me, ma'am," the abigail replied, seeming not at all put out by Lady Preston's bad temper.

"Well, just make sure, when you've finished here, that the stupid maid who brought my breakfast leaves the premises at once. I'm starving. Did you order some more breakfast for me?" Lady Preston demanded, still breathing quite heavily.

"That I did, ma'am. It'll be here any time now," she said as she reached for a wrapper and held it while Lady Preston slipped her arms into it. She pulled out a stool in front of the dressing table and, when her mistress was seated, proceeded to brush the long black tresses until her ladyship was breathing more easily, then she dressed the hair in two coils at the back of the neck, allowing a few curling tendrils to escape on the forehead and around the ears, to soften the effect.

When there was a knock at the door, Yates walked over, took the tray from yet another maid, and set it on a small table beneath the window. As she poured the tea, Lady Preston got up and came over; then, before taking her seat, she deliberately stepped on the abigail's swollen foot with all her weight.

"You're becoming a little too familiar, Yates," she said viciously. "Just remember, you can be replaced just as easily as the others."

Without a word, the old abigail turned and limped out of the room.

Promptly at eleven o'clock, Trevor Downs presented himself at his stepsister's house and was shown into the drawing room.

He was a good-looking and astute young man, but he lacked the breeding of which Angelique so frequently boasted. His mother, Sybil, though genteel, had been forced to seek employment at an early age as nursemaid in the household of a recently widowed baron. She repulsed the baron's advances until he was driven almost crazy. When the baron's babe, Angelique, was barely six months old, he married Sybil.

It was not destined to be a lengthy union, however, for he was a compulsive gambler and within but a few months he lost everything in a wager and promptly killed himself. Though now a titled widow, Sybil was once more without funds and with the added burden of the baby Angelique to care for. In desperation she married a wealthy merchant, Bertram Downs, who had a two-year-old son, Trevor.

Although they were brought up together and had much in common, Trevor's parentage did not permit him to travel in the same circles as Angelique, but rather than being bitter about it, he had always adored her. She was fully aware of this, and used it to her advantage, knowing he would go to any lengths to stay in her favor.

He rose as she entered the drawing room, and she allowed him to kiss her cheek.

"Your note sounded most urgent, Angelique. Is there something I can do for you?" he asked eagerly.

"Dear Trevor," she murmured, looking deep into his eyes and caressing his chin with her fingertips. "I do have another small problem with which I need your help."

Trevor beamed. "Just tell me what you want me to do, my dear, and it will be my pleasure."

"An old acquaintance has recently married, and I am anxious to learn whatever you can find out about his bride," Angelique began. "I'd like you to journey to Colchester Castle in Oxfordshire, stay at an inn in any small village nearby, and ask discreet questions. It's a very large estate and it's more than likely that many of the staff take a drink in the local inn."

"What is her name, and what kind of information are you seeking, my dear?" he asked, his face intent.

"Anything and everything you chance to hear. What she looks like, how she dresses, her likes, her dislikes, her habits, her friends, particularly her relationship with Colchester. She was a widow before she married him, the dowager Marchioness of Dewsbury." She paused. "Do you think you could do it for me right away, darling?"

"Of course, Angelique. For you I would do anything, you know that," he said earnestly. "This is easy compared to snuffing out the old marquess."

Angelique frowned. "He was a very sick man, Trevor," she protested. "If you hastened his demise a little, who's to know? This probably won't take you long, and then, when you get back, we'll go to Vauxhall again. Our last visit was such fun!"

"It was more than fun, it was wonderful. It will give me something to look forward to while I hobnob with the country bumpkins.'' Vauxhall was a treat he hadn't dared hope would be repeated for some time.

She handed him an envelope. "This should cover your expenses and a little more besides. Send me a note just as soon as you get back,'' she said, giving him her cheek to be kissed.

After he had left, there was a bright gleam in her eyes and she felt in a much better mood. In a few days, a week at the most, she would know exactly what she was up against and could plan accordingly.

As Colchester expected, his agent in Dorset had everything well in hand, but he believed in keeping a personal eye on his estates, so he inspected the property, visited the tenants, did a little fishing, and then returned to London.

He was not at all surprised when, the day after his return, he received a note from Lady Preston, asking him if he would care to partake of another fine supper. He was too experienced not to realize she had an ulterior motive, but it relieved the boredom of a stay in London without visiting his club, and he gladly accepted.

"I hope you don't think me forward, David,'' she said sweetly after he was settled once more, sipping a very fine sherry. "I know how lonely town can be for a married man, and though I would dearly love to drive with you through the park in your carriage, I know that such a thing is out of the question for you now.'' She heaved a regretful sigh.

"Quite so,'' he said dryly. "And though I could stay in Hanover Square, of course, conversations with my crazy grandmama would drive me mad, also.''

"The trouble is that you and your sweet mama are too kind, darling,'' Angelique murmured. "Anyone else would have consigned Lady Butterfield to Bedlam years ago. Has your bride had a taste of your grandmama's tongue yet?''

"They have met,'' Colchester said briefly, showing

no desire to have Elizabeth's name brought into any discussion here.

Angelique noted his tone and changed the subject. "One thing we could do is take an excursion to Vauxhall. If we wore masks, no one would know who we were," she suggested helpfully, having visited there many times in the past with men whose wives had been there also and not recogized them.

Colchester felt a stab of something very like pain as he remembered the delightful evening he and Elizabeth had spent in Vauxhall Gardens. "I'm afraid not," he said decisively. "Far too risky. You and I know, my dear, how harmless our relationship is, but if the *ton* got word of it, they'd put a very different construction on it. I assume your staff are extremely discreet?"

"They'd better be," Lady Preston assured him, "or they'll be out of a job and with no chance of getting another position. You have no need to worry in that direction, David."

The dinner was even more outstanding than before, for Angelique was quite familiar with his favorite dishes and this time was able to procure in advance the necessary ingredients. After eating his fill of the delicious food and fine wines, Colchester felt generous enough to allow Angelique to win at cards this time to offset the monies she had expended.

When she invited him once more a few days later, he brought her a small gift in the form of a diamond pin, and although on this occasion she changed into a most revealing gown and stroked his hand playfully, when he made no response, she desisted and they spent the evening playing a game of chess, at which she proved to be surprisingly good.

Angelique was resting on her chaise longue, trying to decide how she could get Colchester into a more romantic mood, when a note came from Trevor that he was back in town. She sent word for him to come to

luncheon, and when he appeared promptly, she
rewarded him with a long kiss and a glass of sherry.

She had planned a cold luncheon, and once it was set
on the sideboard, she dismissed the servants so that they
could talk without any eavesdroppers.

"She is very lovely, a little smaller than you, my dear,
but with the same black hair. She does not, of course,
have your exciting eyes," he allowed, "but just the
usual light-gray ones."

"Is she popular with Colchester's servants?" she
asked, a little put out with his description.

"Very. The report is that she's taken a tight hold on
the household reins and has effected many improvements without treading on anyone's toes," he re-
ported.

"And her relationship with Colchester? Could you
find out anything about that?" Angelique was anxious.

"It was difficult to get the staff to talk, but finally I
plied a groom with gin and found out that they don't get
along at all well. There is some doubt as to whether he
even visits her bedchamber these days, but despite that
fact, the lady is in a most interesting condition." He
dropped the bombshell, then waited for her response.

"What? She's pregnant? But they've not been
married more than four months," she exclaimed.

"And that's just about how far along she is," he
confirmed. "She doesn't show much, but the staff all
know and are taking great care of her."

To Angelique this was the worst possible news, for
she knew that Colchester needed an heir. But what was
he doing hanging around London if his wife was on the
way to presenting him with a possible son? Something
must be done about it.

"I don't like it, Trevor," she said softly. "I don't like
it at all. I wonder if it is his child, but whether or not, we
can't take chances. I want Colchester free to marry, and
right now he has one or more encumbrances inhibiting
him." She looked at her stepbrother, wondering how he

would react to her proposition. "I would be prepared to offer a great deal of money and other things to make sure that Colchester is freed from these encumbrances, if you understand my meaning."

Trevor didn't even stop to think about it. "If that's what you want, my dear Angelique, that's what you shall have. How soon do you wish to put your plan into effect?"

"Let's wait another week," she said thoughtfully, "for I need to be a little more sure of him before he goes rushing back to the country. Two weeks might be better still, I think."

"Very well, two weeks it shall be unless I hear from you in the meantime," Trevor agreed.

Angelique smiled for the first time since she heard of Elizabeth's condition. "How would you like to take me to Vauxhall tomorrow night? It will be a moonless night as before, and we will be completely masked."

"Angelique, my love, it would give me the greatest possible pleasure. I'll rent a carriage and call for you after dinner, if that's all right."

"It's perfect. We'll forget our relationship and have a wonderful time," she promised.

He raised her hand to his lips. "Until then, my love," he whispered, bowing low, then turned on his heel and left.

11

COLCHESTER HAD NOW been away from the castle for almost a month, and in that time he had heard nothing whatsoever from Elizabeth. Of course, he had not written to her either, but she had never been far from his mind, even during the three evenings he had spent with the beautiful Angelique.

He had declined all invitations received at his lodging and had not ventured near his club, but when the Dowager Lady Beresford sent a note begging him to attend a small reception she was giving, he felt unable to refuse.

The first thing he saw when he entered the door was the back of a familiar, fiery head of red hair. There could not be two men with that exact coloring, he knew. His right hand connected with the redhead's shoulder and swung him around.

"Jack Greenwood, by all that's wonderful!" he exclaimed. "It must be at least three years since I saw you last."

"David, I couldn't believe you were here. Your mama promised she would dig you out from wherever you've been hiding, but I had given up hope, for I've been around all your old haunts without success." Lord John Greenwood held his old friend close for a moment, then stood back to take a good look at him.

"You obviously missed one or two," Colchester said with a grin. "I must say you look wonderfully fit. What brings you to these parts, Jack?"

A happy smile lit the sun-bronzed, freckled face. "What else but a lady, my friend," he said happily. "I was here on a brief visit when I met the only young woman I've ever wished to marry. I changed my visit to a lengthier one, remained in town to court her, and considered myself the most fortunate man alive when she consented to be my wife."

"Congratulations, Jack. I'm delighted. Is this lucky lady with you tonight?" Colchester asked as he pumped his friend's hand.

"Of course. Your mama is giving us this reception to announce our betrothal, as she's a great friend of Pamela's aunt . . ." Jack started to say.

"It couldn't be Pamela Trevelyan, by any chance?" Colchester interrupted, and when his friend nodded, he continued, "Then I certainly do congratulate you again, for Pamela is a charming young lady, quite a cut above the usual debutante and will, I am sure, make you a very happy man."

Lady Beresford came over and slipped an arm through each of theirs. "It's time to join the receiving line, you two." She put up her face for a kiss from her son. "I'm so pleased you could come, David, but what a pity Elizabeth isn't with you to enjoy this occasion."

"Had you but told me who the reception was for, I'd have insisted she come to town to celebrate, Mama. She'll be sorry to have missed it. Where is Lady Lavinia?" He glanced around the room but could not see her.

"She'll join us as soon as we start to form the line. She is so excited, but hesitated to present Pamela and Jack on her own, so I, of course, offered to do so. Come along, now. As an old friend, Jack may just allow you to kiss his betrothed," she teased, "now that you are a happily married man yourself."

As they approached the place where the line was to form, Pamela left a group of young ladies she had been conversing with and threw herself into David's arms. "Wish me happy, David, please," she begged, her beautiful face glowing.

"I do, little one, from the bottom of my heart. You couldn't have chosen a better man," Colchester assured her, giving her a brotherly kiss.

They stood in line, receiving their guests, and it was some considerable time later that Pamela managed to get Colchester to herself again. When she did, she asked him about Elizabeth.

"Why didn't Elizabeth come with you when you came to town, David? Her last letter sounded rather strange, and I wrote last week telling her my good news, but she hasn't replied, which is not like her at all. Is something wrong between you?" she asked anxiously.

"Of course not," he lied. "The castle is a mammoth place, and she's thrown herself into bringing it to tip-top condition. I had not intended to be away so long, but I had to make an extended trip to Dorset and was then delayed by some business here." Colchester paused, thoughtfully. "You're right, however, it is unlike Elizabeth not to reply, and I am wondering if your letter could have been put, in error, with the correspondence awaiting my return."

Pamela gave a sigh of relief. "That must be what happened," she said, then asked, "If I beg her to come and help Aunt Lavinia with my wedding, will you mind? As we're to be married in two months, there's such a lot to do, and Elizabeth is so efficient. My aunt tries very hard, but seldom succeeds in accomplishing the tasks Elizabeth performs quite effortlessly."

He felt a surge of relief. This was just the excuse he had been waiting for. How good it would be to see her again, he thought. "I'll send a messenger to the castle first thing in the morning, telling her she *must* come to town right away," he promised.

Pamela gave him a big hug. "Thank you so much, David. You know, it was seeing you and Elizabeth so much in love that made me realize I could settle for nothing less. Now I'm so glad that I waited."

Before she could see the pain in his eyes, he swung her around to face Jack, who was approaching them from the other side of the room. "Just keep him looking at you like that, little one, and you'll have no problems," he whispered to her over her shoulder.

After arranging to meet with Jack the next day, Colchester returned to his lodging. Though the hour was late, he went straight to his desk to pen a note to Elizabeth. A bundle of letters forwarded from the castle by his agent lay there untouched, and he pushed them aside as he sharpened a quill.

As he pondered over the wording, his eyes fell once more on the batch of letters, and he picked them up, scattering them over the desk as he searched for one addressed to Elizabeth. He noticed one with an obviously feminine writing, and grunted with satisfaction when he found it was what he was looking for.

His first impulse was to include it with his own letter, but then he paused. Why not keep it and surprise her with it when she arrives? It was bound to put her in a happy frame of mind.

Having made his decision, he wrote a polite letter, simply requesting that she pack immediately and join him in London. As he applied his seal and sent for one of his staff to deliver it, he realized how much he was looking forward to her arrival, and he hoped she would be able to leave within a few days. It never occurred to him that she would refuse his invitation, and when the messenger returned with her reply, he flew into a rage.

Colchester's message came as quite a surprise to Elizabeth. She had been convinced that he had, for all intents and purposes, left her, and would return to the castle only for short intervals when the London round of activities palled.

However, she was now entering her fifth month of pregnancy and, though feeling extremely well, was quite obviously enceinte. Ladies in her condition usually left London for the country rather than going from the country to London.

She could not imagine why he should suddenly

request her presence, but assumed he was finding it uncomfortable to explain to his family and friends why they were apart so soon after their marriage.

She sat down with pen and paper and composed a reply to his request, then read it aloud to see how it sounded.

> My dear husband,
>   Flattered as I am by your belated desire for my company, I must regretfully decline your invitation. I have much to keep me occupied here and I find the country air more beneficial than that of the city. Your wife,
>
>   Elizabeth.

After sealing the note, she gave it to Shackleton, who would, in turn, give it to the earl's messenger. From her window, she watched the man ride away, and when he was out of sight, she turned back to the christening gown she was sewing. What would she do if, after reading her reply, he came in person? she wondered. She shrugged. She would cross that bridge when she reached it. It was time for luncheon, and these days, she was always hungry. Mrs. Fowler, who had become quite motherly toward her, said she was eating for two now and must keep up her strength.

When, two days later, Colchester's messenger came again, she felt a little anxious and took the letter to her chamber rather than opening it in the drawing room. The messenger had been sent to the kitchen to eat, and would, as before, be given a room for the night.

As she broke the seal, she had a sense of foreboding, and when she flattened the sheet, the words seemed to jump off the paper as though he were standing there shouting them at her.

> Madam,
>   As your husband, I no longer request your

presence in London; instead, I command you to join me without delay. I highly recommend you obey me this time, madam, else I will not be as patient and understanding toward you as I have been in the past.

Colchester

Elizabeth jumped up, her eyes blazing. "He commands me, indeed. How dare he! Patience and understanding. He doesn't know the meaning of the words," she shouted to the empty chamber.

She flung herself on the bed and pummeled the pillow with her fists in frustration. If only he were here now instead of the pillow, she thought, her eyes narrowing.

She wanted to reach for paper and immediately pen an appropriately biting response to him, but realized that to do so would probably bring him here the following day to enforce his orders in person, and that would not do at all.

This matter required calm deliberation, she decided, stretching out on the chaise longue and watching the flames curl around the logs in the hearth. An hour later, she rose and gave the bellpull the two tugs to summon Mrs. Fowler. There was a twinkle in her eyes and a look of smug satisfaction on her face.

"Mrs. Fowler," she said when that lady presented herself, "in order to answer the earl completely, I find that, though he may not at all like it, I must consult with my mama and papa on a certain matter. It is only a half-day's journey," she said with a little exaggeration, "and I plan to leave at first light. Jeannie will pack for me tonight and accompany me."

Mrs. Fowler nodded gravely.

"Once I arrive at Danville Hall, I will consult with my parents, then pen a note that the coachman will bring back to the castle, to give to the messenger. Of course, having journeyed there, my mama and papa will not hear of me coming straight back, so I will stay for a

week or so before returning," Elizabeth said, making it
seem the most normal thing to do.

"The messenger will wonder what's going on, milady,
if he's forced to wait two days for an answer," Mrs.
Fowler cautioned.

"I'm sure he will," Elizabeth agreed, "but it's not for
him to wonder. If someone could drop a hint that her
ladyship is a little under the weather and needs another
day or so to see how she feels before replying, it will
serve as an excuse for him to give to the earl."

"I reckon we can convince him, milady, if it will help
you to get everything decided," Mrs. Fowler conceded.
"And an extra glass or two of ale will make sure he's
still asleep when you leave. Would you like me to pack
a hamper for you so that you won't need to stop on the
way?"

"Yes, please, Mrs. Fowler. How thoughtful of you,"
Elizabeth said with a grateful smile. "And now, if you
can send Jeannie up, I'll get her started on the
packing."

After a restful night's sleep, Elizabeth left shortly
after dawn for Danville Hall. She carried with her the
reply she meant to send to Colchester, which she had
carefully composed before retiring last night. She only
wished she could see his face when he read it.

In her condition, the journey was a tedious one,
despite the comfort of the Colchester traveling coach.
Though she fell asleep for an hour or so just after they
left the castle, Elizabeth awoke with a slight headache
and a stiff back. She was grateful when they were finally
on what she still thought of as Danville lands,
approaching the hall.

The twins must spend much of their time watching for
the arrival of coaches, she thought as they came running
out of the house before she could be helped out of the
carriage.

"Where's David?" Sylvia asked, looking around as if
expecting him to come riding up at any minute.

"He's in London right now, so there's nothing to be gained by looking for him, Sylvie," Elizabeth said with a tired smile. When they started to pull her toward the steps, she laughingly stopped them. "Don't be so rough," she chided. "I'm in what is known as a rather delicate condition."

"I was going to say you'd got fat," Louise said, and they both stood back to stare at her, but Elizabeth did not mind. At their age she, too, would have been fascinated if someone close to her had been expecting a baby.

She looked up to see her mama standing in the doorway, a welcoming smile on her face. "Why didn't you let me know you were coming, Elizabeth?" she asked, beaming happily for once. "And you're going to make me a grandmama?"

"I wanted to surprise you all," Elizabeth said as she started to walk up the steps with a twin on each side of her.

On reaching the door, she kissed her mama and they all went into the drawing room.

"You arrived just in time for tea, Elizabeth, but as soon as you're refreshed, I think you'd better lie down for a while. You look as though you need a rest," Lady Danville said in an unusually motherly voice. "Did I hear you tell the twins that Colchester is in town right now? Is that why you came for a visit?"

Elizabeth tried to sound natural. "Yes, it is, really. He had to go to town on business, and I thought it a good opportunity to come to see you while I was still fit to travel," she said, then added ruefully, "I hadn't realized how tired I would become, however, so when I return, I'll stop at an inn for a meal so that I can stretch my legs."

"Do you want it to be a boy or a girl, Liza?" Louise asked eagerly.

"For myself I don't mind," she replied, then realized it was not quite true. "Perhaps I might like a girl, though. But it's always best if the firstborn is a boy to continue the line. The chances are even, I suppose, for Mama had all girls, while Lady Beresford had boys.''

"If David has a brother, why was he not at the wedding?" Sylvia demanded.

"I understood from Lavinia that he died in some sort of accident just after he came down from Cambridge. It was while David was with Wellington, I believe, but I've never discussed it with him." Elizabeth was thoughtful, for she had suddenly realized that was the reason why David was now under so much pressure to produce an heir.

Louise looked mischievous. "You won't be able to go riding this visit, but if you're very, very nice to us, Elizabeth, we'll let you come to the stable and visit our new mounts," she said with a grin.

Elizabeth's eyebrows rose. "Did Papa win this time?" she asked dryly, recalling that there had been no suitable horses for the twins to ride when last she was here.

"Didn't David tell you?" Sylvia asked. "He bought us two chestnut mares that are so alike you'd think they were twins also. He said they were a present for being bridesmaids at the wedding.''

Elizabeth felt an unexpected rush of warm feeling for David. What a very nice thing to do, she thought. Aloud, she said, "He was probably waiting for you to tell me yourselves. I know he's extremely fond of you both.''

"If you stay here much longer, Elizabeth, your eyes will close before you reach the stairs. Come, let's go and see if your room is ready," Lady Danville suggested. "I assume your doctor said it was all right for you to travel?''

"What. . . ?" Elizabeth started to ask, then corrected herself. "I'm sorry, Mama, I thought you said something else. Of course the doctor said I was fit to travel. Aside from a few weeks of early-morning indisposition, I've been in the best of health.''

Of couse, she hadn't known what doctor to see, with Colchester away, and so she'd just taken Mrs. Fowler's advice. She supposed she'd better do something about finding out who the family doctor was when she returned to the castle. Suddenly she remembered some lines from a work of Walter Scott. "Oh, what a tangled web we weave, When first we practice to deceive." How true, she thought.

It was such a comfort to be in the bedchamber that had been hers as a girl, with a room adjoining where Nanny had slept whenever she was not feeling well. Before she slipped between the cool sheets, she took out her note addressed to Colchester and gave it to Jeannie.

"Take this to the coachman and tell him to be sure to give it to Shackleton as soon as he gets back to the castle tomorrow," she instructed. "Tell him it's very important and he must not lose it or forget to deliver it."

"I'll take it right away, milady," Jeannie assured her, and hurried from the room.

With a satisfied smile, Elizabeth lay back against the soft pillows. Everything was going the way she had planned. She was glad she'd brought Jeannie, for she no longer knew which of the hall's servants could be trusted. Her father did not pay servants at all well, even when he was in funds, and the good ones rarely stayed very long.

"Why are you still in semi-mourning, my girl?" Danville asked when they were seated at dinner. "Just confirms my opinion that the earl is somewhat clutch-fisted. Won't buy you any new gowns."

"But he bought Elizabeth dozens of new gowns, Papa," Louise protested. "We saw them before the wedding. What happened to them, Liza?"

"I have been increasing in size, my love," Elizabeth teased, "or had you forgotten? It was easier for me to have my own things let out, for I can throw them away later, but I hated to damage the ones you admired so much." It was a reasonable explanation, she knew.

It seemed that for the first time, Lord Danville realized his daughter was *enceinte*. "Well, that was fast, my dear. He must be overjoyed enough to buy you the moon, never mind a few gowns," he remarked thoughtfully.

"Of course, Papa," Elizabeth agreed. "I'm the one who chose to wear my old gowns."

"Why isn't he with you, instead of letting you gallivant around the countryside in that condition?" he asked, anxious to put Colchester in as bad a light as possible.

"He's in town on some business or other at the moment," Elizabeth said vaguely, "but I promise you he'll be here within a few days."

"He will?" Louise and Sylvia spoke in unison, as they frequently did. "You didn't tell us that when you arrived. What day is he coming?"

"I don't know." Elizabeth was enjoying being mysterious. "But I promise he will be here, not tomorrow, but possibly a couple of days after that."

"Did he tell you so?" Louise wanted to be certain.

"No, but I just know he will. Believe me, won't you?" Elizabeth asked. "Have I ever let you down?"

They both shook their heads, for she had always been careful to fulfill her promises.

When Lady Danville gave the signal for the ladies to retire to the drawing room, her husband detained Elizabeth.

"Stay and join me while I drink my port," he requested. "Perhaps you'd take a glass with me for once?"

"I'll stay, of course, but it will have to be tea, I'm afraid. Port doesn't seem to agree with me these days," she said apologetically.

When they were alone, he gave her a long, hard look. "Did I hear you say that Colchester will be here in a few days?" he asked.

"Yes, I'm pretty sure he will, Papa. And though I would like to stay here for a few weeks, he will probably want to return to the castle immediately, for a number of problems await him there." She did not look forward to their first meeting, but felt sure he would be somewhat restrained in front of her family, and anxious to get her away from their influence.

Lord Danville loudly cleared his throat. "He must be very pleased with you now you're carrying a possible heir. You can twist him around your little finger these days, I'll be bound."

"I don't know about that, sir," Elizabeth said, "for I've not put such a thing to the test. Is that how you were with mother before I was born?"

"That's too long ago for me to remember, and ours wasn't a love match, but suitably arranged for us." He decided to come to the point. "You remember, I'm sure, how I wanted you to wed a man of my choice?" He waited for her response.

"Yes, Papa, I remember very well," she said calmly, then realized where this conversation was leading. "Don't tell me you tried to get Colchester to buy his bride," she said scornfully.

"I don't like your tone, madam." Things were not going the way he had planned. "In view of our family's financial straits, it would not have been unusual for a wealthy bridegroom to offer a little help," he snapped.

"If he turned you down then, Papa, I would not recommend that you try again, for I'm sure he will be no more receptive to the idea now than he was before." She looked at him with a measure of pity. "And I would not advise you to sell the mounts he bought the twins, for he would be sure to find out and he has quite a violent temper."

"I wasn't thinking of approaching him myself," Lord Danville said. "A wife would be in a much better position to ask favors for her family. You have an obligation to your own kin, you know."

She slowly rose to her feet, a sad expression on her face. "No, Papa," she said gently, "any obligation I might have had was well and truly met when I married Dewsbury. Unless Colchester asks me directly, I will not mention this conversation to him."

As she reached the door, she turned and looked at him, sitting slumped at the table, head in hands, but she felt no compassion for him. One thing she intended to do was to make sure he would not use either of the twins in the way he had used her.

Having commanded Elizabeth to come to town, Colchester was not too concerned when the messenger did not return promptly, for he surmised that she would use him as an outrider on her journey to London. In view of this, he was completely taken aback when the messenger finally returned with another note, and the excuse that she had not felt well enough to pen a letter for several days.

"Did you actually see her ladyship?" he demanded as the servant made apologies for his delay.

"No, milord, that I never did. The butler took your note from me, and it was he who brought back her ladyship's reply," he muttered.

Dismissing the man, Colchester ripped open the letter from his wife and started to read.

> Sir,
>   In light of your limited patience and understanding, I am persuaded that a sojourn in London would not be beneficial to my health at this time. I will, therefore, remain in the country, sir, as your command is not my wish.
>
>   Elizabeth

Striding toward the bell rope, Colchester proceeded to yank at it until, to his surprise, he found himself holding only the end in hand. He had achieved his objective, however, for his valet hurried into the room, somewhat out of breath.

"I'm leaving for the castle immediately," Colchester thundered. "Tell the stables to saddle the stallion right away. You will pack enough for a few nights and follow me in the carriage. And see that this worthless piece of string is replaced before I return." He threw the tassled end of the bell rope in Barnes' direction and strode from the room in a rage the likes of which the valet could not remember seeing.

In less than an hour he was on the outskirts of the city and by midnight he was nearing the castle, having stopped to change horses and sup a tankard of ale, but all he ate was a hunk of cheese between bread, for he would not take the time for a meal.

Only a sleepy stable boy was awake when he first arrived at the castle, but within fifteen minutes servants were scurrying around to take care of his demands as quickly as possible, before they felt the edge of his sharp tongue.

When he had given orders for a substantial meal to be prepared, he headed up the huge staircase and burst into his wife's bedchamber, only to find the room dark, cold, and empty.

This was something he had not reckoned on. Stunned, he went through to his own chamber, where a footman was hurriedly lighting a fire while Mrs. Fowler aired the bed.

As soon as the footman had left the room, he questioned Mrs. Fowler.

"I assume her ladyship is not in the house, Mrs. Fowler," he said in a deadly quiet tone.

"Yes, milord—I mean, no, milord." The tired and flustered housekeeper shook her head. "I'm sorry, sir. Her ladyship left on a visit to Danville Hall two days ago."

Suddenly realizing he was upsetting everyone with his thoughtlessness, he took her arm and led her toward the door. "You've done all that is needed here, Mrs. Fowler. Go back to bed and I'll see you in the morning," he said in a kindlier tone.

Shackleton was in uniform and supervising the laying of the table when Colchester reached the dining room, and the look he received from the old servant was as near a reproof as any he had seen since he was a boy.

He forced a smile. "I'm very tired and very hungry, my friend. As long as the soup is piping hot, I'll make do with a generous helping of cold meat and whatever vegetables you can find. First, though, I need a glass of brandy."

Shackleton brought the decanter to the table and poured his master a glass.

"I assume that none of the inns could accommodate you, my lord," he said as he placed the glass in front of Colchester.

"You are quite aware of the fact that I did not seek a room, but was anxious to get here as quickly as possible," Colchester said irritably.

With a straight face, Shackleton asked, "You thought the castle was on fire, sir?"

Colchester's remaining anger dissolved as he roared with laughter. "No," he finally said, "I'm afraid the fire was under me all the way here."

Satisfied with the admission, the butler left the room to see what had happened to the oxtail soup.

Colchester slept well for what remained of the night, and awoke the next morning, refreshed and ready for his ride to Danville Hall and his encounter with Elizabeth.

He left instructions that when his valet arrived in the carriage, he should be sent after him, but as all the servants assumed he knew her ladyship was with child, none of them thought to mention her condition.

12

"I THOUGHT YOU said David would be here in a few days, Elizabeth," Sylvia said impatiently. "This is your fifth day and still he's not arrived. Are you sure he means to come?"

A strange feeling in the pit of her stomach told Elizabeth that he would be here some time today, but she felt fairly safe until after luncheon.

She reassured the twin. "He's on his way, I know. If you're so anxious, why don't you keep a sharp lookout for him and let me know when you see him in the distance."

"Louise and I will take turns and we'll come and tell you the minute he comes in sight, for I know you'll want to look your best when he gets here," Sylvia promised.

They took up a post at an upstairs window, taking turns only to eat lunch. Elizabeth, watching them, wondered if she had ever been so young and eager and sure that everything would work out well. She doubted it, for she felt that the twins bolstered each other's self-confidence. For the first time she wondered if she might be carrying twins. It was an interesting thought.

"He's coming, Liza," Louise called suddenly. "I can see him in my telescope."

Elizabeth thanked her shakily, then turned toward her bedchamber, but before she reached it, she was suddenly overcome by a sense of panic and she took the back stairs instead. Two maids who were coming in from the kitchen garden stared at her for a moment, then gave little bobs as she hurried past them and out through the back door. Realizing that she was going so fast that anyone who saw her would wonder, she made herself slow down until she was out of sight of the house, then she increased her pace once more. She had to find somewhere peaceful where she could just sit and think.

On reaching the woods, she set off down a familiar footpath. She was forced to tread carefully, for it would not do to trip on a root and fall. She headed for a grassy clearing she remembered lay just a little farther, where she could sit on one of the boulders and try to steady her rapidly beating heart.

As she reached the opening, she heard the sound of snapping twigs behind her and Rusty, the twins' spaniel pup, bounded into view, playfully snapping at flies and pausing to sniff at every suspicious-looking rock.

Smiling at his antics, she lowered herself carefully onto a flat boulder and stretched out her legs in front of her. Rusty, tiring of that particular rock, entered the clearing and gamboled toward her with a puppy's awkward gait, his long, floppy ears almost dragging the ground and his silky tail wagging happily.

As Elizabeth reached out to pat him, he jumped up with his front paws on her lap and tried to lick her face. The swift movement startled her, and clumsy with her added weight, she lost her balance and tumbled onto the soft grass.

Although she heard the sound of a shot being fired, everything occurred so swiftly that she did not know what had happened until she felt the weight of the pup as it fell on top of her. She tried to push it off, then saw the blood and heard screams, but did not realize they were coming from her own lips.

Despite his tiredness, Colchester felt a surge of excitement as Danville Hall came into sight. He knew he would have to stay the night, for Barnes and the carriage would not get here until much later, but the first thing he intended to do was find Elizabeth and make it very plain who gave the orders in his household. Then, on the morrow, they would start out for London.

For a moment he thought the black-haired female coming out of the front door was his wife, but when a second, identically dressed, followed, he realized the twins were coming to meet him.

Dismounting, he submitted to their warm hugs with a broad grin and allowed them to escort him into the house while a stable boy took his horse.

"Elizabeth assured us you would be here today," Louise told him, "but we didn't know whether to believe her or not, as you had sent no word, David."

"As soon as we told her you were in sight, she hurried to her chamber to make herself pretty for you," Sylvia said with a mischievous grin. "It's her old room, the third door on the right of the stairs, and as Mama is out visiting, you don't need to stand on ceremony."

He bounded up the stairs, made for the room, and flung open the door, but to his surprise the twins were wrong and the only person in the chamber was a maid, staring at him openmouthed.

"Do you know where Lady Elizabeth might be?" he asked the girl as she tried nervously to edge around him and get out of the room.

When she did not answer, he reached for a gold piece. "This is yours if you can tell me where she went," he said, tight-lipped.

"She went out the kitchen garden, milord," the maid said, hungry eyes never leaving the coin in his fingers. "And we watched her take the path for the woods. In a big hurry she was, milord."

"Take me through the back of the house and point the way," he ordered, retaining his hold on the coin until she obeyed his instructions.

The maid led him quickly down the back stairs and through the garden, until the footpath came into view. Dropping the coin into the pocket of her apron, he set off at a fast pace.

He had already entered the woods when he heard a
gun shot followed by screams; he started to run toward
the sound and within a few minutes reached the
clearing. Panic clutched his heart when he saw Elizabeth
lying on the ground. He dropped to his knees at his
wife's side, lifting the dead pup and placing it on the
grass. Quiet now, Elizabeth stared at him with fear-
filled eyes.

Colchester gasped when he saw Elizabeth's size, but
made no comment. "Are you hurt anywhere,
Elizabeth?" he asked, looking at the bloodstains on her
gown.

"No," she whispered. "That's from Rusty. Is he
dead?"

"Yes, I'm afraid he is," Colchester said quietly.
"We'll have to leave him here and get you back to the
house as quickly as possible. I'll carry you . . ." he
began as he bent to pick her up.

She shook her head violently. "No, please. I can
walk. It's not very far."

Anxious not to disturb the control she was trying to
maintain, he helped her to her feet and placed an arm
around her, feeling her trembling. "Lean on me and
we'll take it very slowly," he instructed, watching her
closely, ready to pick her up at the first signs of
faintness.

"How did you know where I was?" she asked as they
proceeded slowly along the footpath.

"I bribed a maid," he said briefly. "Don't try to talk
right now. You need all your strength just to walk. You
know, I could—"

"No," she said vehemently. "I don't want to be
carried home again."

Colchester raised his eyebrows at her words, then said
soothingly, "All right, if that's what you want, but keep
quiet now and we'll talk once you're safely tucked in
bed."

It was quicker to go into the house the way they had

left it, through the back door, but when they reached the foot of the steep back stairs, Colchester, ignoring her protests, lifted her in his arms and carried her up and into her bedchamber, laying her gently on the bed.

Two sharp tugs on the bellpull brought Jeannie running.

"Find Nanny and tell her to send someone for the doctor, then both of you come back here," Colchester ordered. "And, Jeannie, leave word for Lady Danville, also, when she returns."

"I'm all right, really, Colchester," Elizabeth said fretfully. "It was such a shock, that's all."

"I just want to know one thing for now, my dear. How close to you was the pup when he was shot?" Colchester's face was grave with concern.

"Very close," Elizabeth said, trying to remember. "He jumped up, trying to lick my face. If I had not lost my balance, it might have been me who was . . ." She broke off, unable to put into words what she had just realized.

Nanny came bustling into the room, with Jeannie just behind, and to avoid embarrassing Elizabeth further, Colchester left the room to see that his instructions had been carried out.

As he reached the hall, Sylvia and Louise came running up to him. "What happened to Elizabeth?" they cried in unison. "Is she hurt?"

He steered them into the drawing room and closed the door. "I'm not sure what exactly happened, nor even what she was doing in the woods." He gave a tug on the bellpull. "I've sent for the doctor. I don't believe she's injured, but she has received a terrible shock and I'm afraid your puppy, Rusty, was killed."

The butler's knock on the door was drowned by the exclamations of the twins. When he entered, Colchester gave him instructions regarding the location and the burial of the pup, then turned back to Louise and Sylvia.

"The little fellow may have saved your sister's life, for she might just as easily have been hit by that stray shot," he told them. "She's in good hands, for Nanny is with her now, and I'll talk to the doctor when he has examined her."

"It's just like last time," Louise said, "when Goliath threw her and Sir George found her in the woods and carried her home."

So that was what Elizabeth had meant when she said she didn't want to be carried home again, he thought. "That was about a month before we were married, wasn't it?" he asked aloud. "Tell me what happened."

Sylvia shrugged. "She'd only arrived the day before and she didn't know that Papa had sold our mounts and bought the stallion. She went to the stables at crack of dawn, and when all she could see there to ride was Goliath, she had him saddled."

"He was always throwing Papa, and no one else was allowed to ride him, even if they'd wanted to. Papa was furious when he found she'd ridden him," Louise put in.

"She couldn't hold Goliath to the bridle path, and he took her into the woods and threw her," Sylvia continued. "She had an awful bruise on her head, and had to stay in bed for a couple of days."

"Who is Sir George?" Colchester asked, suspiciously.

The twins looked at each other, then Louise answered. "He's an old friend of Elizabeth's, Sir George Carlton. And he's always been very fond of her. He was very upset when he heard she was going to marry you," she said slyly.

Had Elizabeth been around, she would have recognized that they were deliberately leading him along, but Colchester was too jealous to realize their childish ploy. When they went out to the stables, leaving him to await the doctor's arrival, his eyebrows were drawn together in a heavy frown.

Danville Hall was still the largest house for many miles, and it was not long before the doctor arrived in his trap. After Colchester had introduced himself, he hurried up the stairs and was closeted with Elizabeth and Nanny for some time, while Colchester paced the corridor outside.

When he came out at last, Colchester led him to the library, helped them both to Danville's brandy, and asked the man how his wife was.

"I would say the worst thing she's suffering from at the moment is fear. She has realized that it might easily have been her and not the dog that was killed," the doctor told him. "She is in her fifth month of pregnancy, and so far all seems to be in order. Nanny is a very sensible woman, though, and I have alerted her to send for me right away should she show any signs of losing the child."

"Have you given her anything to settle her nervousness and help her sleep?" Colchester asked.

The doctor nodded. "I've given her a sedative that should keep her quiet for a few hours, and left more with Nanny in case she has a bad night. Don't fret too much, though. She's fine—there's not even a bruise on her. Not like the last time when, aside from the concussion and the big bruise on her head, she was scratched and scraped all over."

"You attended her then, sir?" Colchester asked casually, carefully refilling the doctor's glass.

"Yes, I did. That stallion must have given her a rough ride before he threw her, for there was even blood on her thighs. It worried me, at the time, for she'd been married several years, but I heard later that he was an old man, so that was probably what it was." He emptied his glass, and as Colchester appeared to be deep in thought and not inclined to fill it again, he rose. "I'll be on my way then, my lord, and I'll drop by again to take a look at her tomorrow."

Colchester thanked him for his help and escorted him

to the door, then went up the stairs to Elizabeth's room.

She had bathed and changed into a nightgown, and her eyelids looked heavy. He touched her soft cheek gently with one finger and instantly her eyes opened wide, flickering with fear as she saw who it was. The sedative was taking effect, however, and the look faded as her lids slowly closed.

"I've just given her the potion the doctor left for her, my lord," Nanny told him, "and I think she'll sleep for a few hours. I'll stay with her for now, of course, and have Jeannie sit here through the night, if you like."

Hearing movements in the next room, Colchester strode to the adjoining door and opened it to find two maids busy lighting a fire and making up the bed. He saw his riding crop and gloves on a chair.

"It won't be necessary to have Jeannie here. I'll leave the door open between and be here in a moment if she stirs," he said with a grim smile. "Campaigning with Wellington turned me into a very light sleeper."

There was a knock on the door and Lady Danville entered. "I think Elizabeth had better stay indoors on her future visits," she remarked after taking a close look at her sleeping daughter. "It seems she gets into accidents every time she goes out of doors."

She came over to Colchester and raised her cheek for him to kiss. "I'm glad you're here, my boy," she told him with a look of relief. "I met the doctor just as he was leaving, and he tells me she's going to be all right. I can't imagine who would be hunting in the home woods without our permission, but Danville will check into it when he gets home, I'm sure."

They went out of the room together, leaving Nanny to nurse her charge, and entered the drawing room, where tea was just being brought in.

"Thank heavens for their promptness. That's just what I need," Lady Danville remarked as Sylvia started to pour. "The only good thing about this accident is that you will now have to stay here a week or so until she's fit to travel, and we'll all have a chance to get to know you, David.''

Colchester knew it to be true and did not relish the thought of spending time in Danville's company. Nevertheless, Elizabeth's mother seemed pleasant enough and the twins were like the younger sisters he'd never had.

As he looked at them now, they seemed more subdued than before, and there were signs of puffiness around their eyes. He hazarded a guess that they had attended the burial of their puppy.

As Louise handed him a cup of tea, he asked her, "Is everything all right?"

She gave him a nod and a watery smile. "He was such a sweet little pup, still a baby really," she said. "Sylvie says we have to get another right away."

"It would be a good idea, I believe," he said kindly. "If you know where there might be a litter, perhaps I can take you to pick one out tomorrow."

"I think Sylvie knows," she said. "I'll ask her later."

A commotion in the hall heralded the return of Lord Danville.

"What's this I hear about Elizabeth having another accident?" he asked loudly as he walked into the room. Then he noticed Colchester and offered his hand. "David, nobody told me you'd arrived, though Elizabeth said you were coming. Did you see what happened?"

"No, sir," Colchester drawled, his manner instantly changing with the appearance of the one member of the family he disliked. "I'm afraid I was a few minutes too late for that."

"But you heard the shot?" Danville asked.

"Yes, I heard it," Colchester confirmed, "but at the time I was more interested in helping my wife than in chasing the poacher or whoever it was." He turned to Lady Danville. "If you will excuse me, my lady, I believe I'll find out if my valet arrived yet. I'll see you at dinner."

With a smile for the twins, he left the room, but before going to his own bedchamber, he stopped to check on Elizabeth.

She was sleeping soundly, and some color had returned to her cheeks. Nanny started to get up when he came in, but he motioned her to remain seated. "Has she awakened at all?" he asked.

"No, my lord, I don't think she will for a while." Nanny smiled fondly as she looked at Elizabeth, and Colchester felt pleased that his wife was being watched over by someone who cared, rather than an impersonal servant.

"I'm going to rest for a while before I change for dinner," he told her. "If you need me, I'll be in the next room."

He closed the communicating door quietly behind him, and was somewhat relieved to find that Barnes had arrived and was busily unpacking his clothes, separating the things that needed to be pressed. He gave his man instructions as to what he would wear this evening, then sat down in an armchair to ponder the events of the day. Within a few minutes he was fast asleep.

Dinner was not very entertaining. The twins were still subdued, and Danville had obviously imbibed too freely beforehand. Lady Danville kept up a conversation with a series of vague trivialities that seemed to interest no one, but even she appeared relieved when she could signal the twins to leave the gentlemen to their port.

Once they had left, Colchester expected his host to expound on how badly scorched he was, but was gratified when the port seemed to have the effect of a soporific on Danville, who lapsed into a quiet stupor. He only blinked and mumbled a good night when Colchester excused himself and went into the drawing room, where he spent a few minutes with the ladies before retiring upstairs.

After dismissing Barnes and Nanny, Colchester checked on the candles in both his and the sleeping

Elizabeth's room, opened the door between them wide, and slipped between the sheets.

He had slept for perhaps a couple of hours when he was awakened by a faint murmur from the next room. Instantly alert, he was at the door by the time Elizabeth called out more loudly in her sleep.

"Don't, David. Please don't shoot!"

She started to cry in her sleep and he sat on the edge of the bed and drew her into his arms, deeply concerned that even subconsciously she would think it was he who had tried to kill her.

"It's all right, my love," he murmured soothingly, holding her close and rocking her gently. "No one's going to shoot you. It's just a bad dream."

The sobs subsided gradually and Elizabeth awoke to find herself in David's arms.

"Where's Nanny?" she asked, remembering that Nanny was sitting knitting when she went to sleep.

"In her bed asleep, I hope," he answered with a grin. "It's the middle of the night."

"I don't remember the dream, but it must have been bad because I was crying. I wonder why," she said, a puzzled frown on her face.

"It was bad, my love. Do you really think I was the one who tried to shoot you?" he asked gently.

Elizabeth flushed. "I don't know. You were the only person around, and you were there just minutes afterward," she said hesitantly, hoping he would deny it.

"The shot came from the north, and I was coming from the east—from the back of the house—when I heard it. I was just entering the woods, and when, a second later, I heard you start to scream, I ran toward the sound as fast as I could. How could you possibly think I would want to shoot you?" he asked.

"I don't believe you felt exactly loving toward me when you got my last letter." She lifted her chin and ventured a look at his face, and what she saw there made her feel weak all over.

"Minx," he murmured, "you knew what my reaction

would be so well that you told your family I would be
arriving just after lunch." He could no longer resist the
temptation and bent his head down to place a tender
kiss on her slightly parted lips.

"I don't know, however, if I can forgive you for not
telling me you were carrying my child." He looked
gravely down at her. "Why did you keep it from me,
love?"

"You were so sure I had lied to you, that I feared you
might not believe it was yours."

"It's mine," he said, "of that I'm sure. As soon as
you're well enough, we'll go home, my dear Eliza, and
this time I'll stay there and look after you."

Her eyelids suddenly grew heavy and she had
difficulty in keeping them open to talk. With a tender
smile he placed her head back on the pillow and drew
the bed linen around her shoulders.

"I'll stay here until you're asleep, and then I'll go
back to my own bed, but I'll hear you, so call to me if
you need anything," he instructed, placing a kiss on her
upturned nose.

Her even breathing told him she had fallen back into
a deep sleep, but still he sat there watching her, thinking
back on their conversation. There was no question in his
mind that someone had tried to shoot her, and he could
not deny that he had been close by at the time. He
silently swore to find the man who had fired that shot
and deal with him as he deserved. Then he would take
her home to the castle, beg her forgiveness, and make a
fresh start.

13

WHEN ELIZABETH AWOKE, she lay completely still for some time, reluctant to open her eyes. She had been dreaming they were back in Colchester Castle, that she and David were no longer at odds with each other, and that she had even seen their small son, a replica of his father, running around the vast hall. But once she was completely awake, she felt a strange foreboding, as if today were going to prove even worse than yesterday.

Her common sense asserted itself, however, and she opened her eyes to find David sitting on the chair beside the bed, looking intently at her.

"Hello, sleepyhead," he said softly. "Do you feel any the worse for yesterday's adventure, or is it too soon to ask?"

She stretched her limbs and found that there was not so much as a tiny ache in any of them.

"Everything seems to be working," she assured him, "and I believe I should get up, for I feel like a sluggard, lying in bed when there's nothing wrong with me."

"You're staying right where you are, young lady, until the good doctor has pronounced you well enough to get up for an hour or so," he said firmly, then his face softened. "I have to ask you a favor. There's something I've wanted to do ever since I first set eyes on you yesterday." He pointed to the slight bulge of her belly under the bedclothes. "May I?"

Elizabeth felt suddenly shy. It seemed to her that it was months since he had desired to look at her, let alone touch her, but she realized most husbands would not have asked. She wanted to feel again the warm glow that spread through her each time his hand even brushed against her. He watched her closely, waiting for permission, so she pushed the bedclothes back, revealing her outline beneath a white cotton shift.

With an expression of awe, he placed his bronzed hand on her softly rounded stomach, and she instinctively quivered at his touch.

"Mrs. Fowler says that soon I'll be able to feel him moving and kicking inside," Elizabeth told him, secretly thrilled at the wonder on his face. Then his expression grew stern.

"Have you any idea how angry I am that you didn't tell me before I left?" he asked, a hint of steel in his voice.

His tone of voice made Elizabeth feel cold and uncertain once more. "I already explained why I couldn't tell you. I thought you understood."

"To some extent I do, but by not knowing, I've missed a very precious time. I don't understand why neither Mrs. Fowler nor Shackleton said anything. Did you by any chance tell them not to?" he asked.

She shook her head. "I wouldn't do that. But they assumed you knew and I told them nothing to the contrary." Her lips quivered in secret amusement as she remembered her note to him. "I also made it a point to keep out of the way of your messenger each time he came, as he would surely have said something to you." A hint of mischief sparkled in her gray eyes.

He picked up her dainty white hand and lowered his mouth to enclose a knuckle. Elizabeth gave a little gasp, thinking he was going to bite down on it as Dewsbury had once done in his frustration, but the only pressure she felt was the soft, moist warmth of his lips. She felt a glow start in her finger and spread quickly through her body.

When he had replaced her hand by her side, he tilted her chin to bring her face closer. "Don't ever think I would deliberately hurt you, Eliza. If I couldn't hurt you when I was so foolishly angry that morning, then you can rest assured I never will."

He touched her lips with his, and as the kiss deepened and became more demanding, her arms slid around his neck and pulled him closer. His hand untied the string of her gown and slid inside to stroke a smooth round breast, caress the tip, and then move onto the other, and she felt swept by an almost unbearable longing.

Neither of them heard the light knock on the door, but Nanny's voice asking to be excused aroused them and Colchester gently released his wife and lowered her onto her pillow while his body screened her from any eyes but his own.

"Come in, Nanny. My wife is much recovered, and I believe she is probably extremely hungry, aren't you, my love?" Colchester gazed at her tenderly, but there was still enough fire in his eyes to reveal the urgency of his feelings.

Elizabeth sighed heavily and started to fasten the top of her gown, suddenly realizing she was indeed very hungry. "I'm starving. I suppose I slept through dinner last night. Can you bring me something, Nanny?" she asked.

"The doctor said nothing about food, but I cannot think that a little gruel would harm," Nanny conceded. "I'll go and see what I can find."

As the door closed, Colchester bent over the bed once more and allowed his lips to explore her upturned face, nibbling on each ear, gently caressing each eyelid, her nose, then settling at last on her mouth.

When he raised his head, they were both breathless and Elizabeth's eyes were starry.

"I'd better leave you to Nanny's care before I reach a point beyond which I must not proceed," he said tenderly.

"I want to go home as soon as possible, David," she told him, her voice husky with passion, "so long as you still stay with me this time."

"I will be closer than your own shadow, and so protective you'll grow tired of seeing me around," he promised. "But I won't take you home until the doctor is very sure there will be no repercussions. I have seen men appear unconcerned after the most ferocious battle, then collapse with shock two days later."

They both heard footsteps approaching along the corridor, and with a quick squeeze of her hand Colchester escaped to his own chamber just seconds before Nanny opened the door.

Louise and Sylvia ran Colchester to earth in the dining room, where he was partaking of a substantial breakfast.

"We just stopped in to see Elizabeth and she was completely recovered, but she says you will not let her get up until after the doctor has been this afternoon," Sylvia said accusingly.

"I think Nanny probably seconded my decision, and I have no doubt Lady Danville will also agree," he said with a grin, "so stop giving me those fearsome looks. Did you go riding before breakfast?"

Louise came back from the sideboard with two plates of food in her hands and sat down, placing one of them in front of her twin. "Yes, and we ate before we left, but we got hungry again. We always do," she said, taking a bite of a piece of toast.

He could still recall how constantly hungry he had been at sixteen, and sympathized with them.

"When you've finished, will you come with us to Dobbs Farm and help pick out another pup?" Sylvia begged. "You'll be back long before the doctor gets here," she added, knowing instinctively that he would want to see the man himself.

He smiled broadly. He was becoming very fond of his two young sisters-in-law. "I would be delighted to accompany you and to see a little of the countryside at the same time. First, however, I would like to take a look in those woods and see if there are any signs of poachers having been around.''

"You need to talk to Smathers, the head groom," Louise told him. "He went out yesterday afternoon to take a look. He wouldn't tell us if he found anything, but I'm sure he'll tell you."

"I'll have a word with him before we start out," Colchester said, "and now, if you ladies will excuse me, I'll check on your sister and be ready to leave in about half an hour."

Elizabeth was sitting up in bed with a lacy wrap around her shoulders, a copy of one of Mrs. Radcliffe's novels in her hands and a mutinous expression on her face. It had been a long time since she was forced to do something against her will.

Jeannie was tidying the dressing table, having brushed and dressed her mistress's black hair so that it framed her face becomingly. At Colchester's signal, she left the chamber.

"I assume that patience is not your strong suit, my love?" Colchester said with a lift of his eyebrows. "Perhaps I should ask Nanny to bring you another of the good doctor's potions and make you sleep this morning," he suggested.

Elizabeth looked alarmed. "You wouldn't do that, David, would you?"

"It might be what you need. Your cheeks are a little flushed," he remarked.

"That's only because I've just been throwing my weight around at Nanny—to no avail, I might add," she said, a little shamefaced.

Colchester laughed out loud, delighted that she was so frank and open with him once more. Then he remembered something. "In all the excitement I completely forgot to tell you why I wanted you to come to London."

"It was hardly because you desired my company, I know," she said tartly.

"It was not entirely for that reason, I agree, though I was missing you more than I cared to believe," he admitted. "If I can trust you to stay right there, I'll get something from my chamber that you'll find most interesting."

He went through the connecting door and was back a moment later with an unopened letter in his hand.

"This was forwarded to me in London, by mistake, of course," he told her as he dropped it on the counterpane, "but it caused one young lady a great deal of worry when she did not receive a prompt reply from you."

Elizabeth looked at the writing. "Why, it's from Pamela," she exclaimed, breaking the seal and eagerly unfolding the pages.

Colchester enjoyed watching the range of expressions on her face, from a perplexed frown, to curiosity and finally complete delight, and wondered how he could ever have thought her capable of deception of any sort.

"This is wonderful news, David, and I only wish I'd known earlier for I would have come up to London at once. You've seen Pamela, of course?" she asked.

He nodded. "Mama particularly wanted me to attend a reception she was giving, and when I arrived, I found it was to celebrate the engagement of a very old friend of mine, Jack Greenwood, to none other than Pamela Trevelyan."

"Oh, David, I'm so glad it's someone you know. Is he nice? Is he good enough for her?" Elizabeth asked excitedly.

"Yes, they're very well matched and incredibly happy," he assured her. "She wanted you to come to town to help Lady Lavinia arrange for the wedding, which is to be in less than two months now, and—"

"Then we'll go to London directly from here, David, and we'll stay in Grosvenor Street, for we have the perfect excuse for not joining your grandmama in your house." Her eyes glowed with pleasure at his news, then turned to dismay as he slowly but firmly shook his head.

"You silly widgeon," he said affectionately. "When I sent for you, I was unaware of your condition. There's only one place you should be at this particular time, and that's at home in the country, not running around London."

"Oh, no!" she moaned. "You mean I can't even go to my stepdaughter's wedding?"

"I'm sorry, love, but both for yours and the baby's sake, it's best that you miss this one," he said gently. "If you like, I'll invite them to stop over for a couple of nights before they go off on their wedding trip."

Elizabeth knew there was no arguing. If she should lose her baby for the sake of attending a wedding, she would not seek forgiveness from him, for she would never be able to forgive herself.

She nodded, then looked at him curiously. "When did you find Pamela's letter? Was it after you had been to the betrothal?"

He grinned. "I found it that night, just as I started to write and ask you to join me in town."

"Why didn't you send it back to me? You know I would have come at once," she told him, then her cheeks turned a soft pink as she thought of the letters she had sent him.

"I wanted you to come because *I* had asked you, not because Pamela had done so," he explained, then suggested, "Why don't you take a piece of paper while you're lying there this morning and make up a list of things for Lavinia to do. I know how much she'll appreciate it, and they'll both enjoy just hearing from you at last," he said, with a sly grin.

"I didn't want them to know how unhappy I was," she said in a low voice.

He was beside her in an instant, drawing her into his arms and holding her close.

"I can't tell you how sorry I am, love, for the way I treated you and caused so much misery for both of us.

Things will be different from now on, I promise you," he vowed earnestly.

His lips caressed her forehead; then, reluctantly, he drew away.

"I have to meet the twins, and as I strongly urged them not to be late, I'd best not be the guilty one," he pronounced.

"Where are they taking you?" Elizabeth asked.

"I'd not meant to tell you, for I didn't want you upset," he said ruefully, "but we're going to Dobbs Farm to pick out another pup."

"I'm not a bit upset," declared Elizabeth. "I think it's the best thing they could do, and I'm glad you're here for their sakes also. They think you're wonderful, you know."

After he had left, Elizabeth concentrated on the detail of planning for Pamela's wedding, making list after list of things that should be done. The time flew as she concentrated on the self-imposed task, and she was surprised when Nanny came in carrying a tray with a bowl of hot broth.

Frowning, Elizabeth said, "Nanny, you know I've never liked broth. I'll wait until luncheon and have something to eat then."

"Broth is good for you," the old servant insisted, "and I wasn't intending bringing you any luncheon until the doctor's been and said what you may have. His lordship sniffed it a few minutes ago and said it was just the thing for you."

"Then his lordship may drink it, Nanny, for I shall not," Elizabeth said sharply. "You can take it away, or have it yourself if you want it."

She turned back to the lists she was making and, when she heard the door close, looked up and gave a smile of satisfaction. Nanny had, for once, taken her at her word, and both she and the broth were gone.

The doctor had seen Elizabeth and pronounced her fit

to get up for a few hours this afternoon. Much to her disgust, he had advised a bland diet for the next few days and definitely no coach travel for at least a week.

Colchester, who had been present this time while the doctor checked on his wife's condition, grinned at Elizabeth. There was no doubt that the man was being overcautious, he felt, but in her condition it was better to be on the safe side.

He was walking toward the door, meaning to escort the man downstairs and then come back to comfort his obviously frustrated wife, when Jeannie came hurrying into the room and dropped a curtsy.

"Begging your pardon, milord, but Nanny's been taken real bad. Cook thought the doctor might look in on her, seeing as how he was here," she said worriedly.

"What is wrong with her, Jeannie?" Elizabeth called from the bed.

"It's her stomach, milady. She's having so much pain she can't lie still, and moaning something awful." The little maid looked at the doctor, who nodded and told her to show him the way.

When she was alone once more, Elizabeth started thinking of the last time she'd seen Nanny, and remembered her leaving with the broth she had refused to drink. She had told her to drink it herself, and it was more than possible that she had. What if it had been bad?

She had thought it strange that Nanny had not returned with a light lunch, for it was now early afternoon. The poor thing must have become ill immediately afterward, if she had indeed drunk the broth. But what could have been in it to make her so ill? What if someone had added something poisonous, intending it not for Nanny but for herself?

She shuddered at the thought, then threw back the covers. The doctor had given her permission to get up, so she carefully eased herself out of bed. Then she went over to the armoire to find something to wear. There would be so much confusion belowstairs that for once she would dress herself.

As she was wondering how she could fasten the tiny buttons on the back of her gown, Colchester returned.

"You're just in time, David," she said, presenting him with her back. "I hope your fingers are not too big for those tiny buttons."

Without a word, he attended to the fastening and then turned her to face him. He was trying hard not to convey to her the deep concern he felt at what appeared to be a second attempt to harm her.

"How did you enjoy the broth that Nanny brought you?" he asked, trying to make his voice sound casual.

"I didn't have any. I hate broth," she said, "and I suggested she have it herself. Is that what made her ill?"

"I've no idea," Colchester lied glibly. "The doctor has given her some medicine to try to clear whatever it is from her system."

"Is she going to be all right, David?" Elizabeth asked quietly, then turned quickly away from him. She had suddenly remembered Nanny telling her that he had sniffed the broth and said it would do her good, or some such thing. If he had been close enough to sniff it, he could have dropped something in it, she thought, then told herself she was being ridiculous. She had heard of women getting strange ideas when breeding, and here was proof indeed.

"I believe so." Colchester tried to sound reassuring. "But she'll probably not feel at all well for a few days. How about you? Do you feel fit to come downstairs?"

"I can't wait," she said emphatically as she made for the door, "and I have to find something to eat. There seems to be a campaign afoot to starve me to death."

"I will personally supervise the preparation of a delicious light luncheon for you, my love," he said, meaning every word, for now he was taking no chances.

A faint suspicion still lingered, however, so Elizabeth pretended to tease. "And I will watch you supervise, sir," she said with a smile, "to ensure that the two of us are fed without delay."

Although Elizabeth had been anxious to get out of bed, within a couple of hours she found herself quite exhausted. Seeing the strain on her face, Colchester insisted on escorting her to her bedchamber, where Jeannie was on hand to help her mistress undress and get into bed.

Before leaving, while Elizabeth splashed her face with rosewater, he took Jeannie on one side and instructed her sternly that under no circumstances was she to leave her mistress alone until he returned.

Having put her in the maid's capable hands, he then returned to the drawing room, where Louise and Sylvia were trying to decide upon a name for their new pup, a black retriever.

"Blackie is too commonplace," Sylvia remarked, "and Midnight sounds more like a horse."

"That is something you'll have to decide for yourselves," David said, "and later, if you please, for right now I have something very serious to discuss with you."

Immediately they were all ears, and they pulled their chairs closer to his in order not to miss anything.

"Something must have been added to the broth that was made specially for Elizabeth. I have talked to Cook and I'm sure it was fine when she prepared it, but some poisonous substance must have been put into it in the kitchen before Nanny took it upstairs," he told them, no longer trying to hide his worried expression. "I want you to try to think if any of the staff, either outside or inside, are relatively new."

"Do you think it was meant for Elizabeth?" they asked, their horrified voices in unison.

"Most decidedly," he confirmed grimly, "but she wouldn't have any and told Nanny to drink it herself if she wanted it."

The twins looked with dismay at each other and then back to their brother-in-law. "There's a new kitchen maid, but she's Bill Chapman's daughter and a timid little thing," Louise offered helpfully.

"And there's a new stable boy and several new gardeners. Papa doesn't pay them as much as other places, so they're always leaving," Sylvia explained.

"How about that footman who was put on about a week ago? You know, Sylvie, the young, good-looking one," Louise remembered, and then added, "I see him in the strangest places where I'm sure he has no business to be."

Colchester looked up sharply. "That sounds interesting. I wonder if he replaced someone who left without notice?"

"How did you know?" Louise asked. "Bertha told me that Henry, one of our footmen, didn't show up one day, and that same afternoon this man came and asked if there were any vacancies. Elizabeth had just arrived, and they didn't want to be shorthanded, according to Bertha, so they took him on."

"Where do you think I might find this enterprising fellow at this hour?" Colchester asked, wondering to himself what had happened to poor Henry.

Louise went to the door and peered out into the hall. "He's out there now, standing by the library door. Can we stay and listen?"

Colchester ruffled her black curls affectionately. "I think I'll get more out of him if we're alone, but I promise to let you know if I find anything suspicious."

"All right," she conceded, "we'll hold you to it. We'll send him in to you. Come along, Sylvie."

They left, and a moment later a smart-looking footman of about twenty-seven or twenty-eight entered the room.

"You wanted something, milord?" he asked.

"Yes," Colchester answered. "First of all, how long have you been employed by the Danvilles?"

"Just seven days, milord," he replied. "I was hired on when one of the others quit."

Colchester watched the man's face carefully as he asked the next question. "How long have you been a footman?"

"Eight years, milord."

"In whose employ were you last?"

"At Sir Philip and Lady Gomersall's, in Northumberland, milord."

"And what is your name?"

"Blenkinsop, milord."

"Where were you born?"

"Just outside London, milord."

"London's a big city. In which direction?"

"South, milord."

"And is that where you acquired that strange accent?"

"I suppose so, milord."

"Have your references been checked?"

"They're being checked now, milord."

"Very well, you may go," Colchester said, and the man swung around and left the room as fast as possible.

Colchester scowled. There had been something very shifty about Blenkinsop's expression as he answered the questions fired at him. And he was too fast with the answers to be convincing. Colchester was sure that if he asked any of the other footmen the same questions at the same speed, they would become completely flustered.

Sylvia and Louise came back. "Is he your chief suspect, David?" Louise asked.

"Shall we say I'm going to keep my eye on him, and leave it at that. There's no proof that he has done anything other than wander into odd places, and that's easy to do in a strange house." Colchester rose.

"I'm going to see if Elizabeth is still sleeping and, if not, persuade her to come down to dinner tonight, I think. If we retire immediately afterward, it won't do her any harm," he said, and thought to himself that it would solve the problem of someone keeping a close eye on her. Also, he intended to take a piece of everything she selected, and taste it first.

Before checking on Elizabeth, however, Colchester stopped first in his own bedchamber, where he sat at the small desk and penned a lengthy note, carefully reread it, then sealed it with wax impressed with the insignia from the gold ring he constantly wore.

A pull on the bell rope brought a surprised Barnes to the door.

"I have an urgent letter to be taken to an address just outside London," Colchester told him. "Did you bring any footmen with you from the castle?"

"Of course, milord." Barnes sounded a little offended that his master felt it necessary to ask. "In addition to the coachman, two outriders, Jones and Berry, are here awaiting your instructions."

Colchester gave him a nod and a grim smile. "Good man!" he growled, holding out the sealed missive. "Have Jones set out right away, and tell him to bring a reply back as quickly as possible."

14

AFTER A SECOND night's sleep, watched over by Colchester, as before, with the door between their rooms wide open, Elizabeth felt physically recovered and back to her normal health. She was, however, extremely tense and found herself watching the movements of the servants who were new to her. On more than one occasion, Colchester caught her looking at him anxiously.

During the morning she had a visit from her old friend, Sir George Carlton, who, having heard his servants gossiping about a shot in the woods, was deeply concerned.

"I don't like it at all, Elizabeth," he said. "If the dog was killed practically in your arms, the bullet could just as easily have hit you. What is Colchester doing about it?"

"He and our grooms walked the length and breadth of the woods yesterday, but found no evidence of anyone having been there, George," she tried to reassure him. "It was probably just a poacher who never saw me but mistook the dog for game."

"I've never seen a dark chestnut-colored rabbit in the local woods," Sir George said dryly, then decided there was nothing to be gained by pursuing the topic. "Is this an extended stay or will you be returning to Oxford soon?"

"The doctor said I was not to travel for a week, but I am persuaded I can convince David to return within a day or two. I'm anxious to get settled once more in my own home, and stay there until the baby is born," she explained.

She looked upon him as a true friend, yet still hesitated before asking the question that had puzzled her for some time. "Why didn't you come to my wedding, George? The regrets you sent gave no reason, and I've wondered if I did something to offend you when I was here previously."

"You could never do anything to offend me, Elizabeth," he declared, regret making his voice rough. "I know you've always loved me as a sister might, but when you were here before, I had hoped there could be something more between us." He shook his head. "It was such good fortune our meeting at the inn and I realized at once how I felt about you. You meant to stay for a week or two, and I thought in that time I could bring you around to it before your father could get you married off again."

"And then I used you to make a quick escape, didn't I?" She took his hand in hers. "I love you dearly, George, as my very good friend, but there could never have been anything more. You see, one of the reasons I had come home was to try to understand my feelings about David. It was very soon after my return that we decided to marry."

"Do you love him, Elizabeth?" he asked, oblivious to the pain he was causing himself.

"With all my heart," she said with a fervor that left no doubt, "and I want this child so very much that I can't bear it when I think of how close I came to losing it because of that shot."

"Then I will wish you every happiness, my dear, and will still stand a true friend should you ever need me. Now don't forget," he cautioned, then bent and kissed her cheek.

At that moment Colchester entered the drawing room. Elizabeth had no idea what, if anything, he had heard of the conversation, but she saw the tightness of his mouth and knew he must have caught some of it.

"David, I would like you to meet my childhood friend, Sir George Carlton. George, my husband, Lord

Beresford, Earl of Colchester,'' Elizabeth made the formal introduction. "George is the one who found me last time I was in strife when I was thrown from Goliath.''

To Elizabeth's dismay, the two men looked exactly as if they were facing off before a fight, and for once, it was a relief when Lady Danville breezed into the room.

"How very nice to see you again, George. It's such a pity you only visit when Elizabeth is staying with us,'' she said, unwittingly adding coals to the fires burning in both men. "When Elizabeth was little, we always knew that where George was, she would be also. I remember thinking how unfortunate it was that you were not here when Elizabeth married Dewsbury. I can't think where you were at that time." She frowned as she tried to remember.

"I was a terribly young and very eager captain, chasing King Joseph back into France, if I'm not mistaken," Sir George said with a self-deprecating smile.

Colchester's eyebrows rose slightly, then his frown deepened as Lady Danville continued to question Sir George.

"How is your dear mother, George?" she asked. "It's such a long time since I've seen her, and she used to so enjoy watching you and Elizabeth dancing together at the local balls.''

"Mama has not been in the best of health in recent years, my lady," George said. "She suffers a great deal in the damp weather and finds it difficult to get around. I'll tell her you asked after her.''

"Please do," Lady Danville said, "and tell her I'll be along to pay her a call as soon as Elizabeth leaves. My best to your father, too. Such a handsome man in his youth!''

George had been slowly edging back to Elizabeth. "Well, must be off. Nice to have seen you, Liza, and glad you're up and around again.'' He bowed low over her hand and then that of her mama.

When he turned to Colchester, the latter smiled grimly. "I'll walk with you to the stables," he said. George protested, but Colchester insisted, saying, "No trouble at all, sir. I need the exercise."

"Oh, dear," said Elizabeth when the two men had left, "do you think I should go with them, Mama?"

Lady Danville smiled at her daughter. "Whatever for? It's nice to see how well they've taken to each other."

Elizabeth looked disbelievingly at her mama for a moment, then remembered how impervious she had always been to anything that did not concern her directly. She broached the subject of her departure.

"I know the doctor said I was not to travel in the coach yet, but I'm going to try to persuade David to take me home tomorrow, Mama. I don't at all like what has been happening here, and I think it would be better for me to leave as soon as possible."

Lady Danville frowned. "I can't imagine what you mean, Elizabeth. But then you always did tend to exaggerate things. I remember how it was when your papa arranged your marriage to Dewsbury. An enviable match, and yet you kept on and on about the difference in your ages, as though that had anything to do with it. And you see how well it all worked out, thanks to your dear papa." She nodded her head vaguely. "You must listen to what David has to say about your departure. He's your husband now and you must do whatever he decides."

Elizabeth sighed. Her mama had appeared so happy to see her a few days ago, but she should have known better than try to discuss anything with her. The twins had stopped doing so years ago, but then they had each other to talk to. She looked up and saw that her mama was gazing at her gown as though noticing it for the first time.

"Surely David cannot enjoy seeing you still in mourning for Dewsbury? He's not tightfisted with you, is he?" she asked in a shocked tone. "You have to be very firm from the start about a dress allowance, Elizabeth, for husbands tend to forget how important it is for a lady to look her best at all times," she said, frowning at her daughter's silver-gray muslin once more and giving a disapproving sniff.

"I have a great many gowns that David bought for my trousseau, Mama, that have hardly been worn, for I hated to ruin them by having the seams let out. After all, my activities will be drastically curtailed in a month or so." Elizabeth saw no point in admitting that she had engaged in no social activities whatsoever since her marriage.

"Just the same, you have to be very insistent about it, for even your dear papa has tried from time to time to curtail my visits to the dressmaker. Can you believe he called me extravagant just a day or so ago?" Lady Danville said, a shocked expression on her face. "As I told him, my nerves just cannot stand such deprivations."

Elizabeth recalled quite clearly how her mama's nerves had frequently confined her to her bedchamber at times of stress and, perhaps for the first time in her life, felt a touch of sympathy for her papa.

Outside, some distance from the stables, a very different kind of conversation was taking place.

Colchester came straight to the point. "I am aware, Carlton, that you and Elizabeth are old friends and probably romped together when you were barely out of leading strings, but I would remind you that she is now my wife. I do not find it amusing to enter a room and see another man kissing her, no matter how close they have been in the past." His aggressive stance and clenched fists served to emphasize his feelings.

George drew himself up stiffly. "If you had but come in a few minutes earlier, sir, you would have heard your wife tell me that she loves you with all her heart. I hardly think you are the one with cause for jealousy."

"Do you deny that you are in love with her and would

have married her in a shot if she had given you the chance?" Colchester demanded.

"No, I don't deny it," Sir George said heatedly, "but a kiss on the cheek is a mark of friendship, sir, nothing more. We were hardly in a passionate embrace."

"You wouldn't be alive now to talk about it, Carlton, if you had been, I can assure you," Colchester stated coldly. His frown deepened. "It is immaterial, anyway, for I intend to get her away from this place the minute she is fit to travel, before a third 'accident' happens to her."

"A third one?" Sir George was instantly worried. "She only mentioned the shot to me. Has something else occurred?"

In his concern, Colchester forgot for a moment that he had been feeling jealous of Carlton. "Yes. Nanny became very ill when she drank some broth prepared for Elizabeth."

"Good God!" Sir George exclaimed. "I don't like the sound of this at all. Look here, Colchester, if there's anything I can do to help, will you let me know?"

Colchester looked at him for a moment, then realized he was sincere. "That's awfully decent of you, Carlton. I hope I have no need for help, but I can't rely on her father. He doesn't even think anything unusual has occurred. It seems to me that the poisoned broth had to be the work of someone inside the house, and I'm keeping a close watch on a new footman."

"A youngish, clean-looking fellow?" Sir George asked, and when Colchester nodded, he continued, "I noticed him hanging around by the door when we came out just now. Thought he was trying to hear what was being said."

"That's the one," Colchester exclaimed. "I'm making sure Elizabeth is never left alone, and as her mother seems to think we're imagining the danger, I'd better not stay out here too long. Thanks for the offer, and if I should need you, I'll send you a message." He paused, then asked, "Inside just now, I was wondering, were you at Vittoria with Wellington?"

Sir George nodded, grinning broadly. "It was my first major battle, though I'd been in a few skirmishes before. I heard your name mentioned frequently, of course, but I believe you had to return for some family problem."

"Yes." Colchester looked pained for a moment. "My young brother died, and my mother did her best to persuade me to buy out, but I couldn't, not when we seemed so near the end."

He held out his hand, and Sir George clasped it firmly. Then they parted, Colchester hurrying back to the house where he was relieved to find Elizabeth still in conversation with her mother.

"I was just telling Mama that I should like to go home just as soon as possible, David. When do you feel we could start out? I know the doctor said a week, but . . ." She hesitated to say she wanted to leave tomorrow, but their departure could not come too soon for her, as she had grown to love the castle in the few months she had lived there, and felt sure that all her worries and troubles would disappear once she was back in her new home..

"I think we could leave in a couple of days. Let's see how you are tomorrow and perhaps we can get away the next day," he suggested. "We can take it a little slower than before, and stop at an inn for the night if necessary."

Elizabeth smiled and nodded. An extra day would make little difference, but she was quite determined she would not stay anywhere overnight. By now, however, she knew better than to tell him this in advance. She would have Jeannie personally pack a hamper for them and be sure that a bottle of champagne was included to put him in a mellow mood.

Luncheon had been announced, so she rose and allowed Colchester to tuck her arm in his own and escort her into the dining room. After the lonely weeks when he had been away, she was thoroughly enjoying his attention, and she had finally convinced herself that he could not possibly have had anything to do with the "accidents."

Since becoming a little ungainly, Elizabeth had acquired the habit, when possible, of resting for an hour in the late afternoon before she changed for dinner. So as not to disturb her mistress, Jeannie would already have the gown she was to wear that night pressed and hanging in the dressing room long before she took her rest.

Elizabeth noticed her lilac chiffon gown was there when she came into the chamber, and it brought to mind her conversation earlier in the day with her mama. She wondered what she was going to do about gowns once she was back at the castle. To please David, she would gladly wear the clothes he had bought, but it seemed such a shame to ruin them by enlarging them. Perhaps there was a dressmaker in the village who could run up a few garments to wear during the next few months.

She went into the dressing room and ran her fingers through the lightweight fabric. It was a lovely color, reminding her of the lilac tree when heavy with blossom. Just then she heard a key turning, and Jeannie entered through the separate door that opened onto the backstairs landing.

"I'm sorry, milady. I know his lordship said I was not to leave you alone, but I thought I'd be back before you came up from luncheon," she said breathlessly. "Will you be wearing the white or the purple gloves this evening, milady?"

"The white ones," Elizabeth said firmly, "and I'll wear white flowers in my hair, I think. And don't worry, Jeannie. Lord Colchester did not know you were not here and I won't tell him."

After removing her gown, Elizabeth stretched out on the bed and fell into a sound sleep while Jeannie busied herself with needle and thread, securing loose buttons and loops on her mistress's clothes. After a while she went down to the conservatory to look for white roses, returning just before Elizabeth awakened.

"How lovely," Elizabeth said when she caught sight of the roses. "I was wondering where you'd been. They'll be just perfect."

She was bathing her face and arms in cool, rose-scented water when she heard the girl cry out.

"What is it, Jeannie?" she asked as she patted her face with the towel and turned to where the maid stood with the lilac gown in her arms.

"I don't understand it, milady," Jeannie said, tears in her eyes. "I'd swear on my mother's grave that this gown was perfect when I left it here this afternoon."

She held out the garment for Elizabeth to see where the bodice had been ripped in the front, as though by a sharp knife.

"You don't have to swear on anything," she said to the maid, her voice little more than a whisper. "I looked at it myself before I lay down, and it was not torn then. You came in through the chamber door just now, Jeannie. I wonder if you forgot and left this door open."

She moved through the dressing room and, grasping the knob, opened the door.

"I must have forgot to lock it behind me, milady." Jeannie was crying in earnest now, and Elizabeth put an arm around her shoulders.

"Now stop that at once," she said firmly. "Let's pick out another gown quickly and you can run down to the ironing room and press it." She went over to the armoire, gathered up a lavender satin, and thrust it into the girl's arms. "Don't worry about it, Jeannie. Just hurry, for you know how I hate being late downstairs."

Elizabeth had, of course, realized that someone must have entered the dressing room and torn the gown while she slept. Her first reaction had been one of panic, but she controlled it quickly and pushed Jeannie out of the room.

Once the girl had gone, she confirmed that all the doors to her chamber were locked, peering into David's room, but seeing only Barnes, who told her his master had already gone down to meet first with Lord Danville. She started to perform as much of her toilette as she could without the maid's assistance, but it was more than half an hour before she heard the key in the lock and Jeannie ran in, the gown over her arm.

"I'm sorry to take so long, ma'am," she said frantically. "But someone had moved all the irons, and with everybody busy preparing dinner, it took me a good fifteen minutes to find one."

Elizabeth knew by now that she was going to be very late for dinner, but it would only make her later still if she sent word to the others in the drawing room, where they would be already drinking sherry.

"Never mind, Jeannie," she said, putting a good face on it. "The sooner we get started, the sooner I'll be out of here."

Lord Danville looked at his watch for what must have been the third time in the last fifteen minutes. "What on earth can be keeping Elizabeth?" he asked the room in general. "Never known her to be so late."

"You mean you've never known her to be late, Papa," Louise piped up. "Elizabeth has to be the most punctual lady in all England. She puts us all to shame."

"If she's not here in five more minutes," Lord Danville growled, "we'll go into the dining room without her."

Colchester, who was hardly aware of Elizabeth's reputation for punctuality, became suddenly quite apprehensive. With a murmured "I'll see what is delaying her," he put down his glass of sherry and left the room.

With some concern he noticed that the new footman was nowhere in sight as he made for the stairs.

Swinging around the newel post, he took the steps two at a time; then, as he was almost at the top, he tripped and sprawled full-length. He picked himself up carefully, glad that none of the footmen had a view of the staircase, then realized that his foot had caught, not on the step itself, as he had assumed, but on a thin piece of wire that had been stretched an inch or two above, from one banister post to the other.

He heard a sound and saw his wife hurrying along the upper corridor toward him, with Jeannie a few paces behind her.

"Stay where you are, Elizabeth," he called.

She stopped, curious as to why he was bending over one of the steps. "What are you doing, David?" she asked impatiently. "We've got to hurry, as Papa gets so cross when anyone is late."

"I'm afraid someone must have been relying on just that," he said quietly, coming to join her at the top of the staircase. He held out his hand, showing her the wire he had just removed. "I came to look for you and fell up the stairs. Someone had stretched this across the one next to the top. Had I not come to look for you, you would have come hurrying along and Jeannie could not have stopped you falling headfirst down the lot."

She gasped and gave a little shudder, and he pulled her into his arms, holding her close.

"You're safe now, but tell me, love," he said softly, his lips brushing her forehead, "was there some reason why a lady who is never late was delayed this evening?"

Elizabeth explained about the gown.

"That does it," he said grimly. "We're leaving first thing in the morning. You'll be far safer at the castle than you are in this house. And I'll have some serious words to say to your maid for leaving you alone. Now we'd better go down for dinner before your dear papa bursts a blood vessel."

Under the circumstances, a shocked Lord Danville delayed his evening meal to allow his oldest daughter a much-needed glass of sherry. Colchester, meanwhile,

had a word with the butler, who hurried off to look for
the new footman. He returned within five minutes with
the news that the footman was nowhere to be found,
and his belongings had also disappeared.

Dinner was a dismal affair as even the twins, realizing
how close Elizabeth had come once more to being
severely injured, could not keep up their usual cheerful
chatter. They tried not to talk about it, but could not
help coming back to the subject foremost in their minds.

"I really don't see why everyone thinks Elizabeth
might have fallen," Lady Danville remarked airily. "I
could have fallen just as easily, but I didn't, and I came
down the stairs."

"But the wire wasn't there when you came downstairs,
Mama," Louise tried to explain. "It must have been put
there after we were all in the drawing room."

"Nonsense," her mama protested. "Who would go
around putting wire across stairs for no reason? It must
have been one of the servants measuring for something,
who forgot to take it away. I'll have a serious talk with
them about it tomorrow morning. I could have broken a
leg."

Sylvia glanced across at Louise and shook her head,
at which they both giggled hilariously, causing their
mother to give them a severe frown.

"I think I'll have tea in my chamber," Elizabeth said,
"for I want to get Jeannie started on the packing."

"Can we have our tea up there with you?" Sylvia
asked eagerly.

As Elizabeth nodded, Colchester said, "No, they
can't, I'll be joining you."

She looked at their disappointed faces, then at David.
"Darling, they see so little of me, and . . ."

He grinned. "When you call me darling, you can have
anything. Not more than half an hour," he warned them,
and as Sylvia passed his chair, he caught her hand. "Don't
leave her alone for a moment," he whispered.

"Don't worry, David. We won't," she mouthed.

15

"DARLING, I HAVE a confession to make," Elizabeth said once they were finally under way, the twins having hugged them both at least five times and extracted promises that they might come to stay and "help" when the baby was born.

Colchester was feeling much more relaxed as Jones had returned during the night with a favorable answer to his urgent request. He leaned back in his corner of the carriage, his elbow against the window and his chin resting on his hand. "I know what it is," he teased, "it was you who put the wire across the staircase just to watch me fall flat on my face."

She laughed and shook her head. "I'm afraid not, for had I done it, I would have been hiding on the corridor where I could really see your downfall."

He pursed his lips as though thinking what else she might have done. "Then, let me see, it was you who fired the shot at yourself. You rigged up a pistol with a piece of thread attached to the trigger, and pulled the thread when you heard me coming through the woods."

His eyes twinkled as she shook her head, indignantly.

"All right, love. Confess whatever dirty deed you have unearthed, and plead with me not to send your father to jail—or perhaps it should be your mother. To tell you the truth, I started to feel sympathy for your father before we left. Has she always been so strange?" he asked, laughing as her eyes widened alarmingly.

Looking as if she were about to explode, she said, "You can talk about my mother being strange when you are Lady Butterfield's grandson?" she asked, leaning

forward and pulling away the hands with which David
had covered his face.

"Don't you know never to mention that lady's name
in my presence? It's instinctive. I always cover my face
when that name is mentioned," he pronounced. "But,
seriously, love. Your mother did not appear so vague at
the wedding."

"She's not always. She seemed perfectly normal when
I arrived, delighted about the baby and very anxious to
see that I got food and rest. I've decided that it's like the
spells she has when Papa won't let her have another new
gown. It's a way of avoiding reality, I believe,"
Elizabeth said seriously.

Colchester nodded. "Many people do the same thing,
but while we're being serious, I suppose I'd better let
you make your confession, if you insist."

"I have to tell you first that I was glad, in a way,
about the staircase thing. You see, until then, I still had
a tiny little feeling that it was you who was trying to get
rid of me." She ended the sentence in a whisper.

He moved over to sit by her side and draw her into his
arms. "You silly widgeon," he said gently. "Did you
imagine I didn't know you still thought it was me? I
could see it in your eyes the very first day, and then after
I pointed out how it couldn't have been me, it seemed to
fade somewhat. When you heard I had taken a sniff at
the broth before Nanny took it upstairs, all the doubts
were back in those expressive eyes of yours. But tell me,
why were you so anxious for me to take you back to the
castle, alone, if you felt so suspicious?"

"Because, despite all my doubts, I love you and I
don't want to be with anyone else. If I can just be near
you I know that all the other worries will disappear."
She bit her lower lip. "I feel terrible, for suspecting you
when you've been so good to me . . ." She broke off as
Colchester put a finger to her lips.

"I've been good to you for several days, but I
behaved abominably to you for several months," he

asserted. "Don't you think I have a lot of catching up to do?"

The corners of her mouth started to twitch. "No, not really," she said, "but if you want to try, I'm not going to complain. Would you like to start right now?"

"You forward minx," he said, pretending to be shocked. "Have you also determined how I should start?"

She gave him a decidedly saucy look. "How about making a further exploration? Nanny interrupted you the other day just at the point where you were discovering how certain parts of me have changed."

Without further preliminaries, he unbuttoned the front of her carriage dress and slipped a hand into the warmth inside. She felt the same thrill as before, when his fingers caressed her breast, but the excitement was enhanced by the very fact that they were in a carriage, in broad daylight.

She sighed happily.

"When we get home I must ask Tom Radcliff how long I may continue to make love to you," he said softly, his warm breath so close to her ear that it caused a heightening of sensations.

She suddenly realized what he had said, and found it very shocking. Who on earth was Tom Radcliff? She wondered.

She started to pull away, but his arms tightened, drawing her back. "I'm sure you got along with Tom, for he's one of the most likable doctors I've ever met. Did he give you any idea when the baby will be born?" he asked.

Elizabeth exhaled with relief, not having known quite what to imagine from his first remark. "I assume the baby will be born exactly nine months after our wedding night," she said firmly, "but I've not yet met your Tom, so I don't know whether I shall like him or not. Why would he have any say over our lovemaking?" she asked.

His strong hands grasped her shoulders and turned her around, holding her away from him so that he could gaze into her eyes. "Are you telling me you have not seen the doctor since you started to increase?" he asked, looking quite alarmed. "Didn't Mrs. Fowler suggest you send for him?"

She remembered now that the housekeeper had asked if she should have him call, but by then David was in London and she was over the bouts of morning sickness.

"I believe she did, but when I said I felt fine, she did not press the matter," she told him hesitantly.

"As soon as we get back, I'll send him a note to call. And if there are any complications, I'll . . . I'll . . . I'll do something to you, but I can't think what at the moment," he ended with a shake of his head and a rueful grin.

Elizabeth sighed. The romantic interlude was obviously at an end, so she buttoned her dress. "Would you like to have something to eat? Jeannie, who was very tearful after the scold you gave her, packed that hamper herself and tasted everything first to be on the safe side." She laughed. "If we go on like this, we will have some very fat servants."

He tapped on the roof and signaled the coachman to slow down somewhat, so that they would not spill the champagne he had just discovered, then they nibbled on cold chicken breasts, pressed tongue, and delicately smoked ham and salmon.

As Elizabeth had anticipated, the champagne put him in a mellow mood, and he did not remember, until it was too late, that he had planned to break the journey overnight.

"You little schemer," he said with some amusement when he saw the satisfied smile on her face. "I can see that I'll have to have my wits about me to anticipate your moves. I may not be used to having a wife, but I have always been an excellent chess player, so just watch out, young lady."

They were no more than an hour from the castle, and Elizabeth could now stop trying to hide her feeling of weariness from him. She closed her eyes and put her head back against the headrest.

"You silly girl," he said fondly, putting his arm around her and drawing her close. "Lean against me and let my body take the impact of the bumps. I think we'll have Jeannie get you bathed and into bed as soon as we reach home. Then, after you're rested, we'll have a light supper served in your bedchamber."

Too tired to protest, Elizabeth just smiled and rested her head on his shoulder. She was indeed happy to let him take over and make all the decisions for once.

Elizabeth liked Dr. Thomas Radcliff as soon as she saw him. For one thing, he was young—about David's age, she supposed—and after expressing mild concern that he had not seen her before, he examined her carefully and seemed pleased about her general condition.

"You seem to be an extremely healthy young woman, Lady Beresford," he remarked, "but just the same, I will make it a point to stop in to see you once a month, and if you have even the slightest concern, you must not hesitate to send for me."

"Thank you, Doctor," Elizabeth said, positively glowing at the confirmation of her good health. "I know you're going to have a word now with my husband and stop him worrying so much. As it is so close to luncheon, would you perhaps be able to join us?"

"I would be delighted to do so, my lady," he said, then added, "This visit is going to prove most profitable to me, for the whole countryside is agog to know what David's countess is like. I shall be run ragged with calls to visit if so much as a lady's little finger aches."

Just then David walked into the room and caught the doctor's final words. "It won't be profitable unless they pay you, Tom, for the gentry around here are notorious for their little economies," he said. "I take it Elizabeth has been forgiven for neglecting your services?''

"It appears, to my chagrin, that your wife didn't need me, David, but I know you'll see that she keeps in close touch during these next crucial months." He walked to the door with Colchester, who turned back for a moment.

"You will join us in a few minutes, darling, won't you? I'd like you two to become friends, and it's much easier to do so over a glass of sherry," he said.

"Of course, David. I'll be down directly," Elizabeth promised.

Jeannie helped Elizabeth into a morning gown, and the two men left, talking of trivialities until they were behind the closed doors of the drawing room, then Colchester poured two generous glasses of sherry and handed one to his friend.

"You really did mean it when you said she's in the best of health, Tom, didn't you?" he asked. "You see, she's had a number of close shaves lately that might have had a damaging effect on any woman's nerves, let alone one in her condition."

"I meant every word of it, my friend," Tom said, putting an arm around Colchester's shoulders. "You're very fortunate to have found such a remarkable woman, though I cannot imagine why you've kept her hidden all this time."

"I had to be away in London," Colchester mumbled with some embarrassment. "But we intend to make up for it and entertain a little now, as long as it won't tire her too much."

"I think that if you confine your dinner parties to no more than a dozen or so guests, it will do her no harm," Tom advised. "In fact, quite the contrary, it will probably do her a world of good, for your staff have always been very competent." He frowned, recalling something his old friend had said. "What did you mean by close shaves? A little clumsy on her feet, is she?"

"No, no, there's nothing clumsy about her gait, as

you'll see when she joins us. I hope we've left it all behind, but at her parents' home someone seemed determined to injure, if not kill, both her and the baby," Colchester said grimly. "By late this afternoon we will have another footman here in the person of my old army batman, Bert Eggers, whose sole duties will be to discreetly guard her throughout the day whenever I'm not with her. Until he arrives, I'm scarcely going to let her out of my sight in case the lunatic might have followed us."

He described in detail the three attempts, and when he was finished, the doctor looked quizzically at his friend. "You've no idea at all who might be behind it?" he asked.

Colchester shook his head. "None whatever. Elizabeth had never seen the new footman before in her life. Everyone there who had anything to do with her seemed tremendously fond of her and delighted that she was to have a child." He grimaced. "I had forgotten about her father. He was none too happy, but I hardly think he would do his own daughter more harm than he has already."

The door swung open and Elizabeth walked in wearing a delicate sprigged-muslin morning dress in a flattering shade of pale blue.

"What have you two been talking so earnestly about behind closed doors?" she asked with a playful smile. "I suppose David has told you that twins have turned up on quite a few occasions in my family, Doctor?"

Colchester looked at his friend with raised eyebrows. "Is it possible, Tom?" he asked as he poured a glass of sherry for his wife.

"Possible, of course, but not too likely. It frequently skips a generation and I recall you did say that Elizabeth has twin sisters. But I'll certainly look out for it now that I have been warned," Radcliff promised.

"I'm not sure whether I would like it to occur this time, or not," Elizabeth said seriously. "If I had twin boys, there might be a great deal of jealousy between them because of the inheritance, and I know I wouldn't like that.''

"That's a good point, my love, but not one over which I will lose sleep," Colchester observed. "And now that the more serious part of your visit is over, Tom, might I suggest that it would be more comfortable for all if you two were on a more informal footing." He turned to Elizabeth. "Tom and I shared tents, batmen, cooks, and on more than one occasion, our last bottle of brandy, when we were on the move in the Peninsula, and I wouldn't mind having a golden guinea for every stitch he's put into my tough hide. It was because of me he agreed to set up practice in this part of the country.''

A gleam came into Elizabeth's eyes. "You didn't tell me that when you insisted on having him take a look at me, David,'' she teased. "I might have had doubts about an army doctor's experience with birthing infants.''

"I've done my share of that, also, Elizabeth,'' Radcliff said with a grin, "for an army is always accompanied by hundreds of camp followers, there for no other purpose but to perform various services for the fighting men.''

Her cheeks tinging a pale pink, Elizabeth said, "Oh, dear, I hadn't thought of that.'' She glanced mischievously at Colchester. "I just realized how upset Lavinia would have been at such an improper conversation. There are some things that are definitely advantageous about being married, particularly to someone like you, David.''

Her voice became husky on the last few words and the look she and David exchanged could not have been shared with anyone else.

Dr. Radcliff gazed discreetly out of the window at the artistically laid-out formal gardens, and did not turn around until he heard David attempting to clear his throat.

"I'm sorry, old—" Colchester began, but his friend raised his hands to stop him.

"Please don't," he said with a gentle smile. "I cannot tell you how extremely lucky you are, David, and how very happy I am for you both."

The two weeks that followed their return were the happiest Elizabeth had ever known. She was at first quite disturbed at the idea of having a guard follow her and stand outside every room she went into, but once she met Eggers, sampled his peculiar brand of dry humor, and became aware of his keen, watchful eyes, she accepted his presence gratefully.

Most of the local gentry had been enjoying the Season in London at the time of their marriage, so little notice had been taken of their reluctance to go out and about together. Now, however, after the good doctor spread the word of their return and hinted that the countess would soon be unable to travel far, they were showered with invitations.

Colchester seemed reluctant to let his wife out of his sight for long, despite Eggers' presence, and Elizabeth finally came to realize this was a great deal more than just concern for her safety. He deeply regretted the months he had wasted without the joy of her companionship, and having been assured that, for now, there was no reason why he should not share his wife's bed, he frequently made tender love to her, and she grew used to falling asleep in the comfort of his arms.

Colchester had never mentioned that Tom Radcliff was the third son of an earl, and therefore socially accepted, and she was surprised to see him at almost every small dinner party they attended. He was that rarity, a good-looking young bachelor, and was, consequently, much in demand by the wealthy families with unmarried daughters.

One morning, Colchester found Elizabeth in the attractively furnished room she had originally set aside for her personal use. She was sitting at the Queen Anne desk, chewing on a freshly sharpened quill.

The worried frown on her face disappeared the moment she saw who it was. He came quickly across the room and dropped a kiss on the tip of her nose. "What's the matter, Eliza, love? Has some merchant tried to overcharge you?" he teased, as he had quickly realized her penchant for strict accounting of all charges.

"They wouldn't dare," she asserted. "But how clever of you to come in just at the exact moment I needed you very badly."

"You need me very badly most of the time, my love, not only now," he corrected her. "But what's so special about the present moment?"

"Oh, David," she said in an exasperated tone, "it's so difficult to keep the number down to the twelve that Tom has specified. And as he will be there, he'll know if I invite any more guests."

"Is this the dinner you're planning for next week?" Colchester asked. "Tell me who you've got down so far."

"Lord and Lady Crabtree, Sir John and Lady Blazer and their daughter, Annette, Sir Alfred Waterhouse, Lord and Lady Foster, Sir Anthony and Lady Horsfall, Lord and Lady Parkinson and their two daughters, and of course, Tom Radcliff. That's fifteen and, with us, seventeen." She sighed.

"Why don't you invite the Blazers and the Fosters for the following week? By then I'm sure you'll have found at least three more people you simply must entertain," he suggested.

"You don't suppose Tom will think two dinner parties are too much for me?" she asked, delighted at his suggestion.

"Not as long as you stick to no more than twelve people, love, and use Mrs. Fowler to take as much work off of you as possible." He stroked her cheek gently. "Despite the Gordons' dinner last night, you look radiant, Elizabeth. I don't know how you do it."

Elizabeth had not fully appreciated the fact that she was one of those fortunate women who look even more lovely when carrying an unborn child. Her skin had taken on a wonderful glow, her black hair shone with blue lights, and her eyes sparkled.

This morning she was dressed in another of the gowns David had bought for her. The fashionable high waist was a great help, of course, to a woman in her condition. This particular gown, a fine apple-green muslin embroidered around the neckline, the sleeves, and the hem's flounce with white and yellow daisies, actually had a drawstring at the high waist, and needed only to be loosened a little to accommodate her increased girth.

"Did I tell you how happy I am that you are finally wearing the gowns I selected for you with such care, my dear?" he asked, looking appreciatively at the charming picture she made. "I wanted to bite off my tongue for my remarks that caused you to pack them away."

"I'm glad you didn't," she said with a chuckle, "for I would have sadly missed it, even though its edge is sometimes rapier-sharp. When it flatters, though, and calls me beautiful, it makes me feel like a queen."

"That's not flattery, love, for you are and always will be very beautiful to me," he told her.

Elizabeth smiled at his words. She had started to worry that the loss of her figure might make her unattractive to him, but now she knew he was sincere and she had no call to worry.

The evening of Elizabeth's first dinner party since their marriage arrived at last. After resting in the afternoon, she had made a final check with Mrs. Fowler to be sure that everything was going perfectly, then had gone upstairs to get ready.

She had selected a gown of deep-pink satin with a large bow tied under the breasts, its ends flowing so freely that it concealed, to a great extent, her increased weight.

Jeannie was dressing her hair when David came into the chamber, looking every inch as elegant as if he were spending an evening at Almack's. Elizabeth saw in the mirror that he was holding a box, but Jeannie inadvertently jerked her head so that the first thing she saw of the beautiful diamond necklace was when she felt his fingers and something cold touch her neck. She pulled away from Jeannie to see what he was doing, and gasped as the candlelit mirror reflected the gems' magnificence.

The maid hurriedly found something to do in the dressing room as David bent over Elizabeth to place a tender kiss on her waiting lips. Her eyes were bright with happiness, and as a single tear escaped and started to roll down her cheek, he reached for his kerchief and caught it.

"I don't know what to say," she whispered. "I've never seen anything so absolutely beautiful."

"Don't say anything, then, love." He sounded a little embarrassed. "It's rather belated actually, for it's the groom's gift to the bride, and this is the first occasion I could present it to you."

She smiled mischievously. "At least I finally got it, but now I'm wondering, if this is from groom to bride, what will be the gift from proud father to new mother?" she teased, trying to ease his discomfort.

He threw back his head and laughed. "You're wonderful, Eliza! I've had more joy these last few weeks than I ever believed possible. Stay as you are, darling. Please don't change, will you?" he begged, on a more serious note.

"I won't as long as you don't," Elizabeth answered quickly before she rose and was swept into his arms and soundly kissed.

A few moments later, he held her a little away from him and observed, with a smile, the warm glow in her cheeks and the way her breasts moved more quickly as she sought to regain her breath.

"I would swear you look more beautiful every day, my love," he murmured.

"That's because I'm so happy, David," she whispered, aware that Jeannie was not very far away. "And since Bert Eggers started to watch over me, I no longer fear that something awful is going to happen to me."

"I know. Sending for him was an inspiration that came to me at your parents' home when I was at my wit's end trying to think how to protect you night and day, and at the same time attempt to find out who might be behind it," he told her. "I was sure that if I mentioned it in advance you'd refuse to have a body-guard, but there's something about Bert that I knew you would take to right away."

"You were right, darling. And now you have a rival, for I adore him," she said. "But tell me, have you had any luck in learning anything about that footman?"

"Not so far, love." He shook his head and frowned. "They found the body of the footman he replaced, floating in the river, and it was assumed that he wandered off the path and drowned when he'd had too much to drink, but I've no doubt whatever that he didn't fall, but was pushed."

Elizabeth leaned her forehead against his shoulder for a moment, then turned back to him with a heavy sigh. "Poor Henry. I didn't know him well, as he wasn't there when I originally left home, but it's my fault he died."

"It's not your fault," David said sternly. "Don't think that for a moment. It's the fault of whoever is behind all this. Blenkinsop, as he called himself, waited only to see that his last attempt had failed, then he took off on the stage to London. That much I do know, but after that, there's no trace of him."

"You think he will try again, don't you?" Elizabeth said quietly.

"I don't know. I can't even imagine why he would

want to kill you. But don't worry, love. Either Eggers or I will be with you at all times." David's eyes held hers until her anxious look disappeared, then his lips returned to trace delicate patterns around the corners of her mouth, and his warm breath in her ear made her forget everything else.

Finally he drew away. "I'd best get out of here and let Jeannie finish your hair, love, or the guests will be here before we know it. I'll wait in my chamber until Eggers gets back from his supper, then I'll go down in case some of our guests come early." With a final salute, he left the chamber and Jeannie hurried to finish her mistress's toilette, looking from time to time with disbelief at the fiery necklace.

After that, dinner was an anticlimax for Elizabeth. She sailed through the evening in a dream, accepting but only sipping at first the sherry, then the dinner wines, and hardly tasting the delicious veal, salmon, squabs, duckling, and numerous side dishes, though her empty plates showed she had done justice to the meal. An immaculate Shackleton was in his element, personally serving the wines and the more important dishes, and keeping the other servants on their toes removing plates and glasses and bringing tureens of food from the kitchen.

The ladies duly admired the necklace, and one of them had even seen it before on the neck of Mildred Beresford. "But never so beautifully displayed," the lady added.

Tom was one of the last to leave, for he wanted a word with David. "Elizabeth looks even better now than when she arrived here several weeks ago. I don't know how she does it, but she is a magnificent hostess," he told his friend.

"I'm afraid we are having a repeat of this in a week's time, for she couldn't stay within your limitation and yet have all here who had dined and wined us," David explained. "I don't think it will do her any harm."

"On the contrary, something's doing her a lot of good, and I can only advise that she continue whatever she is doing," he said. "I take it that there have been no more attempts to harm her since your return to the castle?"

Colchester shook his head. "No, but I have a strong feeling that we're not out of the woods yet," he said.

"I had a word with Bert and he said much the same thing," Radcliff murmured, "and I'm a big believer in intuition, as you know. I'd best be off now, as I've early surgery hours tomorrow, but send word at once if you should need me." He grinned. "Please beg Elizabeth not to put me next to those stupid Parkinson girls when she asks me again."

Colchester chuckled. "I think she's probably going to ask you again next week, and if I'm not mistaken, Annette Blazer will be your dinner partner."

With a loud groan and a wave to Elizabeth, to whom he had already said good night, Tom Radcliff accepted his hat and gloves from Shackleton and stepped into his waiting carriage.

16

TREVOR DOWNS SECURED a seat for himself at one of the small wooden tables in the back of the public bar and pulled out a letter that had just been delivered to him by the coachman of the morning stage. The timbered room was alive with the shouts of travelers ordering tankards of ale and sandwiches, and cups of tea for the women and little youngsters. They were glad to move around and stretch their legs again, if only for a few minutes, for the stage would soon be sounding its horn, ready to set out once more on its long journey north.

A buxom barmaid leaned over him, her generous bosom falling out of her skimpy dress as she plunked down a none-too-clean glass of home brew. Its foamy head spilled down the sides of the glass and onto the stained tabletop. She snatched up the coin he had left for her, then ogled him, but when he ignored her and started to intently read his letter, she flounced away.

The room was quiet by the time he carefully folded the piece of paper and placed it in an inside pocket of his jacket, then drained his glass and strolled leisurely out into the bright sunshine.

His dress was somber enough for him to be easily mistaken for a country parson, but in a town such as Oxford it caused no comment and few who saw him would have remembered what he looked like two hours later—not even the generously endowed barmaid.

Now he made his way to the smaller inn, farther to the south of the town, where he had secured a room some two weeks before, for the purpose, he told them, of doing research on one or two of the colleges. He went immediately to his minuscule room, which was sparsely furnished but unusually clean. He read his missive once more, committing it to memory before setting it afire in the empty hearth. He then removed his watch from the pocket where it was hidden, calculated that he had two hours to wait, then stretched out on the bed.

The carriage was dusty, and Lady Preston had forbidden the coachman to clean it, for she wanted it to appear as though she had traveled far. It was a rather old but beautifully appointed carriage, for the marquess had liked his comfort. His coat of arms was emblazoned on the doors, letting the whole world know that its owner was someone of rank.

When the coachman drew to a halt in a quiet lane just a mile south of the town, she smiled grimly and waited until her stepbrother entered and closed the door behind him before tapping the roof to signal the coach to proceed.

"I'm sorry, my love, but as I wrote you, Colchester has become very protective of his bride, and she has never once been outside the castle without either him or a footman in attendance since they arrived," he said apologetically.

"And what about Danville Hall?" Lady Preston asked scornfully. "How could no less than three accidents all go wrong?"

Trevor shrugged helplessly. "The first time would have been the last, had not the dog jumped up at the crucial moment and taken the bullet instead of the countess." He shook his head as though he could not understand his luck. "She seems to have acquired the art of making servants, both at Danville Hall and here at the castle, completely devoted to her. When her doting nanny couldn't get her to drink the broth I added flavor to, the stupid old woman drank some of it herself."

"Unfortunately, Trevor, you have allowed it to become obvious that someone is trying to do her harm, and so it is bound to be considerably more difficult now," Lady Preston said, her cold eyes glinting dangerously. "However, I have conceived a plan that is so brilliant it cannot fail. What is more, at the crucial moment I will be on hand to offer comfort to the earl."

"And when you are married to the earl, what about me, Angelique? I hardly think that Colchester will be as easy to deceive as the marquess," Trevor suggested, concerned that he would lose her if she married a young, handsome lord like the earl.

"I can handle Colchester," Lady Preston assured her stepbrother. "Once I am his countess, I will persuade him to resume his previous pursuits while I resume mine." She touched his cheek and he grasped her hand and held it there for a moment. "You wrote that they are still accepting invitations to dine with his neighbors and friends?" He nodded, and she continued gleefully. "Then my plan will be positively foolproof."

For more than half an hour she went over the details of the plan and the part he would play, promising to send word to the inn when all was ready. She allowed Trevor to kiss her quite passionately before he alighted from the carriage, then she signaled the coachman to drive on to her destination: Colchester Castle.

Colchester had just joined Elizabeth for tea when Shackleton came into the drawing room and announced that a Lady Preston had arrived and that her coachman and servants were bringing in several large pieces of luggage.

Colchester swore softly under his breath, and Elizabeth looked at him with raised eyebrows. "Is this someone from your past, David? For I have no recollection of ever having met anyone by that name." Amusement curled the corners of her mouth.

"I most certainly know a Lady Preston," he said curtly. "She is a childless widow, even older than I, who was married to an old marquess. But that is probably the only thing the two of you have in common. I have most surely never invited her to pay us a visit."

"Perhaps she was passing and did not wish to travel at night," Elizabeth suggested. "Show her in, please, Shackleton, and you may put her in the east wing." The east wing was just about as far from Elizabeth's bedchamber as possible and still be within the castle walls.

A moment later, Angelique swept into the room and appeared about to throw her arms around Colchester, but he grasped them instead and held her at arms' length.

"My dear Angelique, what a surprise," he said coolly. "Allow me to introduce my wife, Lady Beresford. Elizabeth, my dear, this is an old acquaintance, Lady Preston."

"My dear Elizabeth . . . I may call you Elizabeth, may I not, for I feel as though I know you already?" She did not wait for her hostess to grant such familiarity before continuing, "I hope you will not find it strange, but I have been staying with friends in the north, and I simply could not pass so close without stopping to spend a few days with my dear friend David and his bride."

"Any friend of David's is a friend of mine," Elizabeth said, "and indeed you are most welcome, my dear Angelique. We lead a comparatively quiet life, however, and I hope you will not find our small amusements too tedious."

"I have sometimes found David amusing, but never tedious, my dear," Lady Preston murmured, giving David what could only be called an intimate glance, which he did not return.

"What part of the north were you visiting?" Colchester inquired suspiciously.

It was the first time Colchester had spoken since he made the introduction, and Lady Preston leaned forward to answer him, turning her back on Elizabeth.

"The very north part of Yorkshire—no one you would know, darling—and it was positively dreary, all bogs and moors and such.'' Lady Preston gave a little shudder as she described her visit in languid tones.

Over the top of Lady Preston's discourteous back, Elizabeth had a clear view of Colchester, and while he watched, she made a face, then pointed a finger at her visitor and drew it across her own throat while nodding emphatically.

Colchester had to turn his head away to avoid laughing outright.

"Can I give you a little more tea, Angelique?'' Elizabeth asked sweetly, and Lady Preston turned slowly around, a surprised expression on her face, as though she had forgotten her hostess was even there.

"No, thank you, my dear,'' she said with a deprecating shake of her head, "but after such a trying journey I could be persuaded to have a little sherry, if David will join me.''

In less than a minute, Shackleton appeared with three glasses on a tray. Placing one in front of Lady Preston, he raised his eyebrows to Colchester, who shook his head, as did Elizabeth.

"Why, David. I've never known you to refuse a drink. You're surely not going to force me to drink alone?'' Lady Preston pouted.

"I have abandoned many of my coarser habits since becoming a husband, Angelique,'' Colchester said, a note of warning in his voice. "And I will no doubt change even more when I very shortly become a father.''

Lady Preston turned deliberately toward Elizabeth and allowed her eyes to travel slowly from her head to her toes. "Really, my dear Elizabeth, I had not noticed. You must take great care of yourself, for I understand there can be many problems when an older woman has her first child.''

"Oh, Angelique, I'm so sorry. Is that why you and Lord Preston did not start a family?'' Elizabeth asked, her face all sweet innocence. When Angelique made no reply, she continued, "You need have no qualms about me, however, for my doctor has assured me I have many, many childbearing years ahead of me. I have no doubt David and I will not stop until we have at least a dozen.''

Colchester rose and said a few quiet words to Shackleton, then returned to the ladies. "You're looking quite tired after your long journey, Angelique. I've asked Shackleton to have someone show you to your chamber, as I'm sure you'd appreciate a rest before dinner,'' he said firmly, leaving Lady Preston no alternative but to follow the butler from the room.

Closing the door firmly behind them, Colchester turned to see Elizabeth laughing so hard she had to hold her sides.

"I'll get even with you, you minx,'' he said with a grin. "I'll hold you to that dozen.''

"Oh, David, you must tell me,'' Elizabeth said as she tried to regain her composure. "Is she one of your lady friends?''

"One of my former lady friends,'' he admitted. "And if she should hint, as I'm sure she will shortly, that we have been lovers quite recently, I will tell you now that it is not true. I saw her when I was in London, and I dined at her home, but that is all. Do you want me to send her packing?''

"No, darling, please don't do that. I've never had the opportunity to exchange polite insults with someone before, and I find it most amusing,'' she assured him. "The only trouble is, we'll have to include her in our dinner party tomorrow evening, if she's still here, which I don't doubt for a moment she will be. As I can't have thirteen, we'll have to invite someone else. Let's partner her with Tom Radcliff, and perhaps you can think of another man for Annette, who won't mind a last-minute invitation.''

He held out his hand. "Come along, love. I believe I know just the right man, but now it's time for your rest,'' he said. As they left the room and mounted the stairs, he remarked, "I don't know how I managed to get such an understanding wife, but I had no idea you were so adept at verbal sparring. There were a couple of times when I found it hard to hold back a guffaw.''

He made sure that Elizabeth was settled for a couple of hours, with Eggers on guard outside her chamber, then he went down to the library to work on some estimates he'd received. But he found it difficult to concentrate. At the back of his mind there was an odd feeling. He was pretty sure that Angelique had not been near the north of England, and he wondered why she had paid them such an unusual visit. She never did anything without a purpose, and he would give much to know what her purpose was this time.

Elizabeth was more nervous about her second dinner party than she had been for her first, but the reason was, of course, the presence of Lady Preston. No matter what she wore she felt that, in her present condition, she would be outshone, so she selected a gown more for comfort than for competition. It was in the palest of ice blues, with a wide silver ribbon covering the gathers at the high waist, which had been let out almost as much as it would go.

She was almost ready when David came into her chamber. ''You look beautiful, my love,'' he said, his eyes reflecting his pride in her appearance. ''But you must wear the diamonds once more and watch Angelique's golden eyes turn to green.''

He was right, of course, Elizabeth thought as she took the arm he offered to assist her down the stairs. Against her plain gown, the diamonds looked even more stunning than the last time she had worn them. She saw Lady Preston's eyes widen as she entered the drawing room, though at that distance she could not be sure if they changed color.

As she predicted, Lady Preston was wearing a dramatic gown in gold satin, embroidered with thousands of small gold beads. She carried a large gold fan painted with Chinese scenes. Her talented abigail had artfully applied just enough powders and rouge to her face to make her look ten years younger than her true age. Around her neck she wore an elaborate gold necklace, set with large topaz stones, and matching ear bobs dangled at both ears.

"How charming you look, Elizabeth," Lady Preston said when Colchester was out of earshot. "I've been meaning to ask you, do you have a little dressmaker in the village who makes up new gowns as your size increases?"

Elizabeth was inwardly outraged, but she kept the look of amused indifference firmly in place and replied, "No, my dear, I'm afraid we don't, but if you are in need of such a person's services, I'll be glad to check in Oxford for you."

There was an audible sputter behind Lady Preston, which turned into a fit of coughing as Tom Radcliff tried too hard to refrain from laughing.

Colchester came over to pound his friend on the back, and when conversation was possible once more, he asked quickly, "Have you met Lady Preston yet?" and proceeded to introduce the two. "Dr. Radcliff will be your dinner partner, Angelique," he added.

Angelique pouted. "I had thought, as the guest of honor, that you would be taking me in, David, but I forget that we are in the country now," she said disparagingly.

"But, my dear, how could you possibly be the guest of honor when my dinner party was planned long before I had even heard of you. When you arrived on our doorstep, so to speak, David invited our young minister to make the number even, but I believe you will have a little more in common with our good doctor, who is an old friend of David's." Elizabeth's voice was dangerously soft.

"How thoughtful you are, Elizabeth." Lady Preston looked around to be sure that Colchester had moved away. "But then I knew exactly what you were like before I came, for David told me all about his bride when we were together in London recently. Isn't it strange that he didn't tell you about me?"

Elizabeth managed to look complacent. "Not really, for we had many more important things to discuss," she said, more calmly than she felt. "Of course, since your unanticipated arrival he has repaired that omission. Now, if you will excuse me, I must greet some of our other guests."

Once more, the staff, under the eagle eye of Shackleton, completely outdid themselves at dinner. When the ladies returned to the drawing room, Elizabeth deliberately avoided contact with Lady Preston, for she was now finding their increasingly biting verbal exchanges rather tiresome.

Colchester noticed that she seemed more weary than usual when the gentlemen came into the drawing room. As soon as the guests had left, he wished Angelique a good night, took Elizabeth firmly by the arm, and guided her up the stairs to her chamber.

Fifteen minutes later, he came through the adjoining door, looking very handsome in a deep-blue dressing gown. He removed the hairbrush from Jeannie's hand, dismissing her for the night.

"You're handling Lady Preston very well, my dear, but it's not something you enjoy and it's taking strength you need for other things at this time." He watched her face in the mirror as he drew the brush through her shoulder-length hair. "I will give her two more days, and by then, if she has given no indication of when she plans to depart, I will inform her that she will have to move elsewhere as you are in no condition to cope with guests at this time."

"Would you, darling?" Elizabeth looked extremely grateful. "It would be such a relief to see the back of her. There is a problem, however, for the night after next we are committed to a small dinner party at the

Countess of Reading's, and she's such a sweet, nervous little person who plans everything to the minutest detail weeks ahead, we could not possibly ask if Lady Preston could join us.''

"You mean she won't just invite the local clergy to make an even number as we did?'' he suggested with a chuckle, then he became serious. "There's no reason why we should have to drag her around with us, in any case. She was not an invited guest. I'll let her know we will be out, and if she wants to, she can make separate plans of her own for the evening or, better still, she might just decide to make an early start for London.''

He lifted her chin and bent down to place a soft kiss on her parted lips. "Don't worry, love. She'll not come between us no matter how she tries,'' he assured her. "I had once thought her pleasant company, or at least harmless, but I have changed my mind considerably since she thrust herself upon us so rudely.''

He put his arm around her and guided her to the bed, sliding in after her. Taking her in his arms, he held her fast until she fell asleep. He knew she would have shed her weariness and welcomed him had he shown the slightest intention of making love, for her wanton response to him was something he marveled at, not believing his good fortune. But, though his desire for her was always there, tonight she needed her rest.

Trevor Downs hoped with all his heart that Angelique had given up on the plan she had devised, for he was becoming increasingly bored with walking the streets of Oxford, and if the truth were known, he found his part in her plot to be extremely distasteful and dangerous.

He had thought she might, perhaps, don a disguise one night and join him for a few hours of pleasure, as had sometimes happened when she was out of London. But as the days went by and no message came, he reasoned that she must be having her way with Colchester instead.

It was in a mood of intense jealousy, therefore, that he returned to the inn in the late afternoon and found Yates, Angelique's abigail, waiting for him with a note.

"Is your mistress having a pleasant visit?" he asked the woman as he broke the seal.

"Not as you'd notice," Yates replied. "The feathers really fly when she returns to her chamber alone each night. The lady of the house is no simpering chit and it's my belief she gives as good as she takes."

"Mm," Downs murmured, his eyebrows raised. "How very interesting."

He read the note, folded it, and placed it inside his coat. "You may tell her that all is well," he said, smiling broadly and tossing her a golden guinea, which she caught adroitly and pocketed. She left the inn as Downs mounted the stairs to his room.

Once inside, he pulled out a portmanteau from under the bed, opened it, and started to check the contents, paying particular attention to the pair of pistols hidden beneath the somber garments. He went over to the chipped mirror above the chest of drawers and tried on a black mask that covered the upper half of his face, then he tied a bright-red scarf beneath it. His blue eyes, which were all that could be seen of his face, gleamed with satisfaction.

He carefully packed everything away, concealing it once more beneath the bed, then went below into the front parlor and ordered a glass of brandy. Just one more day, and his vigil would be over. He nodded, pleased at the thought. Looking up, he saw that the barmaid had mistaken his nod for acceptance of her frequent hints. Why not? She wasn't Angelique, but then, who was?

Elizabeth was feeling decidedly out of sorts. She would have given much to have stayed in bed this morning, but despite the fact that David had shown nothing but cool courtesy to Lady Preston, for the sake of a few more days she was determined not to let the scheming harlot get him alone at any time.

By lunchtime, however, it became quite clear that she was in no condition to go out that evening. Colchester, having spent the morning outdoors with his man of business, took one look at her and packed her off to bed right away.

"You silly widgeon," he gently scolded. "Why didn't you stay in bed this morning?"

"Because I have duties to attend to, particularly as our guest is still here," she answered grumpily, knowing she should have had more faith in him and stayed in bed.

"I've got good news for you, love." He smiled, obviously very pleased with himself. "She's leaving for London tomorrow."

Elizabeth looked the happiest she had been all day, though she had pangs of guilt at her inhospitality. She suddenly realized how upset the Countess of Reading would be at their absence.

"Oh, dear," she said, "the countess's dinner will be ruined if we don't go tonight. She's more interested in numbers than people at this stage, so why don't you ask Angelique if she'd like to go with you in my stead?"

Colchester looked pained. "Must I, darling?" he asked. "Are you sure you wouldn't rather let the countess work things out as best she can? After all, if you had the measles, none of us could go."

"But it isn't the measles, and I can afford to be generous to Angelique on her last night here," Elizabeth asserted, saying a silent prayer that he could resist the advances she was sure the woman would make.

"Very well, love, I'll take her if it will make you feel better," he said. "I'd best go down and extend the invitation now, for she'll need all afternoon to get ready."

He plumped the pillows up around her, kissed her tenderly, and went to find Angelique.

* * *

"I've got to send a message to my stepbrother right away, Yates," Lady Preston told her abigail. "You cannot go, for I need you here to help me get ready, but this is very important. Which of my footmen is the most trustworthy?"

"There's no question but that it's Paul, the young one you hired last. He'll do anything for you, my lady," Yates said. "I'll take it to him myself and explain exactly how to get to the inn."

Lady Preston gave a little nod of satisfaction. "Yes, he's the right one for the job. Don't forget to tell him how very important this is," she said as she finished writing, sealed the letter, and handed it to the woman. "Then hurry back, for I must look my very best this evening."

The abigail left the chamber and made for the kitchen, where she knew the Preston footmen would be hanging around, playing cards at this hour.

"Now, you take this right away, mind," she told Paul. "It's a matter of grave importance to her ladyship and might easily lead to promotion if you perform well."

She drew a map of the road he would take, indicating the exact location of the inn where Mr. Trevor Downs was staying. The one thing she forgot to tell him, however, was that if Mr. Downs should be out, he must wait there for his return and hand over the letter to no one else.

When she returned, her mistress had already selected the gown she would wear and was lying on her bed with moistened pads over her eyes. She gathered the gown up and made for the door.

"Press it carefully, Yates, for if I find so much as one wrinkle in it, I'll box your ears so hard they'll ring for a week," Lady Preston warned.

The abigail made no reply, but she did take extra care with her mistress's entire appearance that evening.

When she was finished, Angelique stood preening in front of the mirror, knowing that no one at the dinner would believe she was a day over twenty-one, with the exception of Colchester, of course, who had known her for so many years.

She could not resist going to Elizabeth's chamber before she left, on the pretext of inquiring after her health, but in reality to gloat. She noticed the footman in the hall, but did not hear Eggers open the door again and slip quietly into the dressing room as she approached the bed.

Elizabeth was sitting up, looking a trifle flushed and in no mood to receive Angelique.

"It's such a pity that you had to come down with something this particular evening, my dear." Angelique was all anxious concern in case Colchester should still be in the next room and hear her. "You mustn't worry about Colchester, for I'll take even better care of him than you would yourself," she cooed, bending over a little so that Elizabeth could see how low the bodice of her silver brocade gown was cut, and smell the exotic perfume that she had lavished upon herself.

"I'm sure you will, Angelique," Elizabeth said dryly, wishing she felt well enough to think of something really biting to say. "What time did you say you would be leaving tomorrow?"

Angelique was obviously amused. "I didn't, but as I shall be so very late to bed tonight, I doubt that I'll get away before noon."

With a tinkle of laughter, she swept out of the room and down the stairs to where Colchester was pacing back and forth. Shackleton held out Lady Preston's black satin cape, then placed it around her shoulders, as Colchester made no move to take it.

17

ONCE SHE WAS settled in the Colchester carriage, Angelique set out to enjoy her evening, at the end of which she planned to twist her ankle so that she would be forced to remain at the castle several more days. The injured ankle would serve the double purpose of requiring Colchester to carry her to her bedchamber.

"You know, David darling, it really wasn't necessary for you to take me to this dinner tonight in Elizabeth's stead. Surely, in her condition any host would have understood if you had sent regrets, and you hardly seem to be looking forward to the evening," she said softly. "Was Elizabeth a little jealous, perhaps, that you invited me?"

She leaned toward him and sniffed daintily, wafting a heavily perfumed, lace-edged kerchief in the hope that a whiff of the exotic scent she always wore would remind him of their earlier romantic interludes.

Colchester had been deep in thought, but her last few words drew his attention. "Elizabeth knows she has no cause to be jealous, my dear," he intoned a trifle grimly. "As a matter of fact, it was she who suggested I bring you along, for our hostess is a sweet, elderly lady who becomes completely flustered if everything does not go exactly as originally planned."

"You are fortunate to have such an understanding wife, then, for I'm sure, if you were my husband, I'd be jealous of every beautiful woman who came near you," Angelique said huskily, realizing that she must be careful how she implied criticism of Elizabeth. She tried a safer subject. "Won't you tell me a little about the guests who will be at tonight's dinner, so that I won't seem quite such an outsider?''

He smiled, amused at her attempt to seem insecure. "I did not ask our hostess for a guest list, but am pretty sure that you'll find Tom Radcliffe there, if he has not been called out on an emergency. Sir John and Lady Blazer are bound to be there also, with their daughter, Annette, whom you met the other evening.''

"You mean that insipid-looking girl who had so obviously inherited her father's enormous nose, poor thing?'' she asked. "Tom was trying to be so kind to her that I scarcely had a chance to speak to him. Elizabeth indicated that you and he were old friends, but I'm surprised that a country doctor leads such an active social life.''

"He's a little more than just a country doctor, Angelique,'' Colchester said dryly. "I'm sure you would find him most interesting if you could get him to tell you something about his research into the field of medicine. Unfortunately, however, you won't be here long enough for that.''

"Regretfully, no,'' she murmured with a sigh, "but perhaps on some other occasion.''

Angelique's sigh was heartfelt, for she had not at all liked the way he had advised her that his wife was in no condition to entertain strangers. She had graciously named tomorrow as her departure date when her plans were set for the final "accident" to take place this evening. But now that she had been forced to postpone it, a sprained ankle would give her the few days longer she needed.

One day she would make Colchester pay for his rude dismissal and for the pain of a genuine sprained ankle that she would have to endure, as she dare not simulate the injury when Tom Radcliffe was sure to check. For now, however, she must find out when their next evening engagement might be.

"I hope this will not mark the end of Elizabeth's

social life, for she seems to thoroughly enjoy entertaining and partygoing. Do you do this kind of thing often?"

"I believe we're due at the Crabtrees' the night after next, and then the Horsfalls' next week, and that should be the end of it for a while," Colchester said. "It had better be, for I've never been fond of too much partygoing myself and we have more than fulfilled our obligations by now."

It was exactly what Angelique needed to know. She could probably find out tonight where the Crabtrees lived, send word to Trevor tomorrow, and set everything up for the following night.

The conversation had not been exactly what she had hoped for on the first occasion she had been completely alone with David since her arrival, but it had proved most useful. The ride back was bound to be more romantic, for by then he would be mellowed with good wines and brandy and be receptive, as formerly, to her many charms.

"There are some carriages ahead," Colchester said, looking out of the window into the night. "We must be approaching the house now."

He was right, for within a few minutes they pulled through a large iron gate and started up a private road. Two carriages were ahead of them, so it took several minutes before they reached the front door, but once inside, Angelique was, to her dismay, separated from Colchester and seated between two elderly lords. It was quite a large party and she did not get a chance to speak with him again until the gentlemen, many of whom had become quite merry, rejoined the ladies.

Angelique was an accomplished pianist and actually possessed quite a fine voice, so she deplored the entertainment provided by several of the young girls who gave mediocre performances on the piano and the harp, or sang ballads in either squeaky or strident tones. No wonder Elizabeth became ill at the prospect of such a boring evening, she thought, and was much relieved when Colchester raised his eyebrows from across the room, silently inquiring if she was ready to leave.

It was a moonless night, and though several others left at the same time, they were going in a different direction and soon the carriage was alone, jogging gently along a country lane.

Angelique had insisted on sitting on the same side of the coach as Colchester, claiming that she became dizzy when she rode with her back to the horses. She was just starting to shiver a little and edge closer, and could actually feel the warmth of his muscular thigh against hers, when she heard the sound of a gunshot. They were badly jolted as the carriage came to an abrupt halt, and a voice she knew only too well called, "Don't even move yer 'ands a whisker, guv, but step out 'ere an' let's take a look at ye."

Silently cursing the fact that he couldn't reach his gun with Angelique in the way, Colchester stepped down and waited for an opportunity to somehow disarm the masked rogue, who was still on horseback and holding a pistol in each hand.

"You next, milady, an' let's see wot kinda baubles yer wearin'."

Angelique couldn't help thinking Trevor was over-doing it a little, and she hoped he was still on horseback so that he could get away quickly the minute he recognized her. She put her hand on the door and started to step down when she heard a shot and at the same time felt a terrible burning in her left shoulder.

"No, Trevor," she screamed as she lost her footing and tumbled to the ground.

"How's she doing, Tom? Did you get the ball out?" Colchester asked. "It's a good thing Jake's cottage is quite a way from the castle, for she made enough noise to wake the dead."

"She'll be all right now," Tom said grimly. "You should be glad he hit her left shoulder, or she'd not have been able to sign that confession. If he hadn't turned stag when he thought he'd killed her, she might have gotten away with it. What are you going to do with her now?''

"Send her back to London, of course, with our would-be highwayman, and she'd best secure passages for the Americas for them both within the week, or by God, I'll see her stand trial for both murder and attempted murder.'' Colchester's eyes were like chips of ice. "Downs told me that the old marquess hadn't long to live, but she just couldn't wait. And when I think of what she tried to do to Elizabeth, I want to go into that room and wring her neck.''

Tom put an arm around his friend's shoulder. "She's not worth it, David. Don't even look at her again. Jake will be back soon with Bert Eggers and her carriage and clothes, and I'll stay to make sure they get out of here and on their way. They'll need to carry her into the carriage, for I've given her enough laudanum to keep her under until she reaches London.''

"You shouldn't have bothered. She deserves to suffer far worse than that,'' Colchester grumbled.

"I'm a doctor, David. You've seen me treat the French wounded just the same as the English, many a time,'' Tom said quietly. "My vocation is to relieve suffering whenever I can, and I don't at all like her journeying to London with that wound.''

"I know, old friend, but there's nothing else for it. I think I hear Jake now, so I'll go out and have a word with him and Bert before I return to the castle. I want them to stick like glue to the pair of them until their ship has left harbor and is headed across the Atlantic,'' Colchester stated.

"You'd better get back in case Elizabeth is worrying about you. Tell her I'll stop by and check on her tomorrow.'' Tom looked thoughtful. "I assume you will disclose as little as possible about the events of this evening.''

Colchester nodded, then left the cottage. Half an hour later he entered his bedchamber and started to undress himself, for he had instructed his valet not to wait up for him. He slipped into a brown silk robe, then went into Elizabeth's chamber.

At first he thought she was sleeping peacefully, but as he neared the bed, her eyes opened wide.

"Did you have a nice evening, darling?" she asked drowsily.

"To be honest, it was a very dull dinner, love. So dull, in fact, that our guest decided not to wait until morning, but has already left for London," he remarked casually.

Elizabeth was puzzled. "You allowed her to leave, alone, in the middle of the night, David?"

"Not exactly, love, purely by chance she ran into her stepbrother, and they left together. I wouldn't worry about it if I were you." He bent over her.

"I don't intend to," she replied sweetly, lifting her face up for his kiss, "for I don't mean to let you sleep until you tell me exactly what happened."

"What makes you think anything happened?" Colchester asked with a frown.

"Bert is no longer outside my chamber, and when I sent for Shackleton, he told me that, upon your instructions, my dear sir"—Elizabeth's eyes danced with scarcely suppressed mischief as she repeated—"upon your instructions, Bert and Jake had rounded up Lady Preston's staff and got them out of the house without even allowing them time to pack properly. He said that poor old Yates, her abigail, was screaming that her ladyship would beat her half to death when she saw the state of her gowns. What have you to say to that, my lord?"

Colchester shook his head wearily, but his smile expressed both his love and admiration. "That you're too astute by far, my dear. It would seem that the willful widow turned into a willful wife, and I'd best tell you the whole if I want to get some sleep this night."

Elizabeth's look of triumph evaporated as she saw the lines of exhaustion on his face. She drew him onto the bed beside her, plumped up a pillow for his back, and nestled against his shoulder.

"At first I felt terrible," she said softly, "for I thought that Angelique had been mistaken for me and suffered an injury, but then I realized that you would have brought her back here and sent for Tom."

He looked tenderly at her upturned, flushed face, which had clearly shown remorse at the thought of her rival taking an injury meant for her, and he once more marveled at his own good fortune in having her for his wife.

"It's remarkable how close to the truth you are, and yet so far away," he murmured. Then, as she turned her head sharply to look at him, he added, "Bear with me, love, and I'll explain."

His forefinger traced the line of her jaw as he brought the events of the evening into focus.

"The dinner was pleasant, if a little dull, and I found amusement in watching Angelique's face as she was forced to sit on the other side of the room from me, and endure the attentions of two old roués." He paused, remembering Angelique's efforts to get close to him in the carriage. "We were about halfway home when there was a gunshot and the coach was held up. Can you guess by whom?"

Elizabeth gasped. "Not the man who called himself Blenkinsop?"

"None other, though of course I did not know at the time, for he was heavily masked. I stepped out, as ordered; then, as Angelique stepped down, he took aim and fired directly at her." As Elizabeth caught her breath, he bent and pressed his lips to her forehead. "Don't worry, my love. If he'd volunteered for the army they'd have given him a job cleaning boots, for I've never seen a more ham-handed man with a pistol. He was no more than ten feet away and managed to hit her, but only in the shoulder, whereupon she screamed the words, 'No, Trevor.' "

"She knew him?" Elizabeth had turned completely around to see Colchester's slightly sardonic face.

He smiled grimly. "She knew him very well indeed. He turned out to be her stepbrother, Trevor Downs, and the whole stunt was planned with you as the victim, but when plans changed, Trevor failed to get the message."

"Are you going to press charges?" Elizabeth asked in a small voice, dreading the idea of having to appear in court.

He shook his head. "I've given her a week to sell up and take passages for them both to the Americas. Bert and Jake will stay with them to be sure they sail. I have their signed confessions, so they will never dare return, for they admitted to practicing first on her husband, hastening his demise somewhat."

Elizabeth was quiet, not quite believing how evil the woman really was and realizing that she need no longer fear for her safety. Then a thought occurred to her.

"You have a pistol in the carriage, David. Why did you not reach for it?" she asked, and was surprised when his face became quite red.

"I couldn't get at it. Angelique had complained of feeling sick when riding with her back to the horses and had plumped herself down close to me and was . . ." He broke off, remembering how she had pressed her thigh against his, and his color heightened even more.

Elizabeth started to laugh. "Oh, darling, I never thought to see you so embarrassed. I can just imagine what that awful woman was trying to do to you, and I'm glad she got hurt. You did have Tom take care of her, didn't you?"

"Of course, love," he said tenderly, bending to kiss her.

Some time later, he asked, "How do you feel, by the way? Tom's coming by tomorrow to check on you."

"He doesn't need to," she said happily. "I feel wonderful, you feel wonderful, and our son must feel wonderful too, for he just kicked me. Would you like to join me and see if he'll kick you, too?''

She held up the covers, and as soon as he had doused the candles, he slid quickly beneath and drew her into his arms.

About the Author

A native of Yorkshire, England, Irene Saunders spent a number of years exploring London while working for the U.S. Air Force there. A love of travel brought her to New York City, where she met her husband, Ray, then settled in Miami, Florida. She now lives in Port St. Lucie, Florida, dividing her time between writing, bookkeeping, gardening, needlepoint, and travel.